Dear Diary,

Well…that's a start! Katherine will be amazed to hear that her friend Alexandra Webber, restless wanderer, has settled down long enough to take her advice and write a diary.

But then, for the first time in my life I have really great things to write about, and top of the list is Dr. Ben Jessup, my lover, my friend and soon to be my husband. We've had such a good time together these past few months, setting up the new child care center at the hospital.

If only the rest of the world could be as happy. We're all agonizing over the hospital's mystery baby, whose parents were killed in that dreadful car accident. Who is this beautiful little girl and why hasn't anyone come forward to claim her?

Jaron Dorsey's the cop in charge. Ben said there was real friction between Jaron and the head of E.R., Dr. Annabelle Peters. Jaron even accused Annabelle of withholding critical info from the police.

But something must have happened since then. Last night Ben and I were ice-skating, and who should be there but the doctor and the detective, with Jaron's two little kids in tow. They looked very cozy to me.

Of course, Ben insists I'm a hopeless romantic these days, but that's not such a bad thing. And those two are both long overdue for a little romance in their lives.

So what if I have stars in my eyes these days? It never hurts to believe th... .... After ..., just look at me.

Till tomorrow,
Alexandra

MARION LENNOX

is a country girl, born on a southeast Australian dairy farm. She moved on—mostly because the cows just weren't interested in her stories! Married to a "very special doctor," Marion writes for Harlequin Medical Romance, as well as Harlequin Romance, where she used to write as Trisha David.

In her nonwriting life, Marion cares for kids, cats, dogs, chickens and goldfish. She travels, she fights her rampant garden (she's losing) and her house dust (she's lost). After an early bout with breast cancer she's also reprioritized her life, figured out what's important and discovered the joys of deep baths, romance and chocolate. Preferably all at the same time!

Forrester Square

LEGACIES . LIES . LOVE .

MARION LENNOX
TELL NO ONE

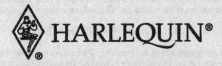

HARLEQUIN®

TORONTO • NEW YORK • LONDON
AMSTERDAM • PARIS • SYDNEY • HAMBURG
STOCKHOLM • ATHENS • TOKYO • MILAN • MADRID
PRAGUE • WARSAW • BUDAPEST • AUCKLAND

HARLEQUIN BOOKS
225 Duncan Mill Road, Don Mills,
Ontario, Canada M3B 3K9

ISBN 0-373-61280-X

TELL NO ONE

Marion Lennox is acknowledged as the author of this work.

Copyright © 2003 by Harlequin Books S.A.

All rights reserved. Except for use in any review, the reproduction or utilization of this work in whole or in part in any form by any electronic, mechanical or other means, now known or hereafter invented, including xerography, photocopying and recording, or in any information storage or retrieval system, is forbidden without the written permission of the publisher, Harlequin Enterprises Limited, 225 Duncan Mill Road, Don Mills, Ontario M3B 3K9, Canada.

All characters in this book have no existence outside the imagination of the author and have no relation whatsoever to anyone bearing the same name or names. They are not even distantly inspired by any individual known or unknown to the author, and all incidents are pure invention.

This edition published by arrangement with Harlequin Books S.A.

® and TM are trademarks of the publisher. Trademarks indicated with ® are registered in the United States Patent and Trademark Office, the Canadian Trade Marks Office and in other countries.

Visit us at www.eHarlequin.com

Printed in U.S.A.

Dear Reader,

Tell No One....

I can't decide whether I like an excellent mystery or a really good romance, so boy, did I jump at the chance to write them both! In *Tell No One* I've given you a gorgeous cop and a delicious doctor—Jaron and Annabelle deserve each other so much! Throw in a mystery baby, a couple of violent deaths, a fire and a little girl gone missing.... Well, I couldn't stop writing. This book wrote itself.

I lost myself in *Tell No One* and I can't wait to see what the ending of the series is. I've just written the first part. The mystery continues....

Thank you for buying my book. I hope you enjoy reading this as much as I enjoyed writing it.

Happy reading,

Marion Lennox

Marion Lennox—who's holding her breath in anticipation of books to come.

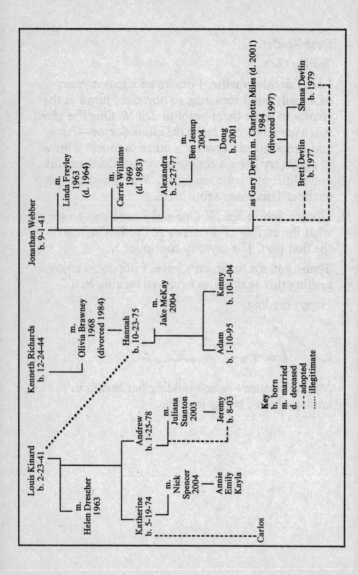

PROLOGUE

TWO BABIES...

If she'd guessed what he intended, she never would have agreed to it. She would have fought him. This was madness.

But the thing was done now, and maybe...maybe it was for the best. There'd been one death already, and she'd been so weak. This one had to live.

But dear God, not this way.

She glanced back at the baby nestled in the car seat. She was just perfect.

Perfect. That was right. What he...what they both wanted was perfection.

But the tiny infant stared back at her with eyes she didn't know, and her heart wrenched with loss. Her baby. Her little one.

She'd love this baby. Somehow she'd make it up to her. But meanwhile...

Oh, please God, where was her own little one? What was happening to her? Was she already dead?

She didn't know. She couldn't know. Not ever. For the rest of her life, she'd have to live with the consequences of what they'd done.

Tell no one.

CHAPTER ONE

"WHAT'S ON this weekend for you?"

Jaron looked sideways at the cop driving the car. Officer Patrick O'Hannassy was twenty-four years old. The kid was smart and good-looking in a red-haired, freckled kind of way. Rumor had it that women fell for guys in uniform, and rumor had it that Pat O'Hannassy made the most of his uniform.

Once upon a time Jaron had been like that.

Ha! A lifetime ago. The memory of what it felt like to be twenty-four made Jaron feel about a hundred.

Maybe he should switch back to uniform.

That was a joke, and a sick joke at that. His face creased into a reluctant grin. He knew how useless such a move would be. As if he had any spare time for dating.

"If I get time off…" Jaron began.

"That goes for both of us." Recently a child molester had been working the Seattle streets. The case was making headlines, and getting time off was near impossible, but they were both due for some.

"My plan is to make Halloween costumes for my kids," Jaron told Pat. "Want to help?"

"Hell, no." Pat steered the patrol car around a garbage truck that was taking up most of the road. It was the afternoon rush hour and Seattle traffic had slowed to a crawl. This was a holiday weekend and everyone had someplace to go. "I've done straight overtime all week and I'm ready for some fun. There's a party at Crane's tonight. Most of the boys are planning to be there, and I have my eye on a lady who just transferred here from Brooklyn. I'm hoping the weekend hots up from there.''

''Well, good luck.''

Pat looked curiously at the man by his side. Detective Jaron Dorsey was thirty-two years old and a damned good cop. But he was still a bit of an unknown quantity. The Seattle Police Department usually knew everything there was to know about its members, but there wasn't a lot of gossip about Jaron.

Except what a good dad he was. Which had Pat intrigued.

''Do you ever date?''

''Nope.''

''Why not?''

There wasn't much subtlety about Pat. Jaron grimaced. ''Too soon, I guess.''

''It's been two years since your wife was killed.''

''Yeah.''

Most men would have shut up at that one bleak syllable, but not Pat. ''She must have been something real special,'' he continued, ''for you to mope for this long.''

Jaron thought about that. *Real special.* That was a good way to describe Cathy, he decided, but lately the images he held of his dead wife were growing blurry. Maybe he was moving on. At last. ''Hey, I'm not moping.''

''Staying home making Halloween costumes on a holiday weekend sounds like moping to me.''

Was it? Jaron thought that through and shook his head. He wasn't moping. Not anymore.

Oh, sure, he'd had his share of being miserable. The night just over two years ago when a teenager hauled open Cathy's car door was still scarred into his memory. The kid was a hophead who'd just robbed a liquor store. He'd screamed at Cathy to get out of the car, but three-year-old Ricky and two year old Tina were strapped in the back seat. How could she have left them?

She couldn't. She'd tried to slam the car door; the kid's gun had gone off and that was that. A perfect life, a perfect marriage, had been blasted to bits by a kid who, when he'd surfaced from his drug-induced haze, couldn't even remember what had happened.

The kid was doing time—ten years. Jaron, Ricky and Tina had been handed a life sentence.

So was he moping now?

"I like spending time with my kids," he said mildly, and watched Pat frown with incomprehension. The idea of spending time with kids when you could be spending time with a hot-blooded woman seemed absurd. To Pat.

"Does that mean you're planning on never dating again?"

"Maybe I will. If the right woman comes along."

"You don't get to meet many women staying home doing Halloween costumes with your kids."

"I meet women at work."

"So how many women have you been out with since your wife died?"

It was time to pull rank. This was getting too close to the bone. "Just concentrate on your driving," Jaron growled. He glanced at his watch. His kids were at Round the Clock child-care center at Seattle Memorial Hospital and they were waiting for him.

They'd be happy. But they'd still be waiting.

Set up primarily to care for the kids of medics working odd hours, the new center was great for Jaron. Round the Clock had been the dream of Dr. Ben Jessup, head of pediatrics at the hospital, and he had enlisted the help of Alexandra Webber, now his fiancée, to set up the center. Alexandra and her step-sister, Shana Devlin, had the place feeling like an extension of home, and odd hours were the order of the day. That meant Jaron wasn't always racing the clock to get there by closing time. Still, he did like to run on schedule. At five years old, Ricky was starting to tell time, and he knew when his dad was expected.

Jaron had told the kids he'd be there about six—if he could. And maybe he could. He'd been out interviewing witnesses to an armed holdup. It was a straightforward case—another hop-head in an armed robbery, but thankfully no one had been injured, and Jaron already had a fair idea who was involved. Luke Sloan, who was also on the case, had volunteered to tie up the loose ends so that Jaron could get back to the station, write up his report and pick up his kids with time to spare.

If this traffic eased.

"Want me to put on the bells and whistles?" Pat asked. He was as impatient as Jaron.

But sirens and flashing lights weren't an option unless there was an emergency. Pat was chafing because he'd been lumbered with a superior with a conscience, but sirens and lights caused people's blood pressure to rise, and there were enough sirens in downtown Seattle without adding one they didn't need.

"No."

"Aw, sir..."

"*No.*" Jaron sighed and stared ahead. An ancient sedan was in front of them—a real rust bucket. If he'd been a traffic cop, maybe he'd be tempted to pull it over for an on-the-spot road-safety check.

But his days of pulling cars over were done. He'd been promoted to detective just before Cathy died, and he'd never looked back. He was good at what he did, and Cathy's death had only served to increase his commitment to fighting crime.

"Jeez, they're jumpy." The car ahead had caught Pat's attention, too. The brake lights were going on and off. The vehicle accelerated in the few moments that traffic eased, and then the brakes were hit hard.

It was nervous driving.

Seemed as if the driver was aware that the car behind was a patrol car.

Both Jaron and Pat had seen this kind of response before. Maybe the driver was over the legal alcohol limit. Maybe he had an unregistered firearm aboard.

Maybe the car was stolen.

Hell!

Neither of them wanted to pull the car over. Doing so meant

hassle. Paperwork. Both of them were off duty as soon as they reached the station. Besides, they weren't traffic cops.

Pat looked sideways at Jaron, and Jaron looked back and swore. They no longer had a choice, and both of them knew it. Having noticed something odd about the car, they had no defense if they found out later it had been involved in a crime. No defense to their superiors—and no defense to their consciences.

They were both decent cops when it came down to it.

Sometimes it paid to be dumb and a bit blind, Jaron thought, but he sighed and picked up the handset to contact Dispatch.

"I'll do a plate check."

"Should I pull them over now or wait till you hear?" Pat asked.

Ahead of them, the car had accelerated again. Heck, was the guy on drugs? It looked as if there were two occupants—a man and a woman. The woman kept glancing back over her shoulder, and even from this distance she seemed frightened.

Something was screwy.

"Pull 'em." There went his plan to knock off early. Pat flicked on the car's flashing light, switched on the siren and flashed his high beams at the driver. That should be enough to make the guy pull over. They were approaching a red light, so the driver had no choice but to stop.

But the flashing light and siren acted like a starting gun. Before they had a chance to react, the car in front lurched forward with a screech of burning rubber.

There was nowhere to go but through the red light.

Dear God...

"Pull back," Jaron yelled...but it was too late. Far too late. The car screeched through the red light and veered straight into the path of an eighteen wheeler.

The truck driver didn't have a chance to stop. Not one chance in a million. He hadn't been traveling fast, but he was loaded up, and eighteen wheelers need time to stop.

There was a smashing, grinding tear of metal and an overriding screech of brakes. Then, before Jaron's horrified gaze, the car buckled and slid right under the massive front wheels of the eighteen wheeler.

"HOLY…"

Jaron was out of the patrol car before it stopped. What fronted him was chaos. All around, cars were slewing sideways, veering up onto the sidewalk to avoid a crash themselves. Blessedly there were no more collisions, but the one was bad enough.

The smell of fuel was immediate and overpowering.

He heard his voice come from nowhere, shouting with authority in an almost instinctive reaction. "Get back. Clear right back. Now!"

Where did crowds come from? He hadn't remembered the sidewalk being crowded, but now there were people everywhere. If the thing blew…

No! Not yet. Please…

He was running toward the crushed car, shouting as he went. "Clear back. You—" He grabbed a guy wearing faded jeans, a stained jacket and leather boots. This guy looked competent and dressed to help, which was more than could be said for the rest of the citizens crowding to see. "Haul the driver out of the truck and get him clear. Switch off the engine and then get away yourself. Pat—" he was yelling back over his shoulder "—get the extinguisher and play it over the engines. Now!"

People were obeying already. They always did when Jaron yelled.

Jaron's graduation report from the police academy said that he had a way about him—when there was trouble, there was no one his instructors would rather have in command than Jaron Dorsey. Which was just as well. This was major trouble.

The car was smashed and had ended up right under the truck. At least, the driver's seat had ended up under the truck. Jaron didn't have to look twice to know that the driver was dead. That section of the car was crumpled beyond recognition.

There was still the woman.

He could see her. Her side of the car had been crushed, but not as badly as her partner's.

There was so much smoke! He was starting to cough, and visibility was dropping by the second. The whole mess could turn into a fireball at any moment.

"Pat, move with that extinguisher!" The guy in the jeans and big boots was hauling the dazed truck driver clear, and Jaron could see that his drafted helper knew as well as he did how urgent things were.

Jaron's responsibility was the woman. He put a hand on the passenger's door and pulled. Nothing. The thing was locked!

For some crazy reason the window was still intact, but Pat was by his side. He'd seen what Jaron was doing and had dived back to their car to grab the heavy flashlight there. Jaron took it with gratitude, and then, as Pat played a stream of foam over the hot metal, Jaron smashed the glass inward. Then he lifted the latch and tried again. The door squealed and heaved. There was the sound of tearing metal, and the whole door crumpled outward.

It didn't take a medical degree to see the woman was in real trouble. She was a petite blonde in her late thirties or early forties. A trickle of blood ran down from the corner of her mouth. A cut beneath her bleached curls was pumping blood, and her chest…dear God, her chest. Blood seeped through the cotton fabric of her dress.

He shouldn't move her.

"It's going to go." Pat still played the extinguisher over the mass of metal, but flames were licking upward as he yelled his warning. The stink of burning fuel was growing stronger all the time. "Jaron, get the hell out of there."

He had no choice. Wise or not, it was move her or let her burn. Jaron put his arm beneath hers and hauled her toward him, saying a silent prayer as he did.

Miraculously, she came free, sliding out of the wreck and onto the pavement.

Then the guy in the boots was with him. Most times crowds were a nuisance, but sometimes they contained pure gold. Like this man. He lifted the woman with Jaron and they hauled her clear of the mess of broken glass and twisted metal.

And as they did, she opened her eyes. Her clear blue eyes gazed up in bewilderment. Obviously dazed with pain and confusion, she met Jaron's gaze and held it.

"You'll be fine," he told her, though as he glanced at her chest, he knew she'd be no such thing. "Just relax."

She took a searing breath. Pain seemed to catch her and she gave a whimper of pure terror. Her hand came up to clutch Jaron's.

"My baby," she said, and slid into oblivion.

MY BABY...

Jaron stared back at the smoking wreck, appalled.

"Get back." Pat continued to spray foam over the wreck, but he was moving back now and shouting at the crowd as he went. The heat was building and he yelled a warning to onlookers. "It's going to explode. Move!" And then his voice rose in terror. "Jaron, no!"

But Jaron wasn't listening. He was diving toward the crumpled car.

"Where..."

The two back doors were twisted beyond recognition. The roof of the car had caved in. Surely no one inside could have lived.

Surely...

He had to be certain.

There was only one way in, through the front passenger seat. The metal was hot to touch. Everything was hot to touch.

Pat was screaming at him. The crowd was screaming at him. *Where...*

He was leaning over the gap between the front seats. Fumbling. He could feel the warmth and the stickiness of blood. He was feeling the driver—or what was left of the driver.

Please...

Where?

There was too much smoke. He groped with his hands and everything was hot.

There it was. A soft cocoon nestled on the back seat. A baby.

If he hadn't had kids of his own he never could have done it, but manipulating the straps of an infant car seat was something he could do in his sleep. Which was just as well, since he couldn't see a thing right now. He could only feel. He grabbed the fastenings. Heat seared his hands. The blankets were starting to ignite.

A click…

The whole infant carrier came up into his arms.

Then Pat was behind him, and the guy he'd called on to help. They were grabbing him from behind, yelling, hauling him bodily out of the car.

They all came out together in a rush, fell backward, rolled away…

The truck and car exploded in a ball of fire.

FOR A LONG TIME nobody moved. They couldn't. To rise above the level of the pavement was to have the fire peel the skin off your face. They lay facedown, waiting for the worst to be over.

Jaron was achingly aware of the baby carrier beneath him. He placed his hands under the little one, cradling, protecting it with his body, and he heard a whimper of protest.

Not dead, then.

Not yet.

He didn't know what the truck had been carrying. This fire was just the truck's fuel. If the load itself was flammable…

It didn't bear thinking about. All they could do was lie and wait for a possible explosion.

The fire subsided just a little. Jaron could hear sirens screaming across the flames. Help was on its way.

He'd be really pleased to see a fire truck.

He lifted his head a fraction and found Pat pushing himself into a sitting position beside him. The young officer's face was stained with smoke. Their Good Samaritan helper was on Jaron's other side, and he, too, was lifting a guarded face to the world.

Three men with smoke-blackened faces cautiously deciding they might live.

It felt…good, Jaron realized. Living. And then he thought, hell, what was he about? Playing the hero when his kids were so dependent on him.

But he knew he'd do the same tomorrow if he had to. He looked across to where the wreck was a diminishing ball of flame, and as he did, he became increasingly aware of the baby wriggling in his arms. He felt sick to the core. So much death and destruction.

But he'd saved a life.

There'd been too much death in Jaron Dorsey's life. It felt good that this time he'd been able to cheat it.

There was still the dead driver. Nothing could help him now. The car was an incinerated shell.

And the mother…her chest… With a wound like that, it'd be a miracle if she lived.

The truck driver seemed okay, though. He was sitting up, rubbing his eyes in disbelief.

The fire trucks arrived then, and an ambulance with para-medics, and more cops. The crowd was being pushed farther back—the population of Seattle seemed suicidal—and jets of water were being played onto the flames.

Jaron could take a deep breath and take stock.

He still had a baby in his arms.

The paramedics had moved straight to the woman and were working feverishly. Their faces were grim, and Jaron lidn't need any explanation as to why. IV lines were being set up, and a mask was over her face to help her breathe, but she was pushing it feebly away.

"My baby…" He heard her terror from where he was lying, and he pushed himself groggily to his feet.

His hands hurt.

Maybe a lot of him hurt.

First things first. He stared down at the child in his arms and the tiny baby stared straight back up.

This had to be a girl, Jaron thought. Pink bunny blanket, pink knitted sweater, pink car seat. He'd hauled the whole bundle free. Here was a baby set for traveling. She'd been tucked securely into her carrier. Her diaper bag was tucked in at the foot, and a tiny pink stuffed rabbit nestled next to her face.

The carrier had saved her life.

Thank God for mandatory car seats for babies.

He couldn't see a mark on the little girl. He stared down at her and she stared right back, eyes wide with curiosity. She was tiny, maybe only a few weeks old, and he felt his heart twist in pain. She seemed so defenseless. Her world had just altered drastically. Her father was dead, and her mother…

Who knew?

"Let's take you to your mommy." He glanced at the still-smoldering wreck, but the firefighters had it under control. There was nothing left for him to do here.

The paramedics were still working over the woman. Jaron approached and looked down. Once more he winced. Even with his limited medical knowledge, he knew she was going to be incredibly lucky to make it.

But still her hands pushed away the mask.

He knelt on the sidewalk, holding the baby close to her face.

"Your daughter's fine," he told her. "I have her here. She's safe."

The woman stilled. Then, "Jim—Jimmy…"

It wasn't hard to guess that Jimmy was her husband. The paramedics were looking questioningly at him and he shook his head. There was no joy down that road.

"We'll take her to Seattle Memorial," the ambulance attendant told him, adjusting the mask over the woman's face. "We need to move fast with this one. We'll call up another car for the truck driver and the baby."

The woman's eyes were still frantic.

"I'll come with you," Jaron told them. "She'll be better if she can see the baby."

"Yeah, all right." The paramedics were already moving her onto a stretcher. The person in charge was a woman of about forty, wiry, gray-haired, clipped and efficient. "Do we know who she is?" she demanded of Jaron, and as he shook his head, she glanced down at the injured woman. "Can you tell us your name?"

The woman gave a tiny shake of her head, and then a moan, as if pain was surging through her.

"We'll get it from the plates," Jaron told them. "Don't worry about it."

"Okay, then, Officer, will you take the baby into the van and step right in out of the way." The injured woman was lifted onto a stretcher in one swift, practiced movement. "We need to move fast," the paramedic said again.

And Jaron knew exactly what she meant. She didn't want the woman dying on board the ambulance—or anywhere, for that matter.

JARON FOUND himself staring out at the noise and stink and smoke of the accident scene. It was like something out of a horror movie. In contrast, the interior of the ambulance was slick and clinical and clean.

Another world.

Outside stood Pat and their helper. They'd assisted Jaron into the van and were now looking at him in concern.

"You helped save this little one's life," Jaron told the man who'd helped Pat pull him free. He gestured to the baby in his arms. She'd slipped into sleep, profoundly oblivious to the tragedy around them. "Pat, get this guy's name. He deserves a medal."

"If there's any medal, it goes to you," the man said heavily. "I just wish..."

He didn't have to finish what he was saying. They were lifting the woman into the ambulance now, and everyone knew exactly what he was wishing.

CHAPTER TWO

THE AMBULANCE TRIP was a nightmare.

They were losing her. Jaron didn't understand all the medical terminology as the paramedics talked over her, but he understood enough to know that their fight was desperate.

He was saying a silent prayer over and over. This scene was one that he was only too familiar with.

When his wife had been shot, he'd been one of the first cops on the scene, and the journey to the hospital had been just like this one.

With its deadly outcome.

Please don't let this be like Cathy. Please let this little one have her mother.

Somehow they managed to keep the woman alive. Somehow. They were pouring in saline and adrenaline and things Jaron didn't recognize, but he recognized desperation when he saw it.

The woman drifted in and out of consciousness, and when she surfaced, it was to terror. "Jimmy," she kept moaning over and over. Jimmy had to be her dead husband. There was no reassurance to give.

"Don't try to talk," the senior paramedic told her. Her eyes were on the monitor. She knew that at any minute the woman could slide away from them. There must be internal bleeding…

"My baby…"

"Your little one's here." The paramedic signaled Jaron to hold the baby so she could see. But the woman gazed at the child with eyes that stared straight through her—as if she couldn't see.

"My baby…my baby. She mustn't die. She mustn't."

"She's safe."

She was fighting the mask. "My baby…my baby…she'll die. I know she will. Jimmy… Mother of God, help me. Please…"

"She's safe." Jaron knelt beside her, taking care not to interfere with the paramedics working over her. But they knew what he was trying to do. The baby was unharmed. If the woman could see…

But it was useless. The injured woman was rolling back and forth, moaning in pain and in fear, and she wasn't focusing on the baby in Jaron's arms.

"Dear God, my baby…"

FINALLY THEY WERE at the hospital, and Seattle's ER team surged through the emergency-room doors to meet them.

Despite the trauma around him, one person clearly stood out. The woman in charge was tall and strikingly beautiful. Masses of auburn curls were caught back in a long braid, trailing a splash of color down her white coat. She was about thirty, Jaron guessed, which was young to be in charge of such a team, but her actions belied her age. She definitely wasn't young in experience.

The doctor's gaze took in the injured mother as she checked the extent of her injuries with a calm, assessing gaze before moving on. Sorting priorities. She also checked Jaron; her gaze traveled over his hands, then rose to the baby still snuggled against his chest.

"Is the baby injured?"

"She looks untouched," the senior paramedic told her. They'd jumped out of the ambulance cab, and orderlies were already pulling the stretcher free. "This guy hauled her out of the car before it burst into flames. He's burned his hands."

Burned hands. Jaron thought about that. Did he have burned hands?

He hadn't thought of himself as a patient, but now he was being helped from the ambulance as if he was injured.

"I'm fine. Look after the mother."

"We will," the woman in charge said coolly. She was assessing the mother as she spoke, adjusting the IV line as the stretcher was unloaded. "Take her straight through to bay five and start cross-matching now," she instructed one of her team.

"She has to have internal bleeding," the paramedic told her. "Broken ribs, query a fractured skull, certainly multiple lacerations."

"What pain relief?"

"Two doses of five milligrams of morphine over the last twenty minutes."

"Let's give it another five." The doctor's voice was clipped and incisive; obviously she was accustomed to issuing commands. "Joel, do it now. She'll be in shock, and the pain will make it worse." The stretcher was out and being clipped to a trolley. A couple of interns were helping Jaron from the ambulance. "Pete, look after the burns. Sarah, take the baby. Call in Ben Jessup." She was directing two younger doctors to Jaron and the baby. "I'll stick with the woman. Does she have a name?"

"Not yet," Jaron told her, and she turned her attention straight to him. Cool hazel eyes caught his and held, and he became aware that he was being further assessed.

"You're a cop?"

"Yes."

"Do you have any further information for me?"

If she could be businesslike, so could he. "Nothing. We don't have any ID yet. The truck driver's coming in later, but it'll just be for shock. He's otherwise unhurt. The baby was in her car seat and seems fine."

"Thanks to you." Then her attention switched back to the woman. "How soon can we get an ID?"

"We'll try and get it from a plate check," Jaron told her. The woman was surfacing again, whimpering with pain.

"There was no one with her but the baby?"

"The driver. Maybe her husband." Jaron caught the doctor's eyes and gave his head an imperceptible shake. He didn't want to be telling the injured woman now that her husband was dead—not when she was fighting so desperately for life—but he needed this doctor to know it.

She understood. The lady was smart—or maybe the lady had seen too much of this type of accident. He got a brief nod in return.

Who was she? Jaron had met a lot of the doctors in Seattle Memorial's ER. As a detective, he seemed to spend half his life here interviewing crime victims, but he'd never met this one.

He'd have remembered that hair.

He'd have remembered those eyes.

Her ID tag said that she was Annabelle Peters. Nice name, he thought inconsequentially, and then decided that was a crazy thing to think at a time like this. He should be thinking that she was a competent doctor—which she surely was. Her actions were confident and precise, as if she'd done this a hundred times before, which she probably had. Her voice sounded as if she'd seen it all.

Jaron might have been focused on Annabelle, but her attention was solely on her patient. "We'll go in without consent," she said.

That was a risk, Jaron knew. They'd be giving her blood, and if she didn't want that—if it were against her religious beliefs to accept a transfusion—they'd be buying themselves trouble.

It couldn't be helped. The courts would uphold the decision, as long as she was unfit to decide for herself and there was no next of kin to sign consent forms.

If they didn't go in, the woman didn't have a hope.

She didn't have much hope, anyway.

"Bay five has X ray set up. Let's move." Annabelle started to turn away, but the woman moaned again.

"My baby…"

"Let her see it," Annabelle ordered. One of the interns moved to take the infant from Jaron's arms, but Jaron shook his head and stepped forward.

The woman shifted her head as if to see, but instead of looking at the baby, once again she seemed to look straight through her. Annabelle's eyes narrowed in concern.

"We'll x-ray for brain damage," she snapped. If the woman wasn't seeing…

The doctor's voice became even more urgent as she motioned to the orderlies at the sides of the gurney. "All right everyone, let's move. Now!"

JARON WAS LEFT holding the baby. The glass doors swung wide to receive the gurney, and Annabelle and her team disappeared. The doors swung closed again, and Jaron was left behind.

There was an instant hush, and it was almost unnerving.

Two young doctors remained—Pete Garner and Sarah Mayle, according to their ID tags. What had Annabelle said? *Pete, look after the burns. Sarah, take the baby.*

He was the burns, Jaron thought. Right. So the guy supposed to be looking after him was Pete.

Pete looked about fifteen.

"I'm fine," Jaron managed to say as they ushered him into the hospital, but there was a chair right beside him, and suddenly he found his knees caving in. The interns helped him sit. A nurse hovered in the background, waiting for orders.

They should all be in bay five, wherever that was, helping the baby's mother. Not here wasting time with him.

"You go. I'll be fine."

"She's in the best of hands," Pete said, and Jaron thought, Okay, not fifteen.

"We have enough doctors to care for everyone," Sarah told him gently. "Can I see the baby?" He was still holding the infant to his chest, as if by doing so he could somehow shield her from the tragedy that was all around them.

"She's okay. She's not hurt."

"I need to check." Sarah was kneeling in front of him, holding out her arms for the baby, and the young doctor wasn't taking no for an answer. "She might seem fine, but she's been in a major car crash. She's been severely shaken. I need to do a complete examination and then get our pediatrician to check on her, as well.''

It sounded reasonable, so why didn't he want to let go of the baby? He was holding her more tightly than ever.

A sudden memory stirred—of him clutching his little daughter in the emergency room while the doctors fought for Cathy's life.

It couldn't happen to this little one, he thought fiercely. She mustn't lose her mother.

He closed his eyes, and when he opened them, they were all watching him—the two young doctors and the nurse. There was sympathy on their faces.

''Do you know who the injured people are?'' Pete asked him.

Jaron shook his head. ''No.''

''But you seem to care.''

''I guess.'' He looked down at the baby. ''Hell. What'll happen to her?''

''I'll take her up to see Ben Jessup,'' Sarah told him. ''He's our best pediatrician. With a child this young, it's best to cover everything.''

''But then?''

The fierceness in his tone startled them all. The young woman took a step back and appeared to think about it.

''You mean tonight?''

''I mean forever. If her mother doesn't make it…''

''We'll contact Keith Hewitt, our Social Services director,'' Sarah told him. ''He'll take her in charge until we can find her people, but that should happen fast. As soon as we have ID, Keith can locate next of kin—or the police can. You'll see. There'll be grandparents, aunts—any number of relatives—here in no time. It's very rare for a child to be completely alone.''

Completely alone.

Jaron looked down at the sleeping child in his arms, and once more he had a jab of remembered pain. Tina waking up the day after her mother's death.

Where's my mommy?

Hell.

"Let me see her." Sarah was lifting the baby, car seat and all, from his arms. And why shouldn't she? It was unreasonable of him to want to keep holding her.

She didn't belong to him. He had his own children. Children who'd be waiting for him right now.

He glanced at the clock and grimaced. "My kids are here," he told them. "At Round the Clock. I'm going to be late collecting them."

"Shana Devlin's in charge tonight," Pete told him. "I know because my kid's there. Kayley. She's four." He motioned to the nurse. "Can you call Round the Clock and tell Shana…" He hesitated. "I need a name."

"I'm Jaron Dorsey and my kids are Ricky and Tina."

"Hey, Kayley tells me her best friend is named Ricky." The young intern was definitely not fifteen, then. Maybe Jaron's view on the world was getting jaded. "We'll put in the call straightaway and we'll contact Keith Hewitt, as well. Now…can we get on with our job? Which is checking the baby and treating your hands?"

"There's nothing wrong with my hands."

"You know, I'm very sure there is." The young doctor was smiling at him and Jaron winced. They were humoring him. As if he was in shock.

Maybe he was.

Jaron had barely handed over the baby when his cell phone rang. Pete was carefully uncurling his fingers. The nurse took the phone from Jaron's belt and answered for him.

"It's Officer Hannassy," she told Jaron, and looked questioningly at Pete.

Officer Hannassy. Pat.

"Let it wait," Pete growled, but Jaron shook his head. He could see Sarah by the door, talking to a doctor who looked as old as Jaron thought a doctor ought to look—that is, older than he was. For some reason it comforted him.

As he watched, they moved out of sight and he looked after

them, still with that fierce reluctance to let the baby go. Which was crazy. There was no reason for him to want to keep holding her, was there?

He had to concentrate on things that might be helpful. Concentrate on the phone call. The nurse was holding his phone and it was Pat who was calling. Concentrate on Pat.

"Pat wouldn't be calling if it wasn't important," he told Pete. "Let me talk to him."

"Your hands—"

"Can wait."

Jaron took the phone. "Pat, what's up?"

"We have a problem. The car's been gutted and the plates are a mess. They must have been rusty to start with. We might get an ID from the engine number, but it'll take a while. Days, maybe. I don't suppose you remember…"

This was a trick Jaron had done since childhood. Close your eyes, relax, and let the scene come back. He had almost complete recall. It was a skill he thought most people had, and he'd been astonished to find that others thought it incredible. His fellow officers knew about it at the station. Pat was depending on it now.

So he let his mind drift, conjuring up the past while Pete and the nurse looked on. He was back in the patrol car again, staring ahead at the rusty sedan. Picking up the handset to radio Dispatch. Looking at the plates.

There it was. He communicated the number to Pat before he opened his eyes again.

Pat whistled. "Brilliant," he said. "How the hell do you do that?"

"That's why I'm a detective and you're in uniform. Practice."

"Yeah, right. Not in a million years. Thanks, Jaron. Do you want me to pick you up from the hospital?"

"I might stay here awhile."

"Fine by me." It meant Pat would be burdened with the entire accident report—but he was young, Jaron thought unsympathetically. He only had a party waiting. While Jaron—

"How are the hands feeling?" Pat interrupted his train of thought, and he forced his attention to his hands. His hands. Right.

"They're fine."

Only they weren't. Of course they weren't. They were becoming more and more painful.

"They're not full-thickness burns," Pete told him as he gently examined and cleaned the angry red palms. "Some salve, some antiseptic, a few days' light use and they should be okay. You've been lucky."

Luck wasn't playing much of a part tonight, Jaron thought bitterly. He considered the drama taking place nearby and thought, Yeah, luck. They could all use some.

They could all use a lot.

ANNABELLE NEEDED more than luck.

In the operating room, she was fighting for a life, and increasingly she was starting to think she was losing.

She hated this sheer, awful waste. Outside was a baby who had every chance of losing both her parents, and who knew? Maybe there were more children waiting at home. The woman looked to be in her thirties. There could easily be more family.

The woman was in such trouble.

There were multiple fractured ribs causing "flail chest"—abnormal breathing. There was blood in her chest cavity from ruptured blood vessels. Her spleen was damaged. Her head injury wasn't as bad as they'd feared, but that was little comfort.

The thoracic surgeon was on his way and Annabelle wished he'd hurry.

"We need more plasma. Has cross-matching come back yet?" The patient's blood pressure was still dropping and she had no way of knowing the full extent of the damage until they went in. She hated operating without knowing exactly what she'd be confronting, but there was definitely internal bleeding and it showed no signs of slowing.

"Prep for anesthesia," she told her team. "And page Jake

again.'' Jake was the best thoracic surgeon they had. She'd assist, but it would take all Jake's skill and more to save the woman. "Oh, and I want a cardiologist on standby. Now.''

Now might not be soon enough. The woman's breathing was growing more labored and her pulse weaker by the minute.

"My baby…"

The whisper made Annabelle pause. The woman was still conscious, then. She shouldn't be feeling pain. Annabelle had erred on the side of caution with morphine, and she was surprised that the woman could open her eyes. But she could certainly feel something. There was such terror on her face.

Did she know her husband was dead? Annabelle wondered. How much had she been aware of?

Annabelle had a few minutes free now, minutes she would normally use to take a deep breath and steady herself before surgery if she was to assist. She needed to scrub, but she didn't want this woman going under the anesthetic without some form of reassurance first.

Who was she? Annabelle really wanted to put a name to her face. Signaling to the doctor beside her to take over, she stripped off her gloves and took the woman's hands.

"Can you hear me?"

"Yes." It was a thread of a whisper.

"I'm Annabelle," she said softly. "I'm the doctor who's taking care of you. Can you tell me who you are?"

There was a tiny gasp and then an imperceptible shake of her head.

Why not? Because it hurt to speak?

"Please…my baby…"

"Do you want us to bring you your baby?"

"Yes." Annabelle could hardly hear what the woman was saying, but she felt the yes rather than heard it. She looked up at a hovering nurse.

"Check what's happening with the baby. If possible, bring her in."

"She's not…she's not…" The woman was conscious enough to hear, then.

"She seems fine." Annabelle's hands were holding the woman's. Around the table the rest of the team worked on. They couldn't hear. The woman's whispers were barely audible to Annabelle, who was stooping so that her face was next to the woman's mouth.

The woman's breathing was ragged and shallow. She was only just holding on to life, Annabelle thought grimly. Her injuries were terrible.

Once more Annabelle felt the familiar dread of impending loss. She should get used to it, she decided. After years of working in the ER, she'd have thought she'd be immune.

She wasn't. She still felt sick at heart.

And now... She'd listened to the woman's chest, and all she could hear was fluid. They could lose her at any time. Well, it'd take a few minutes before Jake was ready, and she'd use that time as she'd want it used if she herself was fighting for life.

"Your baby's fine. We're looking after her, and no matter what happens to you, we'll continue to look after her." She'd seen enough trauma victims to know that this woman would guess that she was mortally injured. Confronting terror was often the best way to relieve it. "Your baby's safe."

Her next words were unmistakable, as was the terror, but it wasn't for herself that the woman was terrified. She was fearful for her baby. "She's dying."

"No." Annabelle's grip tightened and her voice stayed calm. "Your baby is happy and healthy and well cared for." She glanced up and found Ben Jessup at the door. The pediatrician was holding the infant in his arms, and he gave Annabelle a swift nod of reassurance. She wasn't telling any lies, then. The baby was fine. "We'll look after her until you're well enough to take care of her yourself. I promise."

But once again the woman seemed not to hear. Her terror was still palpable. "My baby..."

Ben could see what was wanted. He moved forward and placed the baby in Annabelle's arms and then moved away again, leaving Annabelle space.

Carefully Annabelle held the baby so that one small downy cheek was touching the battered face of the woman on the operating table. Around them the team worked on, fighting against the tide. Ben stood back and waited. Ben Jessup was the head of pediatrics for the entire hospital. He'd have things to do, Annabelle knew, but like everyone, he'd been caught by this tragedy.

He waited.

The baby was a sweetheart, Annabelle thought, but then maybe all babies were cute at this age. Annabelle hadn't really noticed before. She'd done only minimal training in pediatrics, and since then, babies had not been part of Annabelle Peters's life.

Not now.

Not ever.

This was hardly the time for reflecting on her private life, she told herself harshly. But then, this sort of life-and-death drama made her think of the barrenness in her own life. The waste.

But for now she needed to put that aside and reassure her patient. Even if this young mother died, she needed to know that her baby would live and be cared for.

"See," she said gently. "Your little one is healthy and happy. Dr. Jessup's the head of pediatrics here and he's checked her and found her fine. You've done a wonderful job in caring for her till now. She's beautiful."

The woman's eyes were filling with tears. "My baby."

Annabelle lifted the woman's limp fingers and ran them down her baby's cheek.

"She's lovely."

To her surprise the woman snatched her hand away—as if it were burned. "No."

The anesthetist was looking at her questioningly. His hand hovered over the IV cannula he'd inserted into a vein on the woman's wrist. He wanted to increase the sedation, and he wanted Annabelle's go ahead.

Annabelle was staring at the woman in surprise. This was a strange reaction. What was going on?

"You know you've been badly hurt. We're operating to make a few repairs, but your baby will be here when you wake up. I promise."

If she woke up.

"My baby. My baby." The whispering was almost frantic.

"Your baby's here." This wasn't making sense.

"You don't understand. He made me do it. She's not…he said…tell no one. But she…she's going to die. My baby will die."

"Your baby's healthy and well cared for."

She wasn't listening. "My baby. My baby. Oh, God, what have I done? I want her so." Her agitation was increasing by the second. There was a warning glance from the anesthetist. Annabelle looked at the monitor and saw what he was seeing. The woman's heartbeat was fluctuating wildly. She had to settle.

The anesthetist obviously agreed. He'd stopped waiting for Annabelle's go ahead. "The sedative's going in now."

The woman clutched Annabelle's hand.

"Find…find her for me. Don't let her die. Please."

"I won't." Whatever wild imaginings were playing in the woman's mind, now was the time for reassurance. "We'll find her and look after her."

Find her and look after her? Annabelle was holding the woman's baby in her arms right now.

"You'll keep her safe?"

She could promise that. The baby was snuggled into her blankets, her tiny face nestled against the pink fuzz with an expression of pure contentment. Even if there weren't relatives to take over her care, this little one would never be without a loving home.

This child was born to be loved.

"You'll tell…no one…what I said?" The woman's hand was still clutching hers.

What was going on in her mind?

But Annabelle had to move on. She had a job to do. Thinking about the mental state of her patients didn't pay. She'd learned that the hard way. Whatever was going on in this woman's private life didn't concern Annabelle. Her only concern was the life itself.

She needed to scrub. She needed to find out what was keeping Jake. She needed to move.

"I'll tell no one," she agreed, and the woman's terror seemed to lessen.

"My husband…he'll be so angry. But…keep her safe."

"I'll keep her safe." Gently she loosened the woman's hand on hers. The sedative was talking hold.

Annabelle signaled to the anesthetist. "I'll find out where Jake is, and as soon as he's okayed it, we're going in." She handed the baby back to Ben and took the woman's hand in hers again. Damn, if only they had a name!

"We're putting you to sleep so we can make these repairs," she told her.

"Tell no one," the woman whispered again, and then closed her eyes.

CHAPTER THREE

"DO WE HAVE a name yet?" Outside the operating room, Annabelle moved into clipped efficiency, her mind focusing on what lay ahead. She'd met Jake on the way in. The thoracic surgeon had checked the X rays and agreed they had to operate immediately. "Do we have any information at all?"

"Cross-matching's back," a nurse volunteered. "She's AB. There's blood coming up now. Jake's scrubbing and Dr. Forbes is on his way."

Alan Forbes was the best cardiologist in Seattle Memorial, and Jake was the best thoracic surgeon. If anyone could give the woman a chance, they could.

If they could stop the bleeding…

"No ID?"

"The cop might know." Pete was still there. He motioned to the cop they'd brought in with the burned hands. "He's on the phone now."

"How are his hands?"

"Minor burns—nothing full-thickness. He's shaken up, though, about the kid. Oh, and Keith Hewitt's on his way."

Keith Hewitt. The Social Services director. For some reason that made her flinch. "Let's get the family involved. Not Social Services."

"If we can."

The cop had finished on the phone and was turning toward them. As Annabelle made to leave, he raised his hand to stop her.

"Please…"

She paused. "Yes?" Annabelle had been working in Seattle

for a while now, and she'd met many of the local cops. Emergency doctors and the police department seemed to work hand in hand a lot of the time, but she didn't know this one.

He was youngish—a bit older than she was, she thought. Big—at least six-two. Sandy hair with sun-bleached tips, the unruly curls cut into a cop crop. Penetrating blue eyes. A nice open face, but one that showed traces of strain. He'd seen a lot, she guessed. Maybe like her, he'd been in the job a bit long. He'd be used to seeing the dark side.

She'd been told that he'd pulled the woman free of the burning car. Her gaze went to his hands. Pete had bandaged them lightly, but the cop had been using them already, she could tell. She could see moisture seeping through.

"You need to go home," she told him bluntly, and he shook his head.

"I'm fine. I just…" He seemed hesitant. "I need to know. How is she?"

"Not good." There was no point lying. "She'll be lucky to make it. Do you know who she is?"

"I've called in the plates. They shouldn't be long. It's not likely they're local, though."

She grimaced. Hell. Out-of-towners. That made everything a lot more complicated. It'd take time to get family here—time she suspected her patient didn't have.

"She hasn't said anything?" he asked. "Who she is?"

"No." Annabelle was preparing mentally for the procedure ahead and her mind was only half on what the cop was saying.

"Maybe—"

"Look, I need to go." She hesitated. "Officer…"

"Detective Dorsey," he told her. "Jaron Dorsey."

"You don't need to stay."

"I do need to stay."

"Why?"

"Because I care very much about what happens here," he said flatly. "I burned my hands hauling the woman and her baby out of a car that was about to explode. Compared to that, sitting in ER and waiting pales into insignificance."

A cop with a heart. Well, well. Hadn't he learned by now that personal involvement hurt?

But that had nothing to do with her. The fact that her heart gave a solid wrench…well, that was stupid, too. She knew all too well that personal involvement was the way of madness. "Suit yourself." She turned away.

"Doctor?"

"Yes?" She was walking toward the door but turned back. His face was open and concerned. She'd been like that about patients once, she thought bitterly. Not anymore.

"You'll do your best?"

His cell phone sounded then. He lifted it off his belt and listened, and for some reason Annabelle waited. She had a moment or two. And she hadn't answered his question.

Would she do her best?

It was a dumb question, the sort of question that didn't rate an answer, but she knew it was more than that. It was a plea for reassurance. This man had been touched by the tragedy playing out in the past hour. She couldn't reassure, but she could stay for a moment to say, of course—they'd all do their best.

His face would have stopped her in her tracks even if she hadn't decided to stay. His expression had been grim to start with. Now it grew even grimmer.

"Hell!"

What? How could the situation get any worse than it already was?

But Jaron was sliding his phone back onto his belt and his face was thunderous.

"What?" she said.

"The car…" He hesitated and then swore again. "It's stolen."

"Oh." She thought about the woman she'd just spoken to. There were layers of fear, she knew. Was the woman running from something? Was that what she'd been trying to say? *Tell no one…*

Whether the woman was a criminal or not didn't concern Annabelle. Nothing concerned her but the patient's health.

She didn't get involved.

"I need to go," she told him.

"You don't understand," he told her. "Everything's been burned. There're no documents. His wallet, her purse—everything's been incinerated. And I didn't push to find out her name."

"It's a bit late now."

"Ask her," he said urgently. "She's still awake, isn't she?"

"I already tried, but she—"

"We need to know. If she dies…the baby…"

"She's too distraught," Annabelle said. "She's been heavily sedated."

"You could get a name."

Maybe. The sedation was so heavy she'd have to fight to rouse her, but maybe.

She thought back to the woman's terrified whisper. *Tell no one…*

Maybe she could get a name if she tried hard enough, but maybe that would open a whole new can of worms. Confessions. Recriminations. If Ross, the anesthetist, had her settled…

"I'll see what I can do." Her hand was on the door. She needed to scrub.

"Has she told you anything?" His eyes were on her face, searching.

"No."

"But…"

Tell no one, the woman's whisper echoed back. Tell no one what? It was ridiculous. She had nothing to tell that could better the situation here now. "She's told me nothing that can help."

"But she said something?"

"Nothing that's of any use," Annabelle returned flatly. "I need to go."

"Finding out her identity is urgent."

She shook her head. "No. Saving her life is urgent, and that's what my job is. Nothing else."

"You mean you won't try?"

"As soon as she's out of surgery..."

"Ask her now. Before you put her under."

"It might be too late."

"Find out. Delay the anesthetic."

"I'm not delaying anything." They were speaking in fierce, low whispers, and anger was building. "Her heartbeat is all over the place. We could lose her at any minute."

"All the more reason to push now."

"Detective Dorsey, I'm not pushing anyone," she said angrily. "Least of all a seriously injured woman who's fighting for her life. If she doesn't want to tell..."

"She doesn't want to tell. Do you think she's hiding something?"

"I didn't say that. But I did ask..."

"And she said?"

"Her sole concern is for her baby."

"You still think she's hiding something."

"I don't think anything except how to keep her alive," she snapped. She signaled to the nurse. "Claire, can you take Detective Dorsey away and fill out his paperwork? And then, if Pete's finished with his hands, show him the door."

"I'm staying."

"Suit yourself," she told him coldly. "Just don't get in my way."

BY THE TIME she was scrubbed, the team was ready. Annabelle looked around the table and thought there was no one she'd rather work with. This was a great team.

But was it good enough?

The woman was still conscious—just. Ross had given her a heavy sedative but was waiting for the last minute to administer general anesthetic. The anesthetic itself could put more strain on the heart, and the less time she was under, the better.

The woman was draped with hospital linen. Only her face showed, white and strained and dreadful. Annabelle knew death when she saw it, and she was seeing it now. They'd need a miracle to get her through this. She touched her cheek and the woman's lashes fluttered open.

"You're going to sleep now."

"I...yes." A dreamy whisper.

"Can you tell me what I should call you?"

The dreamy look faded to one of distress. "I don't...I can't..."

"Then don't," Annabelle told her. Damn, she shouldn't have even tried. "You go to sleep and we'll worry about everything else later."

KEITH HEWITT, Seattle Memorial's Social Services director, was someone Jaron had known for a while. Jaron liked and trusted the man, and the sight of him arriving through the swing doors lessened his acute anxiety a fraction.

Keith was around the same age he was and the two men had formed a friendship the first time they'd met. Crime and violence had a habit of going together. Cops and hospitals...

Linked cases were almost always heart-wrenching. Parents arrested, kids traumatized. If there was any link with the hospital at all—or even sometimes if there wasn't—Jaron would call on Keith. There was no one he'd rather have onside.

Keith's sympathy for distressed kids didn't come from just studying textbooks. There'd been tragedy in Keith's life, and maybe that was why Keith and Jaron were close. Keith's friendship had been a constant in the awful months after Cathy's death. Now it was good to see him. If this baby needed to be looked after, then Keith was the man to do it.

Hell, would that damned lady doctor do what he'd told her? Jaron asked himself. Why hadn't he pushed the issue?

There had to be someone for the baby. Someone apart from Keith.

Maybe the mother would live, he thought, but he knew in his heart that his wish was hopeless.

Or was it? Maybe he was being too negative, but he'd seen road trauma before, and the woman's wounds meant worse damage inside.

He was going nuts not knowing! For some reason his gut was twisted in a knot of pain. It didn't make sense. He was a cop. It didn't pay to get this involved.

"I heard you were in on this," Keith said as he saw his friend. "Hell, Jaron, you don't need to be here. Go home."

"I need to know the outcome," Jaron said bleakly. "I've come this far." Keith looked as if he'd been heading through the door to the operating rooms. "Are you going in there?"

"I thought I would. Because this is a training hospital, there's a room organized where students can watch. If I shut up and don't faint or throw up, then no one knows I'm there. I don't get in anyone's way." Keith grimaced. "I've just been with the baby. Like you, I need to know what's happening with the mother."

"Can I come with you?"

Keith gave him a sideways look, assessing. "You don't want to watch this."

"The hell I don't." Jaron shook his head. "I'm with this one to the end. How's the baby?"

"Ben Jessup's checking her out." Keith paused, and his concern for his friend showed in the way he was watching him. "The preliminary word is good. Unless of course he finds something in the X ray or scans. But he doesn't expect to. The girl's got a strong pair of lungs," he added. "It seems the young lady's hungry, and she's let the entire hospital know it."

Jaron smiled, but it was a lopsided smile.

"Great."

"They tell me you played the hero to the hilt."

"I didn't have much choice."

"Don't tell me," Keith said wryly. "You were just doing your job." Keith put a hand on Jaron's shoulder and assessed him, taking in the strained look on his face, as well as the injured hands. "You should go home, Jaron. Tuck in your kids and crawl into bed yourself. You don't need to watch this." He glanced down at Jaron's bandages. "You in much pain?"

"Only when I laugh, and I'm not laughing."

Another long look and then Keith conceded defeat. He knew

a hopeless battle when he saw it, and trying to send Jaron home was just that. "I can see that. Come on, then. Let's see how this is going to play out."

He handed Jaron a gown and slippers to cover his outdoor gear, then headed upstairs to a room set up for teaching purposes. Through long glass windows they could see into three of the operating rooms where teams of surgeons were at work. The injured mother was only one of many dramas being played out in the hospital right now, Jaron thought drearily, but it didn't make him feel any better.

"She's in four," Keith told him, motioning to the window before them, and the expression on his face made Jaron feel even worse. Keith would have been speaking to doctors who'd seen the X rays. He'd know...

"Not much hope for her, huh?" Jaron was feeling sick to his stomach, and the nausea intensified as his friend shook his head.

"So what are you doing here?" Jaron asked him.

"I'm here for the family," Keith told him. "There's not a lot I can do, but someone who cares about this woman will eventually land in my office, someone who'll wish they could have been here. For their sake, I'm here."

So he'd watch to the end. Keith went that last mile, Jaron thought. He was one in a million.

"If you want someone who was with her all the way, it'll be Annabelle Peters they should speak to," he said, and tried to keep the harshness from his tone. But it was there. Keith heard it. Jaron heard it himself.

"You don't like our Dr. Peters?"

"She's a bit...cold."

"She keeps to herself," Keith said mildly, looking at the scene below, where the medical team was working on the patient.

They were still working. That had to be a good sign.

There was a monitor on the door, and Keith switched it on. Immediately they could hear voices.

"There's too much bleeding. I'm having trouble locating—"

"Clamp. Now!"

"Blood pressure's dropping."

Hell.

Keith flicked off the monitor. "Maybe we'll just watch. We don't have to hear it."

That was fine by Jaron. The quiet thickened for a moment as the scene evolving beneath the blinding overhead lights played out. Dreadfully.

"So…so how long has Dr. Peters been at Seattle Memorial?" Jaron asked, more to take his mind off what was happening in the operating room than out of interest in the doctor.

"She came from New Jersey a while back, and the hospital was pleased to get her. She's the best head of emergency we've had."

"She seems like a cold fish, in my opinion."

"She's efficient. Gets the job done and doesn't cut corners."

"You don't like her, either?"

"I didn't say that. She just keeps to herself, that's all." Keith shrugged and looked down into the OR, obviously deciding that concentrating on Dr. Peters was better than concentrating on what was happening so close to them. "She hasn't mixed with the rest of the staff in the usual way. She lives in one of the hospital apartments, so there's some interaction off duty with the other in-house residents, but not to the usual extent."

"She's not coming across as a warm and caring human being if you ask me."

Keith frowned. "Why do you say that?"

"She's being less than helpful in this investigation. She won't push…" His words fell away.

"She won't push what?"

"Push for a name. I need to know who this Jane Doe is," Jaron said heavily. "There's a kid involved, and the car they were driving was stolen. It might take weeks to ferret out a name."

"Surely someone will be looking for them." Keith's frown deepened. "A family with a young child doesn't just disappear without someone asking after them. The stolen car could—"

"But if she already knows…"

"Annabelle?" Keith raised his eyebrows. "What are you saying? Are you telling me she knows the woman's identity and isn't telling? That's absurd."

"She knows something."

"Then she'll tell us."

"All I'm saying is that she should have pushed." Jaron turned to look down at the team of doctors working on their nameless patient. "She should have delayed this surgery until we had it."

"And let her patient die? I'm certain you don't mean that, Jaron."

"But—"

Keith's face cleared. "I see the problem. You're kicking yourself because you didn't push more for an identity at the scene."

Ouch. Keith had hit the nail on the head—and it hurt. "I had the chance in the ambulance on the way here," Jaron said bitterly. "I could have pressed…"

"But you didn't because it seemed unimportant in the face of this woman's fight for life. Funny thing is, I'm certain that's exactly the way Annabelle sees it."

"She needs to see the big picture. The woman's dying. The kid—"

"This isn't two years ago," Keith said quietly. "That isn't your wife on that table, and the baby isn't your child."

Jaron sighed and leaned his forehead against the glass. It felt cool. His head was throbbing and he'd only just noticed how much it hurt.

"Go home," Keith suggested again. "Let us do what has to be done."

"Nope. You're here because you care, and so am I."

"Jaron…"

"Leave it. Let's just wait."

THEIR WAIT was nearly over.

"We're losing her!"

"She's going to code!" Ross called out. The anesthetist's

attention was fixed on the blue line of the heart monitor. "Hell, blood pressure's negligible."

The surgeon was still fighting. The intern was handing Jake swabs, and Annabelle was clamping as he cleared, but the blood was surging upward around his fingers. He was fighting…searching…

But the blood flow was beating him. "The aorta…"

There was nothing they could do. There'd been a tear in the aorta, the main vessel pumping blood from the heart. It had been a tiny rupture, which was why the woman hadn't died on the spot. It had been exposed almost the moment they'd opened the chest cavity and was growing by the minute with the building pressure of blood. And now…

The rest of the muscles had given up their fight to maintain blood flow. The tear must be extending. Before their horrified eyes, the pump of blood became a flood.

There was deep silence in the room. Jake was still fighting, but the rest of the team were now just horrified onlookers. They knew…

The fight was lost. Annabelle found she was crossing herself. It was a tiny gesture scarcely remembered from a childhood of church-going with her grandma. A comfort when nothing else would do. Her lips were framing a silent prayer.

Look after her. Please, God.

Jake was standing away from the table, his eyes above his mask grim. "She's gone."

The machines monitoring the patient screamed a warning, signaling the absence of a heartbeat.

Annabelle swallowed, the muscles of her throat struggling with the effort.

"Call it, Dr. Peters," Jake said bleakly. There was no reason for traumatizing this woman's body any further. "It's over."

THEY KNEW IT.

Even without the monitor on, even though they couldn't hear a word, Keith and Jaron knew the minute it was over. The desperate fight, then the collective slump of shoulders. The surgeon standing back from the table.

Annabelle touching the woman's face, a feather touch—almost a blessing—and bringing the sheet up to cover her.

Over.

There was nothing left to do. The two men stood side by side as they watched the team disband. The shape on the table was suddenly nothing.

"It gets to you every time," Keith said bleakly, and Jaron could only agree.

"Now what?"

"Now we get to pick up the pieces," Keith told him. "I'll need to call Seth Nannery on this one. He's our new public-relations director. Hell! The press will have a field day with this. We have an orphaned baby and we don't know her name." He grimaced. "Or maybe we do. Let's see what Dr. Peters has to say."

SHE WAS ANGRY.

She came out fast, shoving the operating-room doors wide. Still in surgical gear, she'd hauled off her gloves and cap. Her bright curls cascaded down her back in a riot of color, but her face was ashen.

"Annabelle?"

Keith's voice stopped her. She wheeled to face him, and the anger in her voice was unmistakable. "What?"

"I'm sorry."

His words softened Annabelle. She checked and caught herself. This wasn't personal, she told herself. It was a patient.

Don't get involved.

"How can I help you?"

"I'm here because of the baby," Keith said. Jaron looked on, saying nothing.

Annabelle took a deep breath, visibly moving on. The baby. Right. The next patient. And the one after that. An endless stream...

The baby.

"You didn't get a name?" Keith asked her, and she shook her head.

"No. Do you know how the baby is?"

"The X rays were being done when I came down here, but all reports look good," Keith replied. "Ben Jessup's seen her and he's happy."

Annabelle nodded. Ben was an extremely competent pediatrician. If he'd checked the baby, then she could relax. But... "Maybe we should still admit her," she said, thinking it through. "If the relatives arrive..."

"There's a problem with admission," Keith told her.

"What?"

"Kids' ward is full. If we want her admitted, she'll have to go on bypass."

"Damn." Bypass meant sending her to another hospital, and Annabelle hated the idea. For a start, if relatives came here, they'd want to see the baby. Second, in some strange way the baby seemed like their baby. Their responsibility. "I want her to stay here," Annabelle said flatly. "I don't want to send her to the other side of the city."

"No."

Jaron was still watching. He looked involved, Annabelle thought, giving him a sideways glance. This was none of his business, but then, they were talking about the baby he'd pulled from the wreck. If she felt somehow responsible for the baby's future, then maybe he did, too.

"What if I take her to Round the Clock for the night?" Keith suggested. "I'll get Social Services involved in the morning, but we don't need to hand her over right away."

Annabelle thought about it and liked the plan. It had definite advantages. It meant that if relatives were found, Seattle Memorial could locate the baby easily and report on her progress without referring to another hospital. She knew from past experience that relatives made straight for the place where their loved ones had died, and she didn't want to be saying, "I'm not sure where the baby is or how she is." She wanted to know.

"Shana Devlin's on duty tonight," she said thoughtfully.

Shana was her friend—or as close to a friend as Annabelle allowed.

Seattle Memorial had been built back in the days when hospitals provided nursing quarters. Now the last thing nurses wanted was regimentation off duty, so those quarters had been converted into tiny hospital apartments—great for single medics—and Annabelle and Shana had been lucky enough to be allocated one apiece. Shana's hospital apartment was right beside Annabelle's. Since she'd moved in a couple of months ago, Shana had tried her best to be friendly, and Annabelle had come to know both Shana and her stepsister, Alexandra Webber, quite well. Between them they ran a first-class child-care facility.

"I know Shana," she told Keith. "But will she be prepared to take on the responsibility?"

"I'll ask her."

"Great." Problem solved. Once more she moved on. "Can you collect the baby from radiology, then, and take her to Round the Clock? Tell Shana I'll check on her before I go off duty." She glanced at her watch. "In about half an hour."

"Will do." Keith looked at Jaron. "What about you, kid? You want me to call you a cab?"

"I need to report back to the station—let them know the mother didn't make it," Jaron said. "Then I need to collect my kids from Round the Clock."

But Annabelle was staring at his hands. Before he said anything else, she'd lifted them and was gazing down at the gauze dressing.

He'd been digging his fingers into his palms. It must have hurt—traces of blood were showing through the dressing—but he hadn't noticed.

"I'll fix these for you."

"There's no need." He tried to haul his hands away, but she gripped his wrists and held on.

"There is a need. You're not leaving like this." She nodded to Keith. "Can you call Seth and let him report the death to the authorities? Take the baby up to Round the Clock and I'll take care of our hero here.''

Jaron flushed. ''There's no need...''

''To be cynical.'' She brought her hand wearily to her face and tucked an errant curl behind her ears. Heck, she was snapping at shadows. She was tired, and maybe the woman's death had affected her more than she wanted to admit, even to herself. ''No. There's not. I'm sorry.''

''Like you're sorry you didn't push for a name?''

She froze. ''Neither did you.'' Anger met anger. ''You rode with her in the ambulance. You had as much opportunity as I did. You know damned well that she didn't want to give her name.''

''Didn't want?''

''Right.''

''So it wasn't that she wasn't able to?''

''I'm not sure.'' She backed off a little, suddenly uncertain where she was headed.

''Then what made you say 'didn't want'?''

''That's...that's just the way it seemed.''

''What else did she say?''

''Nothing.''

''I don't believe you,'' Jaron said flatly, and she gasped.

''Of all the...'' She didn't finish, but she knew very well what she'd been going to say. As did he.

''Arrogant cops?''

''If you like.'' She took a deep breath. ''Yes.''

''I just want you to tell me everything she said.''

''There's nothing to tell.''

He stared at her in baffled annoyance, and she could see he believed she was holding something back. ''I can go to your superior.''

''And I can go to yours,'' she snapped back at him. They were head-to-head, with a couple of nurses watching with interest from the sidelines.

And Keith.

Keith wasn't surprised. In his job as Social Services director, he saw a lot of conflict. These two were taking their frustration out on each other, he thought, and maybe it wasn't such a bad thing. Events like tonight made him want to punch someone. If Annabelle could verbally punch Jaron, and Jaron could do the same back, maybe it'd vent a little spleen and make for better sleeping all around.

But they were glaring at each other with murder in their eyes, and maybe it was time to put in his oar. "Hey, can I find a couple of boxing gloves for you guys?"

"What?" Annabelle wheeled to face him, redirecting her anger at him, and he held his hands up in mock surrender.

"Hey, lady, I'm just the audience," he said mildly. He glanced at his watch. "And as an audience, my time is up. Annabelle, look after Jaron. Jaron, don't punch the nice doctor. Let her fix your hands. Okay?"

Jaron took a visible hold on his temper. "Okay," he said reluctantly, and Keith nodded.

"Okay. Murder averted." For now. He had a baby to see to. "Take care of yourselves," he told them. He gave them a lopsided grin and took off down the corridor.

But Keith's mind was racing. He hadn't been so caught up in the tragedy that he'd missed what had just happened.

Sparks, eh?

Well, he knew more than most that sparks were exactly what Jaron Dorsey needed. And maybe Annabelle, too.

Hmm.

CHAPTER FOUR

HER HANDS were good hands. Skilled and gentle and soothing.

To his surprise, Jaron found himself back on the other side of the beige doors, sitting in a cubicle while Annabelle unwound the gauze dressing and calmly inspected the damage.

It was as the younger doctor had said. Burns, but not too deep. It was the sort of damage you'd get if you put your hands on a too-hot stovetop and hauled them straight away again. A couple of small patches had blistered and burst, but mostly the skin was just red and angry-looking.

His hands looked the same as they had an hour ago, with the addition of a few pressure marks he'd made by digging his fingers into his palms. Which he hadn't even realized he was doing.

Annabelle turned his palms over, carefully assessing. "You got this pulling the baby free?"

"The fastenings were metal," he explained, and didn't have to go any further.

"Lucky baby."

"Yeah?" He arched a brow. "Maybe lucky isn't the first description that comes to mind. She's lost both her parents."

Annabelle wasn't put off by his rebuke. "Kids survive," she said flatly, and he looked at her, and for the first time really saw her.

She kept to herself, Keith had said, and he could see that.

It wasn't her appearance that made him see it. Tall and slim, she exuded efficiency in her starched white coat. Her clear hazel eyes were spaced well and deep-set. She had a neat little nose and a wide and generous mouth. Her eyebrows matched her hair, auburn and attractive.

It was a striking face, he decided—a face that looked as if it could be a model's face. It was made for smiling into a camera. But there was something about her that made him think she didn't do much smiling. She looked...drawn.

Kids survive, she'd said, and he wondered about the sort of woman who could say that. The depth of pain in the words made him think she was talking from experience.

"Do you—"

"I'll put some local anesthetic on this and give you some decent painkillers," she said, cutting across his words just as she was cutting across his thoughts. Maybe she figured she'd exposed enough—she sure wasn't exposing more. "That'll give you a few hours' sleep tonight. You look like you could use it." She narrowed her eyes at him. "You don't plan on digging your fingers into your palms again tonight, do you?"

"No."

"I wouldn't if I were you."

"You don't get involved yourself?" Her calmness was getting to him. How could she not be moved by what had happened?

"No."

"Why not?"

"I've learned...I've learned that no one wins if I get involved," she said, her voice still tranquil. She was stroking cream into his palms and it felt good. Her touch felt good. "I achieve nothing useful and sometimes I even do harm."

"So you stand back and watch. Like the rest of the useless onlookers today. You'd stand and let the child burn..."

"I didn't say that." It was as if she was discussing a cup of tea, he thought. She kept her voice on such an even keel that he had to remind himself of her fury as she'd stalked out of the operating room. She was capable of emotion. But not now. "If there's something useful and practical to do, then I do it," she told him, doing just that. Bandaging his hands.

But he wasn't letting her off the hook that easily. "Something practical and useful. Like fighting for a life?"

"Like fighting for a life."

"How about fighting for a future?"

"What do you mean?" She finished stroking on the cream, and he was aware of a stab of disappointment. Then she picked up the dressing and lifted his palm and he thought, Okay, this was almost as good.

But he was concentrating on what had happened. Or he was *trying* to concentrate on what had happened. It was hard when she was touching him.

The baby. Focus on the baby.

"That baby needs her family."

"That's your job," she told him. "Finding relatives. You're the cop, not me."

"So you—"

"I mend broken bodies. That's my job. If I get distracted, then I just cause trouble."

"How?"

"It doesn't matter." She clipped the end of the dressing in place and lifted his other palm. "But it's like you veering out of your field into something you don't know anything about. Combining being a cop with being…I don't know, a firefighter or something. The two professions work side by side, but they don't mix. Each to his own."

Jaron thought back to today—to Pat holding the fire extinguisher. Without Pat's efforts, the fire would have taken hold sooner. Without Pat's firefighting, the baby would be dead. A police officer's job description didn't include fighting fires, but that hadn't stopped Pat, thank God. "It's a bit hard to compartmentalize," he started, but she wasn't negotiating.

"That's where you're wrong." She wound the dressing, clipped it into place and rose. "It's not hard to compartmentalize at all, and if I don't—" she shook her head as if shaking off a bad dream. "—well, that's the way of nightmares. I'm a doctor, you're a cop, and we have no middle road."

"Maybe we do have a middle road, because we're people. Because we care."

"I don't care," she said neutrally. "I can't."

What on earth was she saying? She didn't care? "What?"

"I do what I need to get by," she told him. She was clearing her equipment, ready to leave. "Which in my case is seeing one more patient and then going off duty. That's it. You can call a cab at reception."

Yeah. Right. He'd been dismissed and he didn't like it.

"About our Jane Doe..." He stood, too. They were face-to-face and the antagonism was back between them, an almost tangible presence. "Can you tell me if she said anything at all?"

She sighed. "I told you..."

"You told me nothing."

"She said nothing."

"I—"

"Goodbye," she said, and looked pointedly at her watch. "We need to clean this cubicle for the next patient. Can you leave, please?"

"But—"

"Now."

KEITH WAS WAITING for him outside the treatment cubicle. Jaron hardly saw his friend through his anger, but Keith caught him by the shoulder. He had someone with him—a youngish guy in a suit wearing hospital ID.

"Can you spare a few minutes?" Keith asked. "This is Seth Nannery. He's the hospital's new public-relations director and we need to make some decisions."

Jaron nodded. He was still fuming. He was weary with the fatigue of shock, but he knew that when he did get home, that he wouldn't sleep. His kids would be asleep already in Round the Clock. He'd have to wake them to go home, anyway, so a few more minutes wouldn't hurt.

"Fine."

It wasn't fine. He was no longer sure what he was feeling, but fine was a long way from it.

Annabelle. She'd made him furious and he couldn't get her out of his head.

Damn the woman. What on earth was she playing at?

He needed to concentrate on something other than Dr. Annabelle Peters. Keith was doing the introductions. "Seth Nannery, Detective Jaron Dorsey."

Jaron held out a hand in greeting and then thought better of it. The painkillers were kicking in, but he wasn't pushing it. He gave a rueful grin and motioned to his bandages. He needed to get his head together if he was to be of any use to anyone.

And he needed to be of use. "Planning a statement for the press would be good," he managed. "It might even be helpful in solving the identity of the parents."

It seemed his words had made sense—to Keith, at least. "Let's go to my office," Keith suggested, placing a hand on Jaron's shoulder again and propelling him forward. That was fine by Jaron. He was almost at the stage where he could be propelled anywhere.

Keith's office was on the third floor. From the main lobby they took the elevator. All the offices were dark except Social Services. Keith ushered Jaron inside. The chairs were plush and inviting, and Jaron let himself sink into one.

"So what have we got?" Seth asked, and Jaron had to force himself to concentrate instead of leaning back in the chair and closing his eyes. He knew the reason for this meeting, and it was important. A mystery baby. They'd all be in the limelight from this moment on and they had to get their stories straight.

Seth was folding his hands in front of him. The man looked nervous, Jaron thought, and then decided, well, why wouldn't he be? This case was going to blaze with publicity the minute the press found out. It had all the elements. Violent death, a mystery and a baby. This case might even make bigger headlines than the child molester the papers had been screaming about all week.

"What have we got?" Seth had asked, and Jaron forced himself to focus.

What did they have? Not enough. Jaron grimaced. "As you know, the driver was DOA and the woman was too far gone to say much of anything." He paused, skepticism shading his expression. What *had* Annabelle heard? "I have my doubts where Dr. Peters is concerned, however."

Seth frowned. "What the hell is that supposed to mean?"

Maybe he'd been thinking aloud. Seth's surge of anger made Jaron jerk back to reality. "Sorry?"

"I think what Seth is asking is what kind of doubts?" Keith had sensed his friend's confusion and was covering for him— but only to a point. "If you're implying that her professional skills—"

"No, no. Nothing like that." Jaron took his time, considering his next words before speaking. From the look of Seth, the man was working up a head of steam. Great, Jaron thought, just what they needed. A PR man with a short fuse. It'd pay Jaron to think about what he intended to say, but he was sure he was right.

"Dr. Peters isn't telling me everything she knows," he said at last. "It's just a gut feeling I have, but I'm almost sure of it."

"That's ridiculous!" Seth snapped.

"I feel certain if Dr. Peters had any relevant information she'd share it with us," Keith agreed. His gaze was direct and steady, warning Jaron to think before he opened his mouth to voice accusations.

Keith was probably right. Jaron was in no condition to be sensible about anything. He shrugged. "Maybe. I've only just begun this investigation. Time will tell if she's holding out on me."

"Why would she do that?" Keith asked, but Jaron shook his head.

"Maybe I'm being stupid. I'm tired and my hands hurt," he confessed. "But I can't stop a gut feeling."

There was a silence while they all thought that through, and then, in quiet consent, they moved on.

"What are we going to do about the child?" Seth wanted to know. "Obviously this won't be cleared up overnight."

"Since there's really no reason to keep her hospitalized—even if there was room in the pediatric ward—Dr. Peters and I have agreed on a temporary solution," Keith said. "The infant will stay at Round the Clock until morning. After that, we'll be stretching the rules if next of kin isn't found."

"We have to do this right," Seth growled.

"By law," Jaron added. By law? The phrase sounded dreadful. He thought of the baby he'd held such a short while ago. *By law…*

"We have to turn her over to Child Services," Keith agreed. "Keeping her at Round the Clock for one night isn't bending the rules, since it's part of the hospital."

Seth scrubbed a hand over his face, looking more agitated by the minute. "We're going to have the press breathing down our necks on this one, I can feel it already. An abandoned baby in a child-care centre. A stolen car. I don't like it."

Jaron couldn't help but agree. "Neither do I," he told them. "And handing her over to Child Services…hell, it's Columbus Day weekend. No kid should be thrust into the arms of strangers, period, but much less on a holiday. I'd want better than that for mine."

"It's my job to follow the guidelines," Keith said, pushing emotion aside and focusing on the facts. "Once released from the doctor's care, the child must be placed with a state-approved foster parent or facility. I don't want her in an institution. I'd rather leave her right here, but I don't see that we have much choice."

Seth pushed himself to his feet, and they could see he was focusing with misgiving about what was in front of him. "Okay." He ran weary fingers through his hair. "I'll go to work on a statement for the press. I'm sure they'll run news of the accident on the front page. If it bleeds, it leads." He shook his head as if he had no tolerance for media machinations. "If we're lucky, our news will reach someone who knows these people." He took a deep breath. "If you'll excuse me, gentlemen, I have work to do."

"Don't we all," Jaron said, then hesitated. "This case seems to be getting to everyone. I'll keep you up to speed on the investigation, but meanwhile…you guys will take care of the baby?"

Once more Keith put a hand on his shoulder. It was a gesture of comfort more than anything, as if he guessed that his friend's thoughts were bleak. "Of course."

"As soon as I've taken care of a few calls, I gotta pick up my kids," Jaron told him. "I'll let you know if I learn anything. If the situation changes, let me know."

"ANNABELLE." Keith caught up with her as she wrote up her last report. He needed to see her before she went off duty. "Can I have a word?"

"Sure." She smiled at him with the smile that Keith was getting to know. It was a distant sort of smile. She didn't connect, he thought, and he found himself wondering about her past.

He didn't have time to wonder much tonight. A baby's welfare was at stake.

"Jaron Dorsey, the cop with the burned hands, tells me you're holding out on him."

"Sorry?"

"He thinks you know things we don't."

"He's wrong," she said flatly. "Why on earth would I hold anything back?"

"That's what I thought." Keith held up his hands as if to placate her. "Fine. Don't worry about it. I just wanted to check." He glanced at his watch. "I'm going up to see the baby now. You want to come?"

"I'll finish up here and be with you soon." Annabelle frowned, thinking about what he'd said and not liking it. "He's a bit emotionally charged for a cop."

"It's a baby," Keith said neutrally. "Plus…"

"Plus?"

"Jaron has kids of his own," Keith told her. "His wife was killed a couple of years back—a senseless robbery gone wrong—and his two little kids lost their mom. I expect there's a certain amount of pain for him to be watching it happen to someone else."

She thought about that and nodded. "Tough."

"It was tough," he said, maybe more roughly than he intended. "Losing your wife like that would be the pits. And then tonight he hauled a baby out of a burning car, saw a couple of deaths and burned his hands. Maybe you can afford to give the guy a bit of slack."

She flushed. "I didn't mean…"

"To be cold?" He was watching her. "No. But you sounded cold."

"I—"

"Think about it," he told her. "Cops bleed, too."

He turned and walked away, leaving her to do what he suggested.

Had she been cold? Annabelle asked herself. Maybe, but it was the only way to survive.

She didn't want to hurt anyone, she thought. Jaron Dorsey had jumped to the wrong conclusions. He needed to butt out of things that weren't his business.

But…he had kids? A dead wife?

Maybe she had been a bit harsh.

Maybe.

HE HAD his kids to collect.

What Jaron really needed was a cab ride home, a stiff whiskey and bed, in that order. But he had a five-year-old and a four-year-old waiting for him and they were his responsibility. What had Annabelle said? Compartmentalize. She should try being a parent.

Hell, he was tired, but he found a washroom and cleaned himself off as best he could, phoned the station to find out if there was any more information about the dead parents—there wasn't—then rode the elevator to Round the Clock. He pasted a smile on his face as Shana unlocked the door for him, then made his way through reception, ready to meet Tina and Ricky as if it was any other evening.

He was glad he'd made the effort to seem normal. Shana led him through to their beds and they awoke to his touch. They were used to this. Almost as soon as their eyes were open, they were gathered into his arms and hugged.

Maybe tonight his hug was tighter than normal. Or maybe there was no maybe about it. It felt great to hold their solid little bodies against his. The awfulness of the day receded slightly in the face of their reality. He couldn't hug the baby he'd saved, but he could hug these two, and that was almost as good.

Compartmentalize.

Yeah, he had his kids. That was his compartment and it would have to do.

"Are you two ready to come home?" He smiled across their heads at Shana. "Have they been good?"

"They've been great." Shana rumpled Tina's curls. The little girl had glossy black hair just like her mom's. Ricky was fair, but you could still see Cathy in his cheeky grin. Jaron loved those curls and that grin to bits. He loved his kids to bits.

But, hugging finished, they'd moved on, taking in his appearance—and what they saw did not apparently, meet with their approval. No amount of time spent in the bathroom could make his appearance respectable.

"What's the matter with your hands?" Ricky demanded. "You've got bandages on."

"Yep."

"Did you cut yourself?"

"I did." That would have to do.

"You should be careful with knives," Tina scolded, and her likeness to her mother was almost uncanny. Jaron felt his smile fading in the face of his children's concern. They'd taken on Cathy's role and it broke his heart.

It wasn't often that he missed Cathy with such a gut-wrenching ache anymore, but he did now. Two years ago, after a day of horror like this one, he'd been able to go home and find his peace in the arms of his wife. Now he had to find peace on his own and it was hard.

At least today was Friday. Tomorrow he'd do some cooking with the kids. Maybe they'd bake their favorite white-chocolate brownies. That always cheered them up.

Who was he kidding? he demanded of himself as he led them out into the reception area. How was he going to bake with bandages?

"Jaron…" He looked up. Keith was standing behind Shana, and behind him was Annabelle Peters. At the sight of the flame-haired doctor, he felt his tension rise again, but he didn't know why. Simply because *she* was here?

Then he saw what she was holding. His baby.

No. Not his. Someone else's. Someone whose name he didn't know—because of this woman.

"I need your okay on this," Keith was saying, and Jaron frowned. The sight of Annabelle with the baby was enough to make him feel even more wretched. Annabelle was cradling the little one just as Cathy had cradled Tina and Ricky. It took a huge effort to focus on what Keith was saying. "Yours, too, Annabelle."

"What kind of okay?"

"I've decided to take the baby home for the weekend," Keith told him. "With the holiday throwing a wrench in the usual protocol, we don't want her in some facility with strangers."

Keith was taking the baby? This wasn't making sense.

"You're doing this alone?" Annabelle asked, sounding as stunned as he felt. "Can you do that?"

"I'm registered as a foster parent, so it's completely legal," Keith replied. "I had myself registered a while back. I needed to because of the work I do."

Keith? Taking kids home? Dr. Peters wouldn't like this, Jaron thought, casting another glance at her impassive face.

"But if she needs medical attention…"

"That's the beauty of it," Keith told them. "Shana will be accompanying me to my cabin. She's had training as a nurse."

Silence. Then, "That'll work," Annabelle said slowly, a furrow appearing between her eyes as if she was still considering the ramifications.

Jaron's mind wasn't working very fast at the moment. He felt as if he was sifting through fog, and it paid him to take his time.

Keith's cabin…

He'd been to Keith's cabin. It was a great little place in the woods not an hour out of town. He let the image settle, and the more he thought about Keith's proposal, the more the fog cleared and the idea felt good. This was much better than leaving his baby in the hospital over the weekend. Or sending her to some institution.

But…Keith and Shana? They'd stay together for the weekend? He looked from one to the other and saw that their body language was tense. This was an arrangement that could be really, really interesting.

Hell, that was another complication he didn't have time to explore. The baby would be cared for, and that was all he needed to worry about.

"You don't have a problem with this?" he asked Annabelle, and she turned her attention to him. Still her face was impassive. Did she ever show emotion?

"It's not the best arrangement. Should the relatives arrive, it'll cause problems, but it's a good solution to the baby's immediate needs."

"If anyone shows up from the family, I'll have her back at the hospital in just over an hour," Keith assured them. "Since the car was stolen from somewhere close to the Canadian border, who knows how long it will take to locate next of kin."

If anyone shows up from the family…

That sounded dreadful. *If.*

If only Annabelle had pushed for a name, Jaron thought. If only either of them had.

But Annabelle had moved on. She was straight back into professional mode. "Shana's well trained," she said, clearly thinking the situation through as she spoke. "She'll call for help if she needs it. Ben Jessup's checked the baby out thoroughly. I don't see any reason not to agree to this."

And this way the baby would have a mommy and a daddy for the weekend, Jaron thought. Keith and Shana. He couldn't think of two better caregivers.

He felt good about it.

Why wasn't Annabelle smiling? Did she know how to smile?

"There was nothing in the diaper bag I pulled out with her that might help in identification?" he asked.

Keith shook his head. "I went through it again."

"And so did I," Shana said. "It only contained diapers, a couple of changes of clothes and formula."

That was no help. "I made a few calls and checked in with the station right before I came for the kids," Jaron told him, trying to divert his attention from Annabelle. What was wrong with him? Why was he focusing on Annabelle? Maybe it was the way she was holding the baby. Or maybe it was her gorgeous hair. Whatever, it was…something. Some indefinable thing. "There's nothing salvageable from the car."

"So we wait until they're reported missing, is that what you're saying?" Keith asked.

Jaron was forced to agree. "Yeah."

None of them liked it. Ricky and Tina were waiting patiently—they were good kids—they knew to be silent when their dad was using his work voice—and the faces around him were strained. This tragedy had affected them all, Jaron thought. Even Shana.

Shana was normally bright and effervescent. She was standing beside Keith, and he thought…what? What were the consequences of their plan? Shana would be staying in Keith's cottage for the weekend. Hmm. He shouldn't have room to be interested, Jaron told himself again, but despite his preoccupation, he was. "You're okay with this?" he asked Shana, and she nodded.

"I'm fine with it," she said in a voice that forbade him to ask further.

Well, if it was okay with Shana, it had to be okay with him. He had too much on his own plate without Keith and Shana's love life—or lack of it—adding to his confusion. He lifted Tina into his arms and took Ricky's hand. They were dressed in their pajamas, but it was a warm night—they'd be fine for the ride home.

If he could get a cab.

"We'll be off."

But Keith was thinking about transport. "Where's your car?"

"At the station," Jaron told him. "But—"

"You're not driving with those hands."

"I'll catch a cab."

"At nine o'clock on a Friday night?" Keith frowned. "I don't think so. Look—I'll take you and then come back for Shana and—"

"I'll take you home."

The offer had come from Annabelle. Everyone stared. It was as if a ghost had spoken, but Annabelle handed the baby to Shana and stripped off her white coat, revealing jeans and a soft white T-shirt beneath. Her voice was clipped and decisive, but there was a trace of strain beneath the carefully chosen words.

"I need to get out of this place for a while," she told them. "I'm off duty and my car's downstairs. I can drive Detective Dorsey and his kids home."

"But you live here, in a hospital apartment," Keith said blankly.

She nodded, still with that strangely decisive expression. It was as if she knew that what she was doing was unwise, but she'd decided to do it, anyway. "That's what I meant when I said I need to get out of this place. After an evening like this…" She sighed. "Hell."

Maybe she wasn't so hot at compartmentalizing, after all,

Jaron thought, a bit stunned. So the ice maiden had cracks. But he didn't want Annabelle Peters doing him any favors.

"I'll be fine," he told her.

Her answer to that was to ignore him. "I bet your kids would like a ride home in my car." She was speaking directly to Ricky and Tina, leaving him to watch in something close to amazement. "Hi," she told them, "I'm Annabelle." She held out a hand and solemnly shook each of theirs in turn. "I have a Noddy car in the parking lot downstairs and I'd like to drive you home in it. Would that be okay with you?"

"A Noddy car?" Ricky asked, and Annabelle nodded.

"Do you know Noddy? He's a little guy with a hat and a bell and he gets into all sorts of trouble."

Two heads nodded in unison. "We've read about Noddy," Ricky said.

"Then you'll know his car. It's yellow and its top comes down so the wind can blow your hair. Wait'll you see it. It's great."

"You have really pretty hair," Tina told her, and Jaron thought, Yes. Yes, she does.

She was smiling, and then it wasn't just her hair that was pretty. "Shall we go?" she asked, and they were all looking at him. Tina and Ricky. Keith and Shana. And Annabelle.

He was cornered. And why shouldn't he accept? he thought, still stunned. Why the reluctance?

He was angry with this woman…

But they were waiting. He needed his bed and so did his kids. Keith was right; the chances of finding a cab at this hour were somewhere around zero.

"Thank you," he said to Annabelle, his voice stupidly formal. "The kids and I would very much appreciate a lift home."

There was still the baby. Shana was holding her now, but Jaron felt a compulsion to stay.

He couldn't. Shana and Keith were taking over her care. He needed to move on.

He ushered his brood toward the door, but then turned back. Sometime over the weekend relatives would likely appear, and this little one would be whisked away to a life without her parents. Maybe he'd never see her again. He paused, took a deep breath and then returned. Shana relinquished her bundle without asking questions.

No one asked questions.

Jaron lifted the pink-wrapped bundle of baby into his arms and looked down at her.

She was awake. Her wide eyes looked into his with an expression that could have belonged to a village elder. She calmly met his gaze and held.

Who was she? Where did she belong?

"I'll do my best to find out," he whispered, and then he smiled.

With Keith and Shana she'd be safe and loved until her own family was found. He couldn't have asked for better.

"Blessings," he whispered, and kissed her gently on the forehead. Then he surrendered the baby into Shana's care and turned to take his own children home.

With Annabelle.

CHAPTER FIVE

IT WAS INDEED a Noddy car.

They caught the elevator to the underground parking lot, and Annabelle's car stood out like a sunbeam among clouds. It was a tiny convertible in bright, sunshine yellow and it was gorgeous. The children saw it and whooped in delight. They were wide awake now. They'd been asleep for almost three hours and now they were charged and ready to go.

"Can we put the top down? We want to ride with the wind in our hair."

"I was hoping you might say that." Annabelle smiled at the kids, and Jaron thought she had a smile that matched her car. Like sunshine.

The thought unnerved him. He was too darned tired, he decided. He didn't have these sorts of ideas about strange women. Not since Cathy had died.

Hell, he *was* tired. There was a stinging behind his eyes he couldn't account for. Or maybe he could. His kids, this car, this woman... The sensation was suddenly family, and it felt unbelievably good.

Which made him feel unbelievably bad. Because it was a mockery of all he was missing.

Annabelle was winding back the folding top. He helped her, then belted the kids into the rear and climbed into the passenger seat.

"Don't you like my car?" She was still smiling, and he forced himself to answer as pleasantly as he could. Which wasn't pleasantly enough. His voice seemed to be stuck in neutral.

"Of course."

"You don't mind the wind in your hair?"

She was laughing at him. The thought was unnerving. "I...no."

"Then give me directions." She hesitated. "Or how about a drive down to the waterfront before you go home?"

"To the waterfront?" His voice still sounded stiff. Formal.

"That's what I intend to do after I drop you off," she told him. "I've had a rotten day and I need to get some fresh air and perspective before I go home. You're welcome to join me."

He let that sink in. The kids had already been asleep. Being out late wouldn't hurt them. It was Saturday tomorrow. They could sleep in.

He'd wanted to go home. He'd been looking forward to a whiskey and bed. But now... The painkillers must be working, he thought. Or something. Because it seemed as if he had a choice.

He could go home and go to bed, or he and this woman could drive down to the waterfront with the wind in their hair and his kids in the back and have...fun?

Fun. After a day like today, the word seemed almost obscene.

But maybe after a day like today fun was exactly what he needed. It was what they all needed—this strange and aloof young doctor, as well.

"We'd love to go down to the waterfront," he told her, and the "Hooray" from the back seat was all the encouragement they needed.

WHAT WAS she doing?

Annabelle never got involved. Never. She kept herself to herself. That was how she'd been trained and it was the way she was. Her one foray outside her rules had led to disaster.

So why was she stepping outside her square now?

This wasn't stepping outside her square, she told herself. It wasn't breaking her own rules. All she was doing was giving this man and his children a lift home. The long way round.

She was sharing her evening with him.

She was sharing her need.

She'd take one quick turn around the closest of the waterfront marinas, she told herself. Twenty minutes and she'd be rid of them, and then she'd go home. Alone.

THIS WAS the sort of evening that happened once in a blue moon in Seattle. Even though it was October, the weather was like midsummer. It was so warm that it was sheer pleasure to have the roof down beneath a full moon and a sky lit with stars. They were driving by the marina and Jaron could see moonbeams trailing over the water. The moonlight was so bright he could see reflections of the masts of the yachts, which were anchored in stately rows.

Tomorrow's weather threatened to be just as good as today's, and every one of these yachts would be out of its berth, making the most of the Columbus Day weekend. But for tonight they rode at anchor, their reflections shimmering gently in the moonlight.

"Do you want to stop and let me buy us all sodas?"

Why the hell had he suggested that? It was the sort of thing he hadn't done since Cathy died. It was almost ten at night. The kids should be in bed. *He* should be in bed.

But the kids had been asleep. Now they were wide awake and the whoops from the back seat said they weren't anywhere near ready for bed again. And Annabelle...

He found himself looking across at her. She was...

She was beautiful, he decided. There was no other way to describe her. Her wonderful auburn curls were flying back in the wind. The jeans and T-shirt she'd been wearing under that awful white coat were crisp and neat, pale denim and the whitest of whites. She looked relaxed and free and...happy.

Maybe it was an illusion, he thought. Like his own happiness was an illusion right at this minute. A form of blocking out the world. Blocking out pain past and pain to come.

But Annabelle was smiling and pulling into a parking lot, and pain was very far from their minds. A group of bars and restaurants were spilling their crowds out onto the pavement, which merged into the marina beyond. It was a night for being outdoors.

It was a night for now.

Did she want to stop and let him buy soda?

"Why not?" she said lightly, and Jaron thought, Why not indeed?

IT WAS A SILLY, happy half hour. They found themselves a table right on the waterfront and ordered sodas and ice cream, and the kids devoured them, big-eyed with wonder. This was a treat that seldom came their way. Their delight went a long way toward restoring Jaron's sense of reason.

He'd been thrown for a loop by the evening's events. Sitting by the waterfront as he watched Tina cope with ice cream and soda, wiping bubbles off her nose, licking the drips from her ice cream and all the while savoring his own...well, it was a saving grace that was as unexpected as it was wonderful.

"Thank you," he told Annabelle, and he smiled across the table at her.

She smiled back, and he thought again that it was quite a smile. "Do you think I'm doing this for you or for me?" she asked.

"You were shaken up by this evening?"

"Why wouldn't I be?"

"But I thought—"

"That I didn't care." Her smile faded. "I do. That's the problem. Okay, I take care not to get involved, but if I say I don't care, I'm lying. I care too damned much."

"It doesn't hurt," he said softly, watching her face, "to care."

"No." Her voice faded and she stared out at the moonlight over the water. "There's always here."

What did she mean by that?

"You come here often?"

"Just…when I finish up at the hospital. When I can."

"In your Noddy car?"

"Or on my bike." She turned back to the kids, who were chin-deep in ice cream. "Do you guys have bikes?"

She received two solemn nods in reply. There was no way they could speak through their ice cream.

"Riding's my very favorite thing. Do you ride with your daddy?"

Two more nods.

"That's great." She grinned. "Maybe we'll meet sometime on the bike path and wave and say hello."

Jaron thought about that. Or he tried to think about it. He was floating a bit. Maybe it was the painkillers. Everything seemed a bit hazy. A bit…special?

He discovered that Annabelle was watching him from across the table, and he had a feeling she was seeing more than he cared for her to see. "I think it's time we got your daddy home to bed," she told the children. "It's his bedtime."

"He doesn't go to bed earlier than us," Ricky told her, but Annabelle shook her head.

"Tonight he does. Do you see his bandaged hands?"

Two nods.

"Do you guys live by yourselves—just you two and your daddy?"

"Yes," Ricky told her. He chewed his lip and frowned in a way that was almost identical to Jaron's. They were very alike. "Our mommy's dead."

"I heard about that," she said softly, and looked sideways at Jaron. "I'm very sorry. But that makes it even more important that you're there to look after your daddy. Tina, tonight you need to pretend that you're the mommy, and, Ricky, you're the daddy. When you get home, I want you to help pull your daddy's boots off and then make him go to bed. I want you to undress yourselves. Can you do that?"

She got an ice-creamy "Mmm" in response. They were fascinated.

"I want you to brush your teeth and tell yourselves bedtime

stories. I want you to make sure your daddy's tucked in and kiss him good-night. Then, Ricky, I want you to be in charge of turning out all the lights and going to sleep. Do you think you can manage?''

Tina placed her half-finished ice-cream cone on her plate and looked at it. It was just too big for one four-year-old. She sighed, but it was a sigh of pure contentment. This was one very happy four-year-old.

''We have to be the grown-ups?''

''Just for tonight.''

''Okay.''

He should say something, Jaron thought, but he couldn't. The night was drifting in an intoxicating haze.

''Let's go.'' Annabelle picked up her bag and took two sticky hands in hers. She grinned at Jaron. ''Can you manage to walk back to the car, Officer Dorsey, or shall the kids and I carry you?''

The idea appealed enormously to Ricky and Tina. They giggled.

But Jaron had his dignity.

''I can walk,'' he said, and only he knew what a mammoth effort it was to give truth to his words.

THE NIGHT wasn't quite over.

Annabelle pulled up outside his home and helped Jaron lift the kids from the car. It was time to say good-night.

But the niggle of worry was still there. Maybe he wasn't thinking straight, but his doubt had returned. He was looking at her and seeing a beautiful and desirable woman, but the events of that evening were still too raw and too dreadful to forget.

If she doesn't want to tell…

Maybe it was just an impression, but he still had the idea than she knew something he didn't. The thought was bitter. She could be as nice as she pleased to his kids, but if she was keeping something back that could reunite the baby with her family…

"You know, our Jane Doe might well have other kids," he said as she started to get back into her car. She stopped and turned to him.

"So?"

"So it's vital we find out who she is." He looked at her, his gaze meeting hers directly. "It's not a criminal investigation I'm holding here. If there are other little ones home alone…"

"You think I don't know that?"

"So why aren't you helping us all you can?"

She took a deep breath. "I am helping you all I can. Everything I know, you know."

"Now why don't I believe that?"

"Because you're tired and you're sore and you're emotionally involved," she said, maybe more harshly than she intended. "You're not seeing straight."

"And you are?"

"I'm seeing…dispassionately."

"You don't get involved?"

"No," she told him, "I don't get involved. I don't offer to take a pigheaded cop and his kids out for sodas on a night when we should all be in bed asleep. Or at least, I won't again. You're right, Officer Dorsey. I don't get involved. Because when I stick my finger in the water, it gets bitten off. Like tonight."

She stooped and gave the kids a swift kiss, sending them off up the path with a tiny push. "Okay, kids," she told them. "Off you go and put your daddy to bed. And tell him he can't get out of bed until he starts behaving like a rational human being. Whatever that is."

HE SLEPT BADLY.

Jaron lay in the big bed and missed Cathy more than he'd missed her for a year. Her side of the bed was unbearably empty. Unbearably cold. He dozed, but whenever he slipped into unconsciousness, his dreams danced with green-draped bodies, blood and mayhem, children sobbing…

At three he rose and took a couple of the little white pills Annabelle had given him. They helped—the ache in his hands eased, but the ache in his heart didn't ease at all.

Don't get involved.

How the hell didn't you get involved? Surely as a cop of ten years, he'd know the answer to that by now.

He flicked a few channels on the TV remote, but there was nothing worth watching. Nothing that caught his interest.

He kept thinking of the baby.

He was going out of his mind.

Tuesday he'd be back on the job, he reminded himself. Tuesday he'd move on. There'd be more tragedies, more human drama, and he couldn't afford to get caught up in each case the way he was caught up in this one. Not if he was to retain his sanity.

He went back to bed, but he didn't sleep. He lay on his back and stared at the ceiling and thought of the baby. And Cathy.

And Annabelle.

ANNABELLE WASN'T doing much better.

Why on earth had she offered to drive them home? she demanded of herself. It was so out of character. She kept herself to herself. Had she learned nothing?

Tell no one...

He said...tell no one.

The whispered terror returned to her with the memory of the woman's last words and she turned those words over and over in her mind. What had the woman meant? What had she been trying to tell Annabelle?

Nothing, she told herself fiercely. It didn't make sense. Simply the confused ramblings of a dying woman.

And Annabelle had promised to tell no one.

To tell no one what?

Maybe she could tell Jaron Dorsey how confused she'd been.

Oh, for heaven's sake, stop it! There was nothing to tell. The woman had been driving in a stolen car and the cops already knew that.

She rose, shoved her feet into the dinosaur slippers her cousin's kids had given her for her birthday and looked ruefully down at herself. She was wearing an oversize T-shirt that was ancient and misshapen. Her hair was tumbled every which way, and with her bright-green slippers, well, she must look truly amazing.

If Jaron Dorsey could see her now...

Oh, for heaven's sake, what was she thinking of? Jaron had nothing to do with her.

She made herself a mug of hot chocolate and perched on her windowsill to drink it. This was her favorite place. From here she could see the lights of Seattle. She could see more lights twinkling out on the water—boats at mooring. Behind every light was a life, and those lives had nothing to do with her, she told herself. Nothing had anything to do with her. That was the way she'd planned it, and that was the way she intended it to stay.

Tell no one...

What could she do with such a statement?

Nothing, she thought. There was nothing to do, and nothing would come from her interference but trouble.

Unbidden, the memory of a girl came to her mind. Angie. Ruthlessly she pushed the image away, but it stayed, as if it were yesterday rather than three long years ago.

Angie had been fourteen years old. Some young friends had dragged her into the emergency room and she'd been terrified. She was pregnant—about five months—and she was bleeding. It hadn't taken Annabelle long to figure that the girl had tried to terminate her pregnancy herself.

The attempt had failed. Annabelle had tried to persuade the child—for that was what she was—to stay in the hospital, but she'd refused. "My parents will kill me if they find out," she'd whispered over and over again, and in the end she'd run, leaving the security of the hospital for the dangers of the streets.

Annabelle should have butted out right there. But no. She'd known who the parents were. They were names in the city.

Surely they couldn't know what sort of mess their daughter was in.

The more Annabelle thought about it, the more she felt she had to do something. The girl could still be suffering from the botched abortion. If infection took hold...well, it didn't bear thinking about.

So she'd interfered. She'd gone to see the parents. They seemed horrified. They'd thought their daughter had been staying with friends, and no, they didn't know she was pregnant. "Don't worry," they assured Annabelle. "We'll find her and we'll take care of her."

The girl was admitted to hospital a week later, beaten to within an inch of her life. She'd lain mute in hospital, refusing to say a word. She'd lost the baby.

A week after she was discharged, she'd killed herself.

"What a terrible thing," her parents had said, and the mother had even shed tears. But Annabelle had seen the parents' cold and formal visits and the way the girl had flinched at their touch.

There was nothing she could do. Angie had said nothing to incriminate her parents.

Annabelle should have followed the safe, rigid rule.

Tell no one.

It was solid advice.

She sat in her window and hugged her knees and waited for the morning. Waited for the sun. She loved Seattle. She loved the fog over the water; she loved the rain; she loved that her few remaining family members were far away, and here she could keep herself to herself.

Tell no one.

She'd promised, and she knew enough not to break her word again.

JARON DIDN'T NEED to go into the hospital. He was officially off duty until Tuesday, but Luke Sloan, the cop who'd been on the armed-robbery case with him, phoned him before he'd decided what to do.

"How are the hands?"

"Sore," Jaron told him. It was eleven in the morning. He'd managed to shower and shave and rebandage his hands. They looked as though they'd heal fast, but they were sore now.

"Too sore to work?"

"I'm not up to catching villains, if that's what you mean."

"Nope."

"So what do you mean?"

"We've got every man available on this child-molesting thing," Luke told him. "We're short about ten bodies. And now Seth Nannery's been on the line from Seattle Memorial. The press is having a field day with this John and Jane Doe. They reckon the hospital's withholding vital information. Is that right?"

"I don't think so," Jaron said cautiously.

"So where did the press get that idea?"

Maybe someone had overheard his argument with Annabelle, Jaron thought, recalling the heated exchange. Hell.

"Do we have anything else to go on yet?" he asked, and Luke sighed.

"Not a damn thing. The car was taken four weeks ago from Glacier—up close to the border. They'd covered some miles."

"Yeah." Jaron thought it over. "Do we have any idea why they were running?"

"Hell, I don't even know who they are, much less why they were running. They could have had a car full of dope for all I know—every damned thing was incinerated."

"The car…"

"Belongs to a couple with little money and no insurance. It was a bomb."

"So why did they steal it?"

"Who knows? That's why I'm calling you. The chief wants you to take this on." Luke sighed into the phone. "Jaron, you know this child molester is freaking everyone out. He's not just molesting kids—he's terrorizing the city. He's popping up in front of schools, play centers, everywhere kids are. He's whispering to kids, scaring the life out of them and then disappearing. But every now and then he goes further. Horribly further. So until he's off the streets, all leave is canceled. The chief wants every warm body on that—but Pat says you'll be off duty for a week or so with your hands.''

"They're not that bad."

"I know you. I got Pat to talk to the doctor who treated your hands. He says a week off. But a pen-pushing case with no outdoor work might be just the ticket. So the chief is putting you on finding out who the hell our John and Jane Doe are. It'll get the press off our backs, at least on the baby angle. It'll give your hands a chance to heal. It solves our problems and yours.''

Wrong, Jaron thought wryly. It solved the chief's problems by handing them over to Jaron.

"Hey, am I reading this wrong?" Luke demanded. "Are you really immobilized? You weren't planning to spend a week in bed?"

"Hardly." Jaron looked over to where the kids were cutting newspapers into a thousand pieces. That'd keep them amused for a whole two minutes.

"There you go, then. Take yourself into the hospital and see Seth. See if you can quiet things down. And have a talk to this Peters woman. If she does know something we don't, then we need to know what."

"The Peters woman?"

There was a pause while Luke checked his notes. "Dr. Annabelle Peters? The rumor is that she's holding out on us. I don't know how the rumor started, but the press is having a field day with it. 'Hospital Staff Refuses to Identify Baby. Mystery Baby. Doctor Won't Tell.' That sort of thing."

Hell, someone *must* have heard him talking to Annabelle.

"The chief said to fix it, Jaron, if you can."

If he could. Right.

Jaron replaced the receiver and then stood for a while looking down at his kids. Sometimes he just liked watching them. Ricky's blond mop of hair, just like his. Tina's gorgeous Cathy-curls.

They gave him strength.

"We're going into Round the Clock," he told them, and gave an inward sigh of relief when they reacted with delight. They liked their time with their dad, but Alexandra and Shana provided a first-class child-care facility, and the kids loved being there, as well. He didn't need to feel bad on their behalf.

He felt bad on his own behalf. He would have liked to stay. He was the one who needed to hug his kids, to hold them tightly. Not the other way around.

The world was waiting. Annabelle Peters was waiting.

Damn, damn and damn.

CHAPTER SIX

SETH NANNERY was in his office when Jaron arrived at the hospital, and Jaron didn't need to ask whether the guy was stressed. He had a pile of newspapers on his desk and his expression was set to kill. He looked up as Jaron arrived and his frown grew darker.

"You."

The single syllable sounded as if Seth was addressing a lower life form. "You have a problem with me?"

"Did you or did you not accuse Annabelle Peters of hiding this woman's identity?"

Nothing like getting right to the nub of the problem. Jaron thought for a moment, glancing at the headlines and not liking what he saw. "No," he said at last.

"You were making accusations in this office last night," Seth told him. "Who else did you make the accusations to?" He lifted the newspaper on the top of the pile. "Listen to this: 'The couple's identity is unknown, although the hospital authorities may have information they haven't yet released. The woman was conscious when she arrived at the hospital and is believed to have spoken to the treating doctor. This newspaper would like to know what purpose there is in withholding relevant information. Surely the publication of any information at all is in the best interests of this orphaned child.'"

"This is just great." Seth raked his hair and groaned. "The implication is plain—the hospital refuses to tell police identity of orphaned baby. This is a public-relations nightmare, and it's your fault."

"Hey—"

"Did you or didn't you blast Dr. Peters for withholding information—in front of at least three nurses?"

Jaron thought back. Hell. Had he?

He had. He might have known word would fly around the hospital at that. This was a high-profile case. People would be talking, and if they thought there were secrets...

"So what basis did you have?"

"Just a hunch," Jaron replied.

"A hunch." Seth sat back in his chair and looked at Jaron as if he'd lost his mind. "You bring this hospital's reputation into question on a hunch?"

"I'm a cop," Jaron said wearily. "It's my job to know whether people are withholding things."

"Well, we'll ask her." Seth jabbed a finger on the intercom. "Kerry, ask Dr. Peters to come in here, please?"

"I thought it was Dr. Peters's day off," Jaron said.

"It's my day off, too," Seth told him. "I have a horde of reporters looking for facts. Until I have facts to give them, no one's off duty."

"Have you heard how the baby is?" It shouldn't matter to him, but Seth flashed him a look that said he knew very well that it did matter to Jaron. That Jaron was personally involved.

"The baby's fine. Annabelle called Keith this morning to get a progress report. You know, it's not Annabelle Peters's fault the parents died," he said more mildly, and Jaron shook his head.

"I didn't say it was."

"She's a fine doctor. Seattle Memorial's lucky to have her."

"She seems a bit...remote."

"Goes with the job." Seth shook his head. "You don't get to be head of an emergency room as big as this one if you burst into tears over a couple of deaths. Annabelle's probably coped with half-a-dozen tragedies this week. She's tough." He raked his fingers through his hair again in a gesture that Jaron was starting to recognize. "She came to us highly recommended, she's been an excellent ER specialist, and we'd be real sorry to lose her. If her reputation's on the line because of an emotional outburst without any foundation—''

"Hey, we're not talking reputations."

"You called her a liar." Seth's face changed as a knock sounded and the door opened. "Ah, Dr. Peters." He rose to greet her with a statement so blunt it took Jaron's breath away. "Annabelle, this guy's called you a liar. What's more, it seems he called you a liar where half the world could hear him, and I now have a dozen reporters wanting to know why the hospital's not telling all it knows about our Jane Doe. Do you want to clear this mess up?''

ANNABELLE HAD BEEN smiling when she walked into the room. She liked Seth Nannery. He was big and capable and good at fielding trouble. She'd used him as a shield when high-profile cases hit the ER, and she was growing accustomed to his support.

But this? His statement made her stop in her tracks and stare in stunned amazement.

"Um…I'm not sure I can." She cast a dubious glance at Jaron. He'd had a shave and a shower and he looked like a million dollars compared with the exhausted figure she'd shared a soda with last night.

He'd called her a liar?

"Tell me what's happened," she said calmly, talking to Seth and not to Jaron. She was effectively sidelining him—doctor talking to colleague, while patient looks on.

Seth flicked the newspaper to Annabelle. She read, her face still expressionless. Finally she nodded and laid the newspaper back on the desk.

"That's nonsense," she said flatly. She looked at Jaron. "Officer Dorsey is mistaken. He was in a highly charged emotional state, he was injured, he was personally connecting with the baby because of a tragedy in his own life and he became irrational. It was unfortunate he was overheard."

"The press is saying you know who the woman is."

"I don't."

"She didn't tell you anything?" Seth was pressing, more for Jaron's sake than his own, Annabelle thought. She knew she had his confidence.

Seth was one who kept himself to himself, too.

"I've told you. If there'd been any information at all, I would have passed it on. Do you really think I'd keep back a name on some crazy whim of my own? If I knew her name, you'd know it."

But Jaron was watching her face. "There's still something…"

"What?" She wheeled on him. "What is it now?"

"You know something."

"I know nothing." She sighed and spread her hands. "We have one Caucasian woman of about thirty, maybe a bit older. The pathology report isn't in yet, but I can tell you what it'll say. I've just come from the postmortem. The cause of death is ruptured aorta and multiple injuries from road trauma. Other significant injuries. Otherwise she seemed to be in reasonable health. The signs are that she gave birth a few weeks ago—at least three weeks back but no more than five, which fits with the age of her baby. By older scarring we know this wasn't the first birth."

Jaron looked stunned. "You mean there could be other children?"

"Yes." Annabelle tilted her chin and met Jaron's look head-on. "There could be."

"We have to find out. If there's a toddler at home—"

"That's hardly likely."

"Why not?"

"Because mothers don't generally leave their children at home alone. Every sign is that this baby has been loved and cared for, and therefore the probability is that any other child would be, too. I have no idea where that other child is. Maybe it was a stillbirth. Maybe it died or was adopted or left home with Grandma. All I know is that there is evidence of a previous birth."

"What the hell did she say to you?"

"Nothing."

"She said something. Ben Jessup carried the baby in. He said she was talking to you. He couldn't hear what she was saying, but she was talking."

"You've been talking to Ben?"

"Yes."

Anger met anger. Jaron and Annabelle were squaring up like two contestants in a wrestling match. The air was tight with tension and Seth tried to ease it. "Hey…"

He was ignored.

"You interviewed Ben to check up on me?"

"I intend to interview everyone who was near the woman before she died," Jaron snapped. "I want to know exactly what she said."

"Why?"

"I want to know who she is."

"I told you—she didn't say."

"Anything she said might give me a clue."

"It wouldn't."

"Try me."

"No."

"Why the hell not?" He was exasperated. "This couple stole the car they were driving. They're criminals."

"Does that mean I'm free to break a confidence? Because they're criminals?"

There was dead silence. Then, "So there was a confidence."

"I didn't say—"

"You did."

Annabelle took a deep breath. She was fighting her own anger here, and in truth she wasn't sure what she was fighting for.

Tell no one.

Tell no one what?

"She was…rambling," she said, more slowly than before, taking time to think her words through. "She was terrified for the welfare of her baby, wanting to know that the little one was safe. She kept on and on. Her baby. That was all she was worried about.''

"Can you remember exactly what she said?''

"No.''

"Anything?''

"Just rambling. It didn't make sense. I was trying to stabilize her, trying to make her see that her baby was safe. The more I tried to reassure her, the more terrified she seemed. That's all.''

"You still haven't told me exactly what she said.''

"And maybe I won't,'' she shot back. "Maybe I don't care to recall it. I don't need to repeat every word my patients say on their deathbed. There's such a thing as patient confidentiality.''

"Not when a child's life is at stake,'' Seth said heavily, and Annabelle flashed him an irritated glance.

"There's no need to be melodramatic. If a child's life was at stake, sure, I'd tell you every last syllable she uttered. If it would help. But a child's life isn't at stake, and even if it was, what the woman was saying wouldn't help. It wouldn't help identify her.''

"But she did say—''

"What she said was rambling and incoherent, mixed with a plea that I wouldn't tell anyone what she saying. She sounded afraid of her husband, and she was terrified her baby would die. And maybe she was concerned about the stolen car. She kept saying, Tell no one. It didn't make sense to me then, but when I heard the car was stolen, that's what I thought it must be. That's all I can tell you. Now—'' she glanced at her watch "—it's my day off. I've already been to the postmortem because you asked me to, Seth, and now I've done my interview with the police. If you don't mind, I'd like to go.''

"Jaron?'' Seth looked at Jaron and he nodded. This was going nowhere.

"Fine.''

"Okay, Annabelle,'' Seth said heavily. "We know where to find you if we need you.''

"Don't need me," she told him. "Not until Tuesday. I'm off duty as of now."

She walked out and let the door swing closed behind her.

"SO WHERE DO WE go from here?" Seth was watching Jaron's face as the door closed behind Annabelle, and Jaron knew he didn't look happy.

"We find out who the parents are. We've got people trawling the police files from here to Vancouver, looking for any couple who could have been involved in a crime."

"And if they stole a car and did nothing else?"

"Then we wait for missing persons to come up with names. Couples don't disappear."

"Families can," Seth said mildly. "If your wife goes missing, you notify the cops. Same for your daughter. But if Mr. and Mrs. X and their daughter take off over the border for a week or so, they likely canceled the newspapers before they left."

"There's another kid."

"There might be another kid. It's not a certainty."

"Yeah." Jaron shook his head, hating the thought. "You know, like it or not, the more publicity we can get, the more likely we are to learn their identity. We'll play the mystery baby for all it's worth here and across the border. We'll put out descriptions and pleas for public help. That way maybe we'll get a lead."

"You're clutching at straws."

"Straws are all we have."

"Meanwhile my hospital staff is being portrayed as less than helpful."

"You can wear it," Jaron told him. "Keep leaning on Peters."

"Why?"

"I'm not convinced—"

"Oh, for—"

But Jaron wasn't letting go. There was something. Something... "Does she have any friends?"

"She's a loner."

"No one she gossips with?"

"Maybe Shana Devlin." Seth thought about that and then shook his head. "Maybe not. Dr. Peters doesn't get involved."

"Make her get involved," Jaron said.

"Yeah? How would you suggest I do that? Boiling oil?"

"Doesn't she have any friends at all?"

"Not that I know of." Seth kept watching his face. "Keith tells me she offered to take you home last night. For our Dr. Peters, that's involvement indeed. Why don't you put on a bit more of that charm and see what you can do? See if you can crack the shell yourself."

"Yeah, right."

"It's not such a stupid idea."

"It's a really stupid idea."

"She took you home last night. Repay the favor by asking her out to dinner."

"I don't…"

"Ask women out to dinner?" Seth rose and pushed the newspapers sideways into the trash. "Maybe not. Keith tells me that, like our Dr. Peters, you don't get involved, either. But this case isn't going to go away. I don't like media attention and you've a kid out there that needs a family. If you really think there's something Annabelle's not telling you, then maybe you can try. What about candlelight and roses?"

"She'd see straight through me."

"Then take the kids."

"Oh, sure. How romantic is that?"

"It might just work," Seth told him. "Stranger things have happened. Go on. Do yourself a favor and try a bit of romance."

"Are you matchmaking for me or for you?" Jaron asked, and Seth had the grace to grin.

"For me, of course. I want this thing wrapped up fast. I don't believe Annabelle knows anything more, but if it'll give you a bit of fun on the side…"

"I don't have fun."

"Then it's time you did," Seth told him. "Think about it."

JARON TOOK HIMSELF off to the mortuary to see the pathology report for himself, only to find it wasn't ready.

"Dr. Peters knows what the results are," he told the officious woman at reception, and she stared at him as if he was stupid.

"Dr. Peters helped with the postmortem. If you were interested in being there, you could have put in a request for police presence."

He wasn't that interested. "When will the results be available?"

"Maybe tomorrow. They'll be released as a pair." She looked at her schedule. "The guy's postmortem is scheduled in an hour. You want to be present for that?"

"No, thanks," Jaron said with feeling.

Baffled, he phoned the station to be told that all leads led exactly nowhere. Apart from the report of the stolen car, there was nothing. No report of a missing couple or baby. No results from an all-out media blitz. Nothing.

He called Keith. "The baby's fine," Keith told him. "I thought Annabelle would have told you that. If you're happy with it, we'll keep her up here in the cabin until Tuesday. Unless you have an identity for her?"

"No."

"Shana's calling her Chris," Keith told him. "Because she arrived on the Columbus Day holiday."

"That's great."

"What's wrong?" Keith was attuned to strain and must have heard it in Jaron's voice. "How are the hands?"

"Terrific."

"You know, I'm almost sure they're not."

Maybe they weren't. Jaron disconnected and thought, What now?

Annabelle. She was his only lead.

She wasn't a lead at all. He was imagining things. But…he could just go and talk to her.

What had Seth said?

She took you home last night. Repay the favor by asking her out to dinner.

Maybe he could try.

ANNABELLE LIVED in one of the cluster of tiny hospital apartments on the tenth floor of Seattle Memorial. It'd be a great spot to live, Jaron thought, if you were a doctor—incredibly convenient. But then he wondered how he'd react to living above the station? Maybe the nurses had it right when they refused to live here anymore. He could understand why Annabelle had to leave sometimes.

So it wasn't hard to locate her, but when Jaron found himself at her front door, he hesitated before knocking. In truth he didn't fully understand what he was doing. Was he asking her out to dinner? And if so, why?

He almost changed his mind, but then a woman came out of one of the neighboring apartments, gave him a bright smile and said, "Annabelle's in. I saw her go in just now. Go ahead, knock."

So he knocked, and then had to fight a ridiculous urge to run away—like a kid pushing doorbells as a prank.

And then she answered.

For a moment he thought he had the wrong place.

Between her standard-issue white coat and angry detachment from the case, he'd thought of her as an ice maiden. That was how she'd appeared. But now…

She'd made a quick change—or maybe she'd had this on underneath all along. There was a stunning thought! She was standing in her open doorway in shorts—*short* shorts—and a tight little crop top that didn't even begin to cover her midriff. And that was all. Her bare legs seemed to stretch forever. Her toenails were painted bright crimson. She'd freed her hair from the ponytail and it was sort of floating…

The only part of her he recognized was her face.

When she saw who it was her features became shuttered. "*You*," she said.

"Hey, I'm not that bad," he told her, but her face stayed closed.

"Yes, you are."

"I can't be. My wife, who I thought was an expert in such matters, used to say that I was cute."

Now where had that come from? He couldn't believe he'd said something so out of character. It sure wasn't cop talking to potential witness. He took a step back, thinking she'd slam the door on him.

But instead, her shuttered look eased and the corners of her mouth twitched.

"Cute, huh?" she said cautiously. "Like…a puppy?"

He thought about that and found it wanting. "Nope. Cute more like Robert Redford."

"Um—" she appeared to consider "—isn't Robert Redford sixty?"

Sixty. How could Robert Redford be sixty? Jaron thought back to the Sundance Kid and felt old himself. Was it so long since he'd been to the movies? He reconsidered and dredged up memories of a video he'd seen with Cathy. "Okay, then. How about Keanu Reeves?"

She shook her head and her fiery mane swished across her back. There was a twinkle in the back of those hazel eyes he found intriguing. "Keanu Reeves isn't cute," she said decisively. "Good-looking, I'll allow. Maybe even heart-throb, but not cute. How about Heath Ledger?"

"You think Heath Ledger is cute?"

"Yep. Did you see him in *Ten Things I Hate About You?* Definitely cute."

Ten Things I Hate About You was one of their favorite movies. After Cathy's death, home videos became a family lifesaver. Watching movies over and over was their time-out. The kids sat cuddled against him. Some movies were too advanced for the kids, but there was only so much of Bambi a man could take. So some movie bits they understood, some bits they didn't, but they all had fun.

The scene in *Ten Things I Hate About You* where Bianca

slugged Joey was understood and enjoyed by all of them. Tina had watched it and giggled over and over again. Maybe his daughter's view on dating would be a bit warped, but he figured that the parts of the movie she understood were giving her all the right messages.

But Heath Ledger… "He was only about seventeen in that movie," he objected, and she definitely grinned.

"So you reckon you're more in the Robert Redford age bracket than Heath Ledger?"

"Hey! I'm only thirty-two."

"But you still think you're cute?"

This was a ridiculous conversation. He paused, wondering where to go from here. At last he said, "Um…I was wondering if I could ask you out." That didn't help at all. The silence stretched on. He had her really astounded. He had *himself* really astounded.

Maybe she was more astounded than he was. The last thing she'd obviously expected was an invitation. "Am I supposed to say yes because you're cute?" she said at last, and he sighed.

"Can we give 'cute' a rest?"

She wasn't letting go easily. "So you don't think you're cute?"

"No."

She nodded, apparently seriously considering. "Okay. I'm not saying there's no cuteness about you, but if a guy *thinks* he's cute, then a girl's in trouble."

"You have this all sewn up," he muttered, pissed off, and she grinned.

"Yep. Anything you want to know about dating, just ask me. Like you, I watch all the movies."

"So…" He was swimming against the tide and had no idea where he was headed. And her amazing appearance didn't help. He wasn't the one who was cute, he conceded.

He had to force his thoughts back to the conversation they were attempting to have, and it was really hard. What had she said? *Anything you want to know about dating, just ask me.*

Like you, I watch all the movies. "Um…you've learned about dating from the movies?"

She was looking at him sort of sideways—as if she wasn't sure where he was coming from. "That's right. I've never bothered learning about it anywhere else. I don't date."

This was making less and less sense. "Why not?"

"I'm thirty years old next June. I'm a doctor. I have a life. I don't need a man to keep me happy."

He thought about that some more and came to an obvious conclusion. "You're a lesbian?"

She grinned. "Nope."

She had the best grin! Whew! He looked at her again—really looked—and the sensation he felt was as if he was waking from a sleep he'd been in for far too long.

Since Cathy died, he hadn't looked at anyone else. Not like this. He hadn't wanted to look at anyone else. But now…he was definitely looking, and like Keanu Reeves, cute didn't cut it.

He wasn't thinking cute. He was thinking gorgeous.

And here he was, like a dimwit, asking if the lady was a lesbian. Maybe he was getting old, he decided. Maybe he needed to see a shrink. As a pickup line, his could definitely use some improvement.

"We don't have to call it a date," he said slowly, trying to get his thoughts in order. Heck, that little top she was wearing was far too…well, little. It made a man forget what he was concentrating on altogether.

"What could we call it?"

"Dinner."

"Dinner means a date in my rule book."

"What if I bring my kids?"

Her lips twitched at that. "Okay. Maybe that's not a date. You have great kids."

That felt good. He did have great kids, and he liked it that she thought so.

Was she just saying it to be polite?

No, he decided. She didn't have to say it. She could have just slammed the door in his face and been done with it.

"So...you will come out to dinner with me and the kids?"

"How are your hands?" she asked abruptly, changing the topic at a speed he couldn't keep up with.

"Fine."

"They hurt?"

"Not more than you'd expect."

She searched his face. "They do hurt. Can I check them?"

"They're fine."

"I'm not going on any date with a masochistic male who'll let his hands drop off from infection because he has too much pride to let me check."

Whew. He definitely couldn't keep up. He felt as if he'd fallen right off the rails.

"They were fine this morning."

"Did you change the dressing?" She lifted his hands and glared at him. "These dressings haven't been changed."

"I put plastic bags over them while I was in the shower."

"Gee, that'll help. Why are the dressings damp?"

"I made peanut-butter-and-jelly sandwiches. You try doing that without spilling a little jelly. It was either sponge them off or come out looking like they're dripping gore."

She smiled again. She had the best smile, he thought. She was holding his hands lightly in hers and the sensation was weird. Weird but...good? "Do you have anyone who can help you for a couple of days?" she was asking, and he had to haul his thoughts back into order to concentrate. "Someone to give you a hand with the kids?"

"The kids and I are fine."

"You don't get any medals for independence."

"Says she who doesn't date," he said derisively, and to his astonishment, faint color flushed her cheeks. The lady wasn't as cool as she made out to be. Interesting.

She was concentrating on his hands again, and he thought, it's a defense mechanism. When you're in doubt, concentrate on medicine. "Let me check these," she said, and he blinked.

"What—here? Now?"

"You sound scared." She looked at him thoughtfully. "What are you afraid of? Me? 'Come in to my parlor, said the spider to the fly.'" She still had that tone of self-mockery. It was a protective shell, he thought, but maybe it was more brittle than she'd like. If he tried, maybe he could get past it.

What the hell was he thinking? He didn't want to get past anyone's shell. He had a shell of his own to protect!

"Don't worry. I'm not about to tackle you to the floor and have my wicked way with you," she told him, and maybe she was better at reading his mind than he was hers. She released his hands and pushed the door wide, ushering him in. "I'm asking you to sit at my kitchen table and let me change your dressings. Nothing more."

Pity, Jaron thought, and then he looked into her eyes. They were overbright but challenging.

What had she just said? *Nothing more?* For now he'd take what he could get, he decided, and he might even enjoy it.

CHAPTER SEVEN

HER APARTMENT was different from what he'd expected. Actually, he wasn't sure what he'd expected—clinical and neat, maybe? Chrome and white and sleek and expensive? That was the air she gave off in that damned white coat of hers. But the Annabelle who'd opened the door to him, the Annabelle of the bare midriff and bare toes and tousled curls, yep, maybe she fitted in with her apartment perfectly.

Her tiny unit was a riot of ordered chaos. She obviously had a talent for making herself at home.

There were books as far as the eye could see. Plush Persian carpets covered the floor and there was an ancient settee, worn and saggy and covered with a riot of squashy cushions. An obviously much-used piano sat against the far wall, a heap of sheet music scattered around.

And on the walls were photographs. Not just any photographs, but pictures that were truly stunning. The subjects were diverse and wonderful: an ancient fisherman sitting dreaming into the sunset, a ripple on a rock pool at low tide, a baby's fingers curled around one much larger, raindrops on a window...

They were magical, transporting pictures, and in the corner behind the settee was a jumble of cameras, pedestals, lenses—everything to declare that the person who'd taken these pictures was right here.

"You took these?" To say he was shocked was an understatement.

"Mmm." She seemed embarrassed.

"They're fantastic." He moved from picture to picture.

"They're like... Do you know Faith Marshall? Sorry, Faith Dunn. She's a local photojournalist. She and her husband, Ethan are a great couple, and her pictures...they're different to yours but no better. You two would hit it off. I'd introduce—"

"Thank you. But I don't need friends."

It was a blank, harsh statement of fact, and it stunned him. "You don't?"

"No." She wasn't allowing him to go down that track. She motioned to her dog in an attempt to distract him, and she succeeded. An ancient golden retriever was snoozing on the settee. He looked up as Jaron approached, gave his tail a perfunctory wag and then settled back to the serious business of sleeping.

"You keep a dog in a hospital apartment?" he asked incredulously, and Annabelle nodded.

"Of course. Why shouldn't I?"

"Doesn't he get bored with you gone all day?"

"Harold is sixteen years old," she told him, crossing to give the dog's ears a loving stroke. "As long as he has a patch of sunshine and a comfy chair, that's all he needs. I was given Harold when I was fourteen. He's my best friend and it seems like he's been a part of me forever."

"I didn't think you'd be permitted to keep him here."

She grinned at that. "I have special permission. When I applied for the job, I explained that if they employed me, then they got Harold, too. We're a package deal."

He couldn't believe it. He couldn't believe this whole setup. These photographs. This dog. Her!

Concentrate on the dog, he told himself. He couldn't take everything in at once. This apartment was on the top floor. How could she cope with a dog this size? "Do you walk him?"

"We take the elevator down to the garden three times a day. Even that's a bit of an effort for Harold now. We're thinking of getting him a bath-chair."

"Or a trailer for your bicycle?" That was another astounding thing. Her bicycle was parked beside the piano—a splendid crimson machine that looked as if it was built for comfort, not for speed.

"Well, actually—" she grinned and motioned to a tiny box cart in the porch "—we've already thought of that, though Harold far prefers limousines. He quite likes my Noddy car, but really, he's an Aston Martin type of dog. He has a penchant for padded leather."

"Don't we all." Jaron shook his head in disbelief. She was fascinating. Gorgeous, effervescent...wonderful!

His eyes wandered on. "So you play the piano?"

"Badly. But I enjoy it."

He lifted a sheet of her music and saw what she'd been attempting. His very brief encounter with a piano, between the ages of eight and eight and a half, had taught him enough to know that she was playing at a level he could only dream of.

"Wow," he said inadequately, and she smiled.

"Sit."

"I beg your pardon?" Was she talking to the dog or to him?

To him, apparently. "Keep Harold company while I find what I need."

"What do you need?"

"Dressings for your hands." She disappeared and was rummaging in the bathroom while he sat in her delightful living room, staring around him as if seeing a glimpse of another life.

"Do you keep a complete medical kit in your bathroom?" he called.

"Yep." She was out of sight, but her voice carried. It was a great voice, he thought, sort of husky and a bit musical. "I have enough here to cope with everything from heart attack to snakebite. I made up a comprehensive medical kit for my last car, but since I bought my Noddy car, every inch of trunk space is precious. I've left a fire extinguisher in there and basic life-saving stuff so I can leap into the breach whenever I need to, but I've had to shift my ordinary stuff like dressings up here. I should get rid of it, but you never know."

"Do you get to leap into the breach often?" He was fascinated.

"Never." She returned then with a handful of salve and dressing. "Ever since I was nine years old I've dreamed of someone yelling, 'Is there a doctor in the house?' But no one ever has."

"I'm sorry."

"I'm not." She laid her gear on the table and started unwinding his bandages. "I thought it'd be dramatic, but now...well, it'd be like it was with you leaping into the breach yesterday. When it's a real-life drama, you realize it's mostly just plain tragic. This hero stuff isn't all it's cracked up to be."

It wasn't. The echoes of yesterday came back. The little girl was safe for now—with Shana and Keith—but she needed someone to love her.

"Block it out," Annabelle said gently, and again he realized she saw far more than he wanted to reveal. "It's work. You do what you must, but when you've finished work for the day, you walk away and you don't look back."

"Is that how you operate?"

"Yes." She lifted the dressings away from his hands. "The jelly doesn't seem to have penetrated. This is looking good."

"So if you don't look back, what are you doing dressing my hands when you're not working?"

"It's a way of getting rid of you," she told him. "I retreat to my medical self, I slap another dressing on your hands, I tell you you're doing as well as expected, and I send you on your way."

"Without a date for dinner?" he said cautiously, and she nodded.

"Right."

"Because you don't date?"

"No."

"Never?"

"Never."

She had him intrigued. "Can I ask why not?"

"Nope."

"But there is a reason. I don't date because my wife died

two years ago and I haven't gotten over it. There's always a reason.''

"If you haven't gotten over your wife's death, what are you doing asking me out?"

"Professional reasons."

"So—" she was concentrating on his hands while thinking out loud "—you still believe that our Jane Doe told me secrets. Your plan is that you'll ply me with food and drink, and when you have me nicely plastered, instead of having your wicked way with me, you'll ask me what she said."

"Something like that," he agreed with a grin.

She didn't notice. She was still concentrating on his hands. One of the blisters had burst and she was removing the dead skin. Her touch was so light it didn't hurt a bit.

She smelled nice, he thought suddenly. Her head was bowed over his hand and her hair smelled citrusy, like tangerine...

What on earth was he thinking? He was starting to feel like some lovelorn teenager, fantasizing about what he could never have.

"She didn't tell me any secrets," Annabelle said, and he had to remind himself of what they'd been talking about. His normally incisive mind was doing all sorts of nonincisive things.

"You're sure?"

"I'm sure." She looked up then and he found that her clear hazel eyes were only inches from his. The look she gave him was direct and true. "I don't lie." She was meeting his challenge head-on now. Giving him the truth. "She was distressed and confused and terrified about her baby. She was rambling and incoherent. She made me promise to tell no one what she was saying—and I made that promise—but she said nothing that would help your investigation in any way. Do you think I'd withhold information that might find your baby a family?"

Their eyes were only inches apart, and her gaze never wavered. She'd told him the truth, her look said; now it was up to him to accept it.

"If you'd just tell me..."

"There's nothing to tell," she said, exasperated. "What she made me promise not to tell was meaningless ramblings of terror for her child. She was frightened that the baby might die. Ben and I tried to reassure her, but she was too badly injured to absorb the fact that the child was unhurt. I think she realized her husband was dead, or at least seriously injured, and she was linking the two."

Jaron stared back at her. She had him confounded. He just didn't know how to take her.

What was going on with him?

Did he believe her? He did, he decided. She was being direct. But...

"You won't tell me exactly what she said?"

"I promised not to and there's no need." She shook her head and a wisp of auburn curl trailed across the V where her crop top scooped down to her breasts. He had the craziest urge to...

Um, maybe not.

"You're not wondering about the baby yourself?" he managed to ask, and only he knew what an effort it was to keep his voice normal.

"I don't wonder about my patients." She broke eye contact then, bending back to apply salve, and he was aware of a sharp stab of loss.

Heck, he didn't react to women like this.

"Is that why you're an ER specialist?" he asked. "So you don't have to get close?"

"If I didn't want to get close, I'd be a radiologist. Or a pathologist. I'd spend my life looking at X rays or microscopes, rather than warm bodies."

"You know what I mean," he objected. "ER specialists see people as they walk in the door covered in blood or screaming in pain. They do the first-off stuff like stopping the bleeding or clearing the airways, and then it's over to the specialists for long-term care. You never get involved."

"And you do?"

"That's why I'm a detective," he said with just a trace of

smugness in his voice. He liked his job. He was good at it—and it did involve following through.

"You're saying you do more good in the world than I do?" she asked curiously, and he thought about it while she wound fresh gauze around his palms.

"Nope. But I'm not afraid of commitment."

"You sound like you're married to your job."

"Maybe I am."

"Well, I'm married to Harold." She clipped on a couple of smart little fasteners and stood back. "There you are, Detective Dorsey. Hands all better. Keep them clean and dry for another couple of days and you should be fine."

"You won't reconsider on the date?"

"You have all the information I have," she told him. "There's no need to bother plying me with strong drink."

"I hadn't actually thought of liquor," he said.

"But you were asking for a date to get information?"

"Yes." There was no use in denying it. With those eyes she could see a lie from twenty paces.

"There you go, then." She shook her head. "A wasted night saved."

"It wouldn't be a wasted night."

"No?"

"No," he said slowly. He shoved himself to his feet and stood, meeting those incredible eyes again. They were almost translucent. "It wouldn't be wasted. I wouldn't mind finding out what makes Annabelle Peters tick."

"It's you who should be the pathologist, then," she told him. "I've been to enough postmortems to realize that what makes me tick is exactly the same as what makes everyone else tick. A nice little mass of muscle called a heart—which is about as romantic as a fistful of spleen." She crossed to the door and held it wide. "Goodbye, Detective Dorsey."

"You won't reconsider?"

"Why should I reconsider?"

"My kids want to see you again."

That made her pause. "You were serious, then, about taking the kids?"

"I don't date without them." He didn't date, but she wasn't to know that.

"You asked me to dinner?"

"If you'd agreed, I would have gone, but I would have thought of it as work. Now I'm asking you for a proper date." It was true, he realized. Things had changed.

She chewed her lip. "What were you thinking of doing?"

She was wavering, he thought incredulously. She was wavering because of the kids.

"Ice-skating," he said. It was the first thing that came into his head. Ice-skating was something he and the kids often did on weekends, and he'd promised the kids they'd do it again soon. In truth, ice-skating was about the sum of his social life, so maybe…maybe a date should center around that. At least he'd know what to do.

"Ice-skating." She was staring at him as if he'd grown another head. "Are you out of your mind?"

"Why do I have to be out of my mind?"

"With those hands…"

"You're assuming I'd fall," he said, swelling his chest out a little. A man had some pride. "I don't."

"And if you do…"

"Then I'll need someone to catch me, apart from Ricky and Tina."

"So I'm invited to play catch."

"That's the plan. Hamburgers, fries and ice-skating. Take it or leave it, lady. As dates go, you can't get much more romantic than that."

She hesitated. She was still wavering, he thought, and felt astounded. This lady who kept herself to herself, content with her piano and her dog, seemed to be tempted by his kids and hamburgers and ice-skating.

"Not a late night," she said cautiously, and he nodded, full of virtue.

"The kids need to be home in bed. I only had them out late last night because they'd already been asleep."

"You can't ice-skate with those hands."

"I can. I told you. I don't fall. I'm not about to miss out on giving my kids a good time because of a few blisters on my hands."

"You're a dope."

"No." His voice was suddenly serious. He was serious. "I'm a single dad. I do what I need to do to survive. There are thousands of us out there, coping with kids when we feel lousy because there's no other choice. Now, if you'd like to come with us, you're very welcome, but we're going, anyway." He rose. "Thank you for fixing my hands."

She chewed her lip. "You really want me to come?"

"Yeah." He did.

"Not because of your Jane Doe?"

"I accept that you're telling the truth."

"So no more pressure?"

"Not tonight," he promised. "If I get any more desperate, I may resort to using a bit of boiling oil to make you tell every last syllable—just in case there's anything there we can use— but for tonight I'll leave it alone."

"And you'll come home early?"

"You scared you'll turn into a pumpkin?" he teased, and she flushed.

"It's just...I'm not accustomed..."

"I don't understand why the hell not," he growled, and then held up his hands. "Okay. I accept you're not gay." He thought of something and frowned. "You're not married, are you? There's no ex-Mr. Peters around?"

She grinned. "No way."

"There's no 'no way' about it," he told her. "Will you come?"

Would she? She chewed her lip some more and stared at him as if he were some sort of puzzle. Jaron wasn't sure he liked it. He wasn't sure of anything, he decided. This lady had him thoroughly confused.

But finally, she made up her mind.

"Okay," she said grudgingly, and he grinned.

"Gee, that's a gracious acceptance."

"You asked me for the worst-possible reasons," she told him. "You can't expect me to be grateful."

"I do expect you to relax enough to enjoy yourself. You think you can do that?"

She considered, and he could see that it was a really big request.

"I'll try," she said, and he couldn't expect any more than that.

"I'll pick you up at five?"

"I'll meet you at the skating rink."

"What sort of date is this, anyway," he grumbled. "I'll pick you up."

"It's the only sort of date available if you want me," she said. "I'll meet you there. Take it or leave it."

WHAT HAD SHE done?

Annabelle watched until the elevator doors closed after him and then retreated back into her apartment and closed the door. Harold looked up at her, his wise old eyes questioning.

"You're thinking I'm losing my mind," she said to him. "Maybe you're right." She crossed to the settee, heaved her dog's backside up so she could sit down, then let his rear end flop over her knees. This was her comfort position, as it had been for sixteen years, since her mother's friend had given her the dog in an attempt to make her feel loved.

She hadn't felt loved by the gesture—its consequences had left her appalled—but the eight-week-old Harold had wrapped himself around her heart and he'd been there ever since. Her one constant.

"I don't date," she murmured, and Harold gave her a soothing lick as much as to say, *Very wise, too. Dating's a bad idea.*

"I'm only going ice-skating with his kids."

"I wouldn't even do that."

"The guy's lonely." She was chatting to Harold but answering herself. It was the sort of conversation she was used to.

"Just tonight. Never again."

"What's wrong with dating?"

She sighed and rose and walked over to her piano. Some Rachmaninoff, she thought. Something sober.

What was wrong with dating?

Dating was for people who were looking for commitment. Annabelle had learned the hard way what commitment led to. She'd never had anyone committed to her, and she'd discovered early on that loving only led to heartbreak.

She played a few bars but it didn't sound right. She didn't feel sober enough for Rachmaninoff. She felt...different.

"He's nice," she told Harold, and Harold's old eyes regarded her with concern.

"You think I'm being a fool?"

There was silence, but Harold didn't sink into sleep again. He kept looking at her, sensing her trouble as only a dog can, but not knowing what to do about it.

"Okay, I'm being a fool," she whispered. "But it might just be fun."

Fun. Fun didn't play much of a part in Annabelle Peters's life. She worked, she studied, she kept to herself.

For thirty years.

"So out of thirty years, maybe I can afford one night of fun?"

"If that's all it is," she answered herself.

Oh, for heaven's sake. Ice-skating with a cop and a couple of kids. It'd be fun.

What else could it possibly be?

THE RINK was crowded. On Saturday nights, this was one of Seattle's favorite places to be, and it seemed as though every family in the downtown area was putting on skates.

Which was a problem.

The kids had put on their skates and so had Jaron, but the laces were beyond him. They should have been laced tightly, but as he hauled on Tina's laces, he winced. Hell, it hurt. And he had his own and Ricky's to go.

"So *this* is why you invited me?"

Jaron's head jerked up and Annabelle was laughing down at him.

"Hi."

And all he could think was *Wow!*

She was dressed all in white. White sweater with a huge turtleneck that hung loosely like a wonderful shawl. Tight, tight leggings that made her long legs look wonderful. White skates with gleaming silver blades. Her wonderful hair was caught back in a white ribbon and she looked for all the world like an ice princess.

She'd obviously been here for a while. She'd already been out on the rink, and her cheeks were flushed from effort. She was smiling and her gorgeous eyes were dancing, and Jaron darn near dropped the skate he was holding.

"Can I help?" She didn't wait for an answer but stooped to lace Tina's skates. Her hands brushed his and it was all he could do not to yelp. It was as if she packed an electric charge.

"You've obviously been here before," he said inanely, and she nodded, still intent on laces.

"Ice-skating's one of my very favorite things."

"You do it often?"

"Whenever I can." She moved on to Ricky's laces. "Hi, Ricky. Hi, Tina. Who's the best skater? You or your daddy."

That was easy. "We are, of course," Ricky told her. "Daddy sometimes sits down."

"Does he now?" She looked sideways at Jaron and grinned. "I can see that about him. He looks like a sitting-down sort of guy."

"Hey!"

But the kids were giggling. "I'm glad Daddy invited you," Tina told her, and she smiled at the little girl's confiding expression.

"I'm glad he invited me, too. I hope I get to see him sit down. Do you think I will?"

"He does it a lot," Tina told him.

"Do you mind?" Jaron was feeling out of his depth. They were all laughing at him—his kids and this gorgeous creature who seemed almost to have materialized out of nowhere. "A man has some pride."

"Of course he does," Annabelle said amicably. "Now sit back, Detective Dorsey, keep still and let Annabelle do up your laces."

SHE SKATED like a dream.

Jaron wasn't sure what he'd anticipated when he'd invited her to skate, but it certainly wasn't this. Maybe he'd had some idea that she'd be a rank amateur and he could help. Hold her up. Instead, she was gliding around him and the kids as though she'd been born on ice.

The place seemed to be full of people he knew, and most of them recognized Annabelle. He could see blank amazement on their faces as they watched her fly by. She must skate at times when families weren't there, he thought, or maybe this was a childhood skill never forgotten.

She had Tina in one hand and Ricky in another—encouraging them, swooping round and round the rink, skating in circles around him...

Making his head spin!

"What have you done with our Dr. Peters?" Jaron turned to see Ben Jessup beside him. Clutching Ben's hand was his little son, Doug, and on Ben's other side was Alexandra Weber.

Jaron knew this couple well. He'd met Alexandra when his kids were at Forrester Square Day Care and she'd been instrumental in setting up Round the Clock. Although she seemed to have delegated most of the responsibility for running Round the Clock to her stepsister, Shana, Alexandra was often there and the kids knew and loved her.

Ben was a pediatrician with a special interest in the troubled kids Jaron so often found himself dealing with. Like Jaron, Ben had lost his wife in tragic circumstances.

When Jaron heard that these two were engaged, the news had pleased him. They were two special people. Doug was beaming with all the confidence of a kid who knew these grown-ups were his. With Alexandra and his dad beside him, he could conquer the world.

"It's great to see you out," Alexandra said softly, smiling at him and then following Ben's gaze to where Annabelle was playing with Jaron's kids. "Annabelle. Wow!"

"You know Dr. Peters?" Ben asked, and she nodded.

"Her apartment is next to Shana's. But she doesn't mix much."

"She's thought of as definitely frosty by the medical staff," Ben said wonderingly. "She doesn't so much as have a cup of coffee with us if she doesn't have to. And here she is tugging Jaron's kids around the rink like she's a mommy. What gives, Jaron?"

"I asked her out and she came," Jaron said, trying not to sound smug. Which was impossible.

"Well done." Ben was watching Annabelle swoop around them in a wide semicircle. "She's quite something!"

"Hey," Alexandra said, and swiped him with her scarf.

"I mean she would be quite something if I wasn't happily settled with the lady of my dreams," Ben amended, grinning. "But Annabelle's only seen in white coats at work. She keeps that amazing hair pulled back, and I don't think I've ever seen her smile. This is some transformation."

"Tell me what you know about her," Jaron said.

"Why?" Ben's eyes narrowed in interest. "Are you working on a crime together, something to do with our mystery baby. Or is it the lady you're interested in?"

"Shut up, Ben." Alexandra was grinning. "Look at her. You think he's interested in a crime scene?"

"Maybe not." Ben followed Annabelle's progress for a while longer. They all did. "She came from New Jersey with a string of references like you wouldn't believe," he said at last. "Since she's been here, she's gone from strength to strength. The powers that be are still patting themselves on the back for getting her.''

"Why?"

"She's ambitious, she's smart, she works herself to death, and she lets nothing stand in the way of her medicine.'' He hesitated. "Except her dog. We had to have a special meeting of the board to get permission for her to keep that damned dog in her hospital apartment. You see how much we wanted the lady?''

"I've met the dog,'' Jaron told them. "It's more a throw rug than a dog. I can't see the board taking exception.''

"You've met the dog?'' Ben's brows rose in astonishment. He opened his mouth to say something, but caught Alexandra's eye and shut it again.

"We need to keep going, Ben,'' Alexandra said serenely. "Doug's getting bored.'' The little boy was tugging the grown-ups' hands with impatience.

"The things we do.'' Ben gave a theatrical groan. "Come on, my soon-to-be wife.''

Jaron's gaze went to Alexandra's hand and the sparkling diamond on her finger.

"Have you two set a date?''

"We've decided on a June wedding,'' Ben told him. "We'd like to have the reception outdoors.''

"That's fantastic!'' Jaron smiled at the pair of them, his pleasure genuine. Alexandra was a lovely person. She'd been through a hell of a time over the past year or so, and she deserved all the happiness in the world. And now, by the way Ben was looking at her and Doug was clutching her hand, it seemed she'd finally found it.

But overriding his pleasure at his friends' happiness was something else. He was aware of his gut twisting into something that could only be envy.

He and Cathy had been like this. Once.

His eyes strayed back to the rink. Annabelle had caught Tina and was whirling her around and around, making giant circles with her on the ice. Ricky was squealing for his turn, and the three of them were laughing and alive and…

And it was only transitory, Jaron thought. Ben and Alexandra were a family forever. He and Annabelle, they were a family for the night. Tomorrow he'd be back to being on his own again.

Somehow he switched his attention back to Ben and Alexandra, and he found them watching him with more than a hint of curiosity.

"Are your hands stopping you from skating?" Ben asked.

Jaron shook his head. "Nope. I'll join them now."

"Don't let us stop you," Ben said lightly, but Jaron realized; it wasn't just Ben and Alexandra stopping him and Annabelle from playing happy families. They had nothing in common. Annabelle was a loner and he was a widower.

And never the twain shall meet.

Ben, Alexandra and Doug skated on, leaving Jaron looking after them with a deep feeling of longing.

He really missed Cathy.

He turned and looked back at his kids. Annabelle was squatting now, crossing her arms Cossack style and spinning and spinning while Ricky and Tina squealed in wonder.

"Come and see," Tina yelled to him. "Daddy, come and see us. Isn't Annabelle wonderful?"

Yes, he thought. Yes, she is.

The vision of Cathy receded. Annabelle was waiting.

THEY SKATED until hunger drove them from the rink. They ate hamburgers and fries, and then, after such a nutritious meal, Annabelle decided they needed to skate some more.

"Or I won't fit into my skating outfit," she told him, and Jaron looked at her gorgeous leggings and thought she barely fitted into them now. There wasn't a spare inch of room for anything.

"Do you want to skate again?" Annabelle asked.

"I don't know whether I can," he confessed. "Maybe that second hamburger was a bad idea."

"You can watch from the side," Annabelle told him kindly, "if your hamburgers are weighing you down." Her eyes creased in concern. "Or if your hands are hurting."

"My hands aren't hurting." He was no longer noticing his hands.

"Or if you're feeling a bit frail."

"You make me sound like I'm a hundred," he complained. "Just tuck me up in my blanket and park my wheelchair on the side."

"But you are rather old," Annabelle said, considering. "Isn't he, kids?"

"He's really old," Tina agreed. "He says he used to be able to do loop-the-loops when he was a boy."

"But that must have been centuries ago," Annabelle declared. "Did they have ice-skating rinks when you were a boy, Mr. Dorsey, or did you tie bear hide on your feet and skate on the river?"

How could he sit on the sidelines and watch after that? Goaded, he returned to the rink and found himself doing loop-the-loops and things he'd almost forgotten he ever learned.

And he didn't think of his hands once.

EVERYTHING HAD to end.

The kids started stumbling, their fatigue showing, and it was time to go. Annabelle unfastened everyone's laces, which did exactly nothing for Jaron's state of mind. How could a woman unlacing his skates seem so damned erotic? They made their way to the parking lot, Jaron carrying Tina, while Ricky stumbled gamely beside him, clutching Annabelle's hand and trying not to let on how tired he really was.

They'd had a wonderful night, Jaron thought gratefully. The kids would remember this forever. But then he asked himself, Why? Why had tonight seemed so different from the nights when he'd brought the kids here alone?

It was Annabelle, he decided. Of course it was Annabelle. She lit up places he didn't know had been dark.

How could he bear to leave?

They'd come separately and he expected to walk her to her car, but she turned toward the cab rank.

"You didn't drive?" he said.

"Some cowboy parked behind me in the hospital parking lot," she confessed. "It was catch a cab or stay at home."

"I could have collected you."

"I'm fine."

"Well, you're not taking a cab home," he told her firmly. "Is she, kids? Last night you took us in your car. Tonight it's my turn."

THEY WERE SILENT until he pulled up by the hospital entry. The children were verging on sleep. Tina seemed to have succumbed, but Ricky was holding on to the ends of his glorious day.

Like his dad, he didn't want it to end.

"Can we see you again?" Jaron asked, and Annabelle hesitated. They were sitting in his ancient wagon—much more sensible than Annabelle's Noddy car, but not nearly as much fun. Seattle had remembered that it was October, and tonight was misty with rain. The car seemed warm and intimate, but Annabelle had to leave.

"I don't date," she said at last, and he thought about that for a while before responding.

"What about tonight?"

"Tonight wasn't a date."

"No?"

"No."

"Then tomorrow isn't, either," he told her. "It'll be just me and the kids. The forecast's good again. How about coming for a bike ride?"

"Ooh, yes," Ricky murmured, and for a moment Jaron thought Annabelle would agree.

But she glanced back at the child's eager face, and it seemed as if something within her closed down.

"I can't," she told him. "I need to look after Harold tomorrow."

"Who's Harold?" Ricky asked.

"Harold's my family."

"Your family's pretty small."

"It is," she said gently. "That's the way I like it. Good night, Ricky. When Tina wakes up, tell her I said goodbye."

She climbed from the car, with Jaron standing in the misty rain holding the door for her.

"There's no need to play the gentleman," she said, and he smiled.

"I can't help it. I am one."

"Of course." Once more that gorgeous smile. "Sorry. How silly of me to imply otherwise."

"You really can't come bike riding tomorrow?"

"No."

"Annabelle…" He paused. The hospital entrance was brilliantly lit and humming with activity. Saturday night was normally frantic and tonight was no exception. There was the scream of distant sirens. A couple of ambulances were pulled up in the entrance. While they stood watching, an ER team hauled someone from one of the ambulances. Another trauma case.

Annabelle's world was pulling her back in.

"I need to go."

"You're off duty."

She smiled, but the smile had changed. She'd moved on. "Yes, but I still need to go. Thank you for tonight."

"No." He lifted his bandaged hand and touched her cheek with the back of his fingers. She had the softest skin. She felt…

He didn't know how she felt. How long since he'd touched a woman like that?

He felt a shudder ripple right through his body. Heaven knew whether she could feel it, but it was uncontrollable.

She didn't move. His hand was tracing the contour of her cheek. Her face was tilted to his, a mute invitation.

His need was reflected in her eyes.

The kids were waiting in the car. A misty rain was falling

on Annabelle and him. The lights of the hospital entrance were garish and intrusive.

It didn't matter. Nothing mattered. At this moment only the two of them existed. One man and one woman.

His hands cupped her face, she looked wonderingly into his eyes—and he kissed her.

CHAPTER EIGHT

IT BLEW HIM AWAY.

Jaron felt her mouth under his and he thought, quite simply, that nothing had ever felt so wonderful.

Once maybe…with Cathy.

No. What he had had with Cathy had been fantastic, but memories don't stick around for as long as you'd hope. The way Cathy had felt, had tasted, had blurred into the mist of a loving past. There'd been nights lately when he'd lain awake and tried to conjure up the feel of her, the wonder…

Now wasn't Cathy. Annabelle was a far cry from his wife, but that was the wonder of it. She was so different. A whole, sweet, new beginning.

She wasn't his past, memories laced with pain, as well as pleasure. She was now.

The future? Who knew? He didn't care. For this moment there was only now.

She was so soft. So sweet. Her hair was silky under his hands. Her curls had fallen forward and were brushing his fingers as he deepened the kiss. Her mouth was pliant and lovely. Her lips were parting, welcoming him as he searched deeper, wanting to know all of her. Her body was molding to his. He could feel her breasts against his chest…

Yes!

His whole body was screaming its needs. He'd been alone too long. Too damned long.

Annabelle…

His hands dropped to her waist, pulling her in tight against him, and she stirred and lifted her hands to run her fingers through his hair. As if in wonder.

That was what this whole night was. Wonder.

That was what this woman was.

It wasn't enough. He was kissing her, teasing her, wanting her, but the hospital was bustling behind them. It was almost as if the building itself was waiting for her, and his kids were in the car behind them waiting for him.

He broke away, somehow, and felt a sharp jab of loss as she drew back and gazed up at him.

"Come home with us," he managed to say, and his voice was hoarse with a passion he hardly recognized.

She smiled then, but her smile was tremulous. She was as shaken as he was, he thought, and felt almost triumphant. Whatever he was feeling, it wasn't one-sided.

"No."

He was holding her around the waist, searching her face.

"No?" He'd expected it, he realized, but he didn't have to like it now he had it.

"You must see it's impossible." She cast an uncertain glance toward the car. "You have kids. I don't think one-night stands are an option."

"I don't think," he said huskily, "that this is any one-night stand."

Her face closed at that. He'd almost forgotten the barricades, the no-dates decree she'd given. It had receded in the night as if it didn't exist. But here it was again, inexplicable but real.

"It was a lovely night," she said softly, but there was a hint, or maybe more than a hint, of reserve in her voice. "I enjoyed it. I enjoyed meeting your kids." She gave the ghost of a smile. "I've even enjoyed kissing you good-night. But that's it, Jaron. I need to go. Harold's waiting for me."

"But—"

"I don't get close."

"Annabelle—"

"Leave it, Jaron."

"I need to see you again." He was still holding her, loath to let her go. Thinking of reasons to prolong the moment.

And he thought of the wrong one.

"I need to interview you again about our Jane Doe."

Mistake. On a scale of one to ten it was right up there at number one hundred. Her face shut down as if he'd slapped her.

"What do you want to know about our Jane Doe?"

"Nothing. I mean…" She'd hauled herself out of his grasp, and her color was mounting. She was standing under one of the huge entrance floodlights, where he'd parked to let her out of the car. Dressed all in white with that amazing hair and two splashes of angry crimson on her cheeks, she looked stunning, he thought. And he'd made her angry. It was hardly the way he wanted this evening to end.

"Good," she told him. "Because there's nothing to tell. I'm tired of it, Jaron. I hate that she died. I hate that her baby's orphaned. But I've moved on. I must."

He took a deep breath and blotted out the fact that she looked beautiful. "I can't move on."

"Why not?"

"My job is to find out who she is—why she and her husband were driving a stolen car, who the family is that'll take on the long-term care of the baby."

"And my job is to take care of the next Jane Doe who comes through the door of the emergency room. I might have a dozen heart-wrenching cases a day, Jaron. I can't afford to get involved with a single one of them."

"And that's why you're an ER specialist? Because you don't want to get involved?"

She thought about it, her face still and expressionless. Whatever passion she'd felt for him had been put firmly away.

"Yes," she said at last.

"You don't ever get involved."

"No."

"It makes for a pretty barren life."

"Look after your own life," she snapped. "Leave mine alone. It suits me."

"You'll let a baby suffer..."

"I will *not* let a baby suffer." She was practically shouting at him. "Will you get it into your thick skull that I know nothing? Everything I know, you know. I might not be a bleeding heart, but I do care. I gave you every piece of information that could possibly be useful."

"Maybe it's me who should decide what's useful."

It was almost as if he was driving her away, he thought, somehow dispassionate in the face of her fury. He'd held her and he'd kissed her but...

But what was between them had no future. Not now.

Was that why he'd made her angry?

"Thank you for the evening," she said stiffly, controlling her temper with visible effort. "I enjoyed it. But as for anything else, if you want to interview me, you'll have to make it official. Do it through Seth and I'll answer any questions the hospital tells me to. Nothing more."

"So it's back on a business footing?"

"What else did you expect?" she said bitterly, and turned and walked away from him—back into the hospital where she belonged.

He was left staring after her, wondering why he'd done what he'd done.

"Why did you make Annabelle mad?" Ricky asked, and Jaron had no answer to give him.

No answer at all.

ANNABELLE'S NIGHT wasn't over yet. Seth was in the hospital foyer. He'd been talking to the hospital porter, but when he saw her, he pushed himself to his feet and intercepted her on the way to the elevators.

"Hi."

"Hi." Her tone was wary. It was late on a Saturday night. This wasn't the normal time for the hospital's public-relations officer to be here.

It meant trouble.

"Can I talk to you?"

"You've been waiting for me?"

His smile didn't reach his eyes. "You weren't answering your phone and word is you don't stay out late on Saturday nights. I hoped you'd be in soon."

Word is that you don't stay out late on Saturday nights. Annabelle bit her lip. She knew she had a reputation for being aloof. She hadn't realized, though, that her social life—or lack of it—was talked about, as well.

"You've been waiting long?"

"Half an hour." He gave a rueful grin, falling into step beside her as they walked on to the elevator. "It kept me away from my office."

"What's wrong with your office?"

"It's inundated." He grimaced. "Half-a-dozen reporters and cameramen seem to have taken up residence in the corridor."

She thought about that. "Because of the baby?"

"Because of the baby."

"And you think I can help?"

"You dropped us into this mess in the first place."

She shook her head. "No. Jaron Dorsey dropped us into this mess by implying I know things I don't."

"Jaron accused you publicly of withholding information." Seth punched the elevator button and Annabelle thought, he's planning on coming up to my apartment. She didn't like it. She kept work and home separate, but more and more the boundary was blurring.

"I'm not withholding any information at all." The elevator arrived and she stepped in, decisive and formal. Dismissive. But Seth was in no mood to be dismissed. He walked right in after her and hit the button to the tenth floor. Her floor.

"Look, I don't know what you want," she said, but he shook his head.

"Time."

"You're planning an inquisition?"

"I'm planning on coffee," Seth told her. "So you're going

to give me some. Look, Annabelle, I know you wouldn't with-hold information that could help, but I do know that between the pair of you, you've given the public the impression that the hospital's being less than helpful. The press can't get near the baby—Keith's taken her to his cabin…''

"You're saying you'd rather she was here so the photogra-phers could spend the weekend taking photographs?'' Her tone was incredulous.

"No.'' He lifted her hand away from the Open button and pressed Close. The elevator started its smooth path to the tenth floor. "Of course not. We took a couple of pictures before Keith left and we've distributed them.''

"That's not enough?''

"Nothing's ever going to be enough in this case,'' he said wearily. "It has everything the press loves. A baby no one knows. A stolen car. Mystery parents. Violent death. And now a bit of corporate cover-up.''

"I didn't cover anything up.'' She spoke through clenched teeth, her anger building.

But Seth was unmoved. "I know that, but it doesn't matter anymore whether you did or you didn't. That's the way they see it.''

She shook her head in confusion as the elevator arrived at the tenth floor and she stepped out into her lobby. This nor-mally felt like coming home. She wanted to open her apartment door, walk inside and slam it after her.

She wanted out—but Seth wasn't letting her off the hook.

"Jaron says you made a promise.''

"To tell no one?'' She sighed. "I did. But I honestly can't think of anything she said that I haven't already told you.''

"It's a pity no one else overheard.''

"Why?'' She glared at him. "Men! You think you're so dispassionate.''

"And you're not passionate?'' He was waiting for her to open her door. "Maybe you're too close.''

"And you're too pressured. You want the press off your

back—otherwise you wouldn't be pushing me to give you information I don't have.''

"You're right of course." She'd put her key in the lock and now he pushed the door open and held it for her. "Just give me a break, Annabelle," he told her. "Give me a cup of coffee and breathing space until I have to face them again." He bent to pat Harold, who'd roused himself for a welcome. "Introduce me to your dog. Be nice for a change."

"I'm always nice." She wasn't feeling nice. She was feeling furious.

"No," he told her thoughtfully. "No, you're not nice, Dr. Peters. You give the impression of being as cold as ice. That's certainly the impression you've given Jaron Dorsey. Is that deliberate? Is that the impression you want him to keep?"

Annabelle thought back to ten minutes ago. Was it only ten minutes? It seemed as if she could still feel the pressure of Jaron's mouth on hers, the way his hands had tugged her body into his, the way her breasts had molded against his chest...

The feel of him. The arrant maleness. The sensation of tying his laces while his kids giggled. The feeling of eating burgers and fries as a family would. The warmth...

What had Seth said? Cold as ice? Was that the impression she wanted Jaron to keep?

It had better be, she told herself. Otherwise she'd be in deep trouble.

Maybe she was in trouble, anyway.

"Annabelle?" Seth was talking to her and she was a million miles away. She forced herself back to what he was saying.

"I want a press conference," he told her. He was looking at her oddly. As if he'd thought he knew who she was, but now wasn't so sure. He might well be confused, she thought. She wasn't making much sense to herself.

"A press conference?"

"Tomorrow morning," he told her with exaggerated patience. "Ten o'clock. With you and Jaron both available for questions."

"I'm off duty tomorrow."

"Where this case is concerned, you're never off duty," he said grimly. "I don't know what sort of isolated world you're living in, Dr. Peters, but in this instance, isolation is a thing of the past. This hospital is in this up to its neck, and if you value your job, then that means you."

"I—"

"Just give me a coffee," he said wearily. And then he gazed around at the apartment walls. "And tell me who the hell took all these pictures?"

DAMNED WOMAN!

Why couldn't he go to sleep? Jaron stared at the ceiling and swore to himself. She'd gotten under his skin—and women didn't get under his skin. Not since Cathy. He'd hardly been aware there was another sex since Cathy's death, and why this particular woman had the power to wake him up out of his sexless indifference...

She was cold. She was coolly professional. She wasn't the least bit like Cathy.

But the thought of her as he'd seen her at her apartment slipped back into his mind. Annabelle, with her long, bare legs and her hair floating free, with her muddle of sheet music, her fantastic photography, her ancient dog and her delightful, jumbled apartment...

He stirred uneasily, aware that more than just his mind was being disturbed by the memory.

That kiss...

He clenched his hands and released them, trying to make himself relax. He'd kissed her and she'd tasted wonderful. He'd let that fabulous hair slip through his fingers, silky and beautiful. He'd felt the soft yielding of her body.

He wanted her.

And he'd made her furious.

"Yeah, good one, Dorsey," he muttered to himself in the dark. "You're attracted to a woman so you make her hate you. You imply she's a liar."

Maybe she was.

But he knew damned well she wasn't.

He didn't want to see her again, he thought, but then, that was impossible. Seth had rung just before he'd gone to bed and told him he'd set up a press conference at ten the next morning.

With Annabelle.

"Damn." He thumped his pillows and then groaned, got up and crossed to his window, where he stood and looked out over the city. It wasn't far from here to the hospital. If he could just crane his neck to see around the couple of skyscrapers in between, he could even see Annabelle's window.

Dear God, what on earth was he thinking?

"You're losing your mind, kiddo," he told himself. "Cathy's been dead for too long."

She had.

But while he tossed and turned in bed for an hour or so longer, it wasn't Cathy he was thinking of.

It was very definitely Annabelle.

SUNDAY MORNING. Annabelle awoke and let her mind drift for so long that Harold put his front paws up on her bedcovers to investigate why his breakfast and early-morning walk weren't happening.

"I'm sorry." She rumpled his old ears and hugged him close. "I'm a million miles away."

Harold was less than impressed.

"Okay." She threw back the bedcovers and looked out the window. The sun was breaking through a light scattering of clouds, and weak rays were already drifting into her window. It promised to be a gorgeous autumn day.

She had to go to a press conference. With Jaron. The thought made her feel ill.

"How about we go for a drive in the country as soon as I'm finished?" she asked her dog. "That should cheer us up."

Harold looked at her, a pained expression on his face, and she nodded.

"Yeah, right. Cheering up isn't in the cards for either of us."

OBEYING SOME BASIC instinct of self-preservation, Annabelle decided to go formal for the press conference. She arrived at the hospital auditorium wearing ER clothes—plain pants and shirt covered with a crisp white coat. Her stethoscope was dangling from her pocket, her hair was braided and neat, and she looked cool, efficient and entirely professional.

Her appearance was a shield, she decided. But maybe she needed as strong a shield as she could find.

Jaron and Seth were waiting in the auditorium.

The men were wearing dark suits and ties. Maybe they'd had the same feelings she'd had. Seth normally wore a suit, but it was the first time she'd seen Jaron in one.

He cleaned up well, she thought, her stomach doing a queer little lurch at the sight of him. He'd removed the dressings from his hands and he looked businesslike and entirely professional. A cop in charge of his case, promising a smooth investigation and every hope of a successful outcome.

Maybe it was a front, but in this environment, with a hostile press—there must be twenty or thirty cameramen and journalists, Annabelle realized—they'd need all the veneer they could manage.

"Hello, Annabelle." Seth smiled warmly across at her, but whether the smile was for her or for the benefit of the cameras already being pointed at them, she couldn't tell.

Jaron was smiling, too, but his smile was strained and it didn't reach his eyes. What had been between them the night before seemed light-years away.

He'd kissed her? Ha! There was nothing between them at all.

She could be politely pleasant, she decided, and maybe that was the only way to play this. "Mr. Nannery. Detective Dorsey." She aimed a perfunctory smile at the pair of them and sat down at the prepared table, afraid her knees might buckle beneath her. Jaron sat down beside her, her shoulder brushing his sleeve. The contact made her feel even colder and she gave an involuntary shudder.

She felt ill.

It didn't get any better.

This was what might well be termed a hostile press. It wasn't just Seattle press, she discovered. There were journalists here from most of the major national dailies. They didn't let up—and it was Annabelle they were aiming for.

"You were the treating doctor. You were there as she died. What were your impressions of the woman? You must have some impressions."

"What did she say to you?"

"Did she give any idea that she knew her husband was dead?"

"Did she seem as if she could have a criminal background? Was she hiding something?"

"What did she say to you about the baby?"

This was like a barrage from an automatic rifle, Annabelle thought helplessly. One question after another, leaving no chance for her to catch her breath between volleys.

Seth and Jaron were seated on either side of Annabelle, but the journalists seemed focused only on her. Maybe they saw her as the weakest link. She was aware of flashbulbs going off all the time. She couldn't focus on the questioners—her eyes hurt.

"I don't know anything more. You must believe me." She wasn't used to this. Any minute now she'd burst into tears, she thought, and how professional would that be?

"I think it's time to back off. Dr. Peters has had enough." For a moment she couldn't believe she'd heard right, but the interjection came from Jaron. He leaned over and put a hand on hers, as if to stop her from doing something she might regret.

Like what? she thought wildly. Bursting into tears in front of the press? Yes, she would regret that.

"Dr. Peters has been given a hard time because of an inadvertent comment of mine," Jaron was saying smoothly. "As you know, I was involved in the accident itself. I helped pull the woman and her baby from the burning car, and by the time I reached the hospital, I was emotionally involved and I was entirely unprofessional. I harangued Dr. Peters to demand the woman give us her name, and Dr. Peters responded, quite rightly, that her first priority was saving the woman's life. As far as I know, Dr. Peters did try to get the woman to give her a name, but when a name wasn't forthcoming, she didn't press it. Dr. Peters decided, in conjunction with her colleagues, that they couldn't wait any longer to operate. The woman died under anesthesia. That's all there is to it.''

"We have inside information that there was conflict," one of the reporters said. "You were heard arguing."

Annabelle flinched, but Jaron nodded, as if the question didn't disturb him at all.

"Yes. I was demanding Dr. Peters hold the anesthetic until we had an identity. As I said, I was entirely out of line. There's not a doctor in this hospital who doesn't agree with the decision Dr. Peters made. She had a woman dying under her hands and she was trying to save her."

"Do you believe Dr. Peters is withholding information?" the reporter asked, and Annabelle caught her breath.

But Jaron was shaking his head.

"Dr. Peters wishes very much to find the baby's family. As we all do. To that end there's not a single one of us who's not pulling out all the stops, pooling all known information, to get a lead. You guys can help by headlining it. I'm sending detectives upstate to sift through information. By this evening we'll have artists' impressions of the mother and a rough description of the father. We'd like as much publicity as we can get on this one."

"The picture Nannery's given us of the baby is useless," one of the cameramen complained. "Hell, it could be one of thousands. If you want headlines, we need something better. Give us access and we'll take some decent pictures."

"The baby's been traumatized and she needs quiet," Seth interjected. "I'm afraid I can't permit access."

But Jaron was formulating an idea. This could get the press back onside. Maybe…

"Dr. Peters is an excellent amateur photographer," he said thoughtfully. "I imagine she'll be checking on the baby today. How about if she runs off a roll of film and lets you people have it by this evening? You can do whatever you like with the shots."

"How do we know she's any good?"

"Oh, she's good," Jaron said softly. His eyes were resting on Annabelle's face, and they were suddenly warm. So warm she felt her face flush with heat. "She's very, very good. Believe me."

"I'd agree with that," Seth added. "I've seen her work and it's fantastic. And now, if that's all, ladies and gentlemen, we'll wind it up."

"BRILLIANT, JARON," Seth closed the door of the auditorium, blocking out the press, and let his breath out in a gusty sigh of relief. "You took the heat off us and you made Annabelle helpful. If she takes good shots of the baby, the hospital just might get back to being the good guys in all this. You two go up to Keith's cabin right away and make sure the shots are excellent. Use a variety of backdrops—that way each publication can have a different one. And not just formal shots. Informal. Nice. Shots to make people want to look at the kid." He thought about it and grinned. "Hey, maybe we can charge for them."

"Maybe Annabelle can charge for them," Jaron told him. "She's the one with the talent."

"She got us into this mess. She can get us out again."

"That's hardly fair." Jaron suddenly felt Annabelle's strained silence. He looked at her face and found it white and drawn.

"Are you okay?"

"I'm fine," she managed to say, and then, because she really had appreciated it, she added, "Thanks for coming to my rescue in there."

"Rescuing maidens in distress is my specialty," he said, smiling. "Like photography is yours."

"I've never taken pictures like this."

"No?"

"No. My photography's private."

"You'll get the hospital out of a hole if you can do it," Seth told her bluntly. "In fact you don't have a choice. If you can't do it, then buy some baby photos…I don't know, anything. Just keep the press off my back. We've got a philanthropist sniffing around at the moment, just aching to give us a really healthy donation, and I don't want him put off by this."

"But no pressure, right?" Annabelle said, and Seth had the grace to grin.

"Don't mention it." He nodded formally to Jaron. "You'll go with her? Cop holding rescued baby? They'll love it."

"Hey, you're not taking pictures of me." Jaron backed away. "I don't need to go."

"You do need to go," Seth said bluntly. "You owe us. You agreed that your public comments about Annabelle's lack of cooperation got us into this mess. From now on I want police and hospital staff working in full cooperation. Publicly. Where are your kids? I know Sunday's a bad day for you, but maybe they could go with you?"

"They're at Cathy's mother's until after lunch." There was a note of strain in his voice and Annabelle cast him a curious glance. Things were going on that she didn't understand.

But Seth wasn't worried about undertones. "Well, where's the problem, then? Go now. The pair of you. Scoot."

"Scoot?" Annabelle echoed, and Seth smiled again.

"Yep, scoot. That's an order."

Jaron sighed. So he needed to scoot? With Annabelle? He glared at Seth, but Seth wasn't giving an inch. "Fine, then," he snapped. 'I was going to wash the car."

"You can't wash your car with those hands," Annabelle told him, and he glared at her, too.

But he conceded. What else was a man to do? "I need to

get out of my suit first." He yanked his tie loose and still felt hot, but Seth wasn't in a sympathetic mood.

"Go home and get changed," Seth told him, "but be quick."

"I'll be in pathology." Annabelle sounded bemused. "I want to go over the autopsy reports."

"There you are, then." Seth even smiled. "What could be better? Jaron, meet the lady outside the morgue. As a dating service, I can't think of a better place to start a relationship, can you?"

HE'D BEEN OUTMANEUVERED. The last thing Jaron wanted today was to drive up to Keith's cabin with Annabelle beside him. At least, he *thought* it was the last thing he wanted. Was it really?

He didn't know.

Hell, he didn't know anything!

CHAPTER NINE

BY THE TIME he returned to the hospital, Annabelle had changed into jeans and a windbreaker. She'd left her hair braided—which was a pity—but the rest of her...she looked cool and casual and very, very lovely.

Jaron took this all in through the glass doors leading to pathology. She was seated alone at a desk, and her long braid of flaming hair fell forward on the table. She was sifting through a pile of papers, chewing a fingernail with intensity.

She looked about eighteen, he thought. Untouched.

Untouched but very, very desirable.

Put your hormones back in place, he ordered himself sharply. What wasn't needed today was emotional involvement of any sort. The kiss last night had been an aberration, to be forgotten before things got out of hand. Professional things.

He pushed the doors open and gave himself another mental kick when she smiled up at him. That smile was enough to knock a man sideways.

Stay professional!

"H—hi." His voice sounded ridiculous even to him. Like a schoolboy on his first date.

She glanced at him again, but in an absent way. She, at least, had her mind on work. "Do you want to see the autopsy report?"

"Summarize it for me," he growled, hauling up a chair. He knew autopsy reports. He'd read a lot in his time—he'd even sat in on a few autopsies—but he'd never gotten better at keeping his squeamishness under control. The pathologist wouldn't miss a thing. It'd all be there right down to what…well, it'd all be there.

He might be a case-hardened cop, but he didn't have to like this sort of stuff.

"There's not much we don't already know," she told him. She was concentrating on the report, not on him, and her detachment let him get his thoughts back into some sort of order and concentrate on what she was saying. "I checked in and saw John Doe on the slab. It wasn't pretty, but it gave me an idea of the type you should be trying to identify."

"So?"

"So as a couple we have an IC1 male and female. Male late thirties, five-eleven or so, wiry, lean, lantern-jawed type. There's an old hip fracture. He might well have walked with a slight limp. The cause of death was multiple injuries—the severity of the skull fracture means death would have been instantaneous."

"And the mother?"

"Mid- to late thirties. Five-seven. Fine-boned, a bit like her husband in build, only shorter. Fair hair curling to her shoulders, blue eyes, freckles, pierced ears but no earrings, a wedding ring but no other jewelry, appendix scar, scarring from a past birth, signs that she gave birth again about four weeks back. The staff have taken photographs of her—I gather that someone from your office collected the pictures and is using an artist to draw up a likeness."

But Jaron was concentrating on what he'd heard.

"The older birth scars are confirmed, then? There's definitely another child somewhere."

"Mmm."

"I don't like it."

"You think I do?"

"How old?"

"Tricky to say. The pathologists say that by the look of the scarring, maybe two years or more."

"If there's a kid out there with no parents… Hell, if they left the kid at home while they took off…"

But Annabelle was shaking her head. "If the parents were the type who'd leave a toddler uncared for, they'd hardly have snuggled their new baby into a car seat, taking as much care as they obviously had. Our baby's been loved and cherished. These parents weren't neglectful. It doesn't make sense."

"But the car was stolen..."

"It doesn't matter. They still took good care of their baby."

"You don't know that for sure."

"No. But I can comfort myself by accepting it as probable. Meanwhile we'll do our darnedest to find out who they are."

We'll do our darnedest. He thought that through and found it ludicrous. "You..."

"Contrary to what you think of me, I care," she flared. "I'm doing what Seth suggested—driving up to Keith's cabin to take some pictures. And I'll even—" She took a deep breath. "I'll even put up with you for the morning."

"Gee, thanks."

"Think nothing of it," she snapped, laying down the autopsy report with a loud thump. "Let's get this over with, shall we? Now."

THEY TOOK Annabelle's car, "because it's more fun than your wagon and Harold loves it."

"We're taking Harold?" It was a stupid question. When Jaron came down to the parking lot, Harold was already settled in the back seat of the Noddy car, looking thoroughly appreciative of the treat in store, and Annabelle was at the wheel.

"Of course we're taking Harold. Harold wouldn't miss a drive in the country for the world. Why can't we take your kids? Wouldn't they enjoy it, too?"

"I told you they're at their grandmother's."

She glanced at him as she steered out of the parking lot. "So your kids are having lunch with their grandmother. Aren't you invited?"

"No." The single syllable was clipped and hard and she thought about changing the subject. The old Annabelle would have. The Annabelle of two days ago.

But Annabelle had changed a bit in the past couple of days. She'd had Seth and Jaron into her apartment. She'd gone skating with this man's kids. She'd become involved, like it or not.

"Cathy's mother doesn't like you?" she asked cautiously, and got a grimace in reply.

"She hates me."

"Because?"

"Because I'm a cop but I didn't protect my own family. Hazel thinks it's my fault that Cathy died. Of course. I was out chasing other villains when villains were killing my wife."

"But…you could have been at the pub or gone out for a quart of milk. It's hardly fair."

"Grief isn't fair," he said flatly. "Hazel has to blame someone and I'm here. I'm alive and her daughter isn't."

"Oh, Jaron—"

"Leave it. I'm over it."

"I'm sure you're not."

He shrugged. "Well, I've learned to put it on a back burner. Like you've done with your shadows."

"Shadows?" she said, startled.

He nodded. "Shadows. Try telling me that you had a Brady Bunch upbringing and I won't believe you."

"Why not?"

"Because you're gorgeous, you're funny, you're sensitive and you're clever—yet you've built yourself an armor thicker than mine."

"How can you say that?"

"It's not true?" He eyed her closely. The wind was blowing her hair. Her braid was working free and he loved the way her curls wisped around her face. She looked carefree and unfettered, but he knew that the impression was a long way from the truth.

"When you graduated as a doctor," he said carefully, watching her face, "who came to the ceremony?"

Silence. Her face closed down.

"Who?" he pressed.

"I have a cousin…"

"No one else?"

"That's none of your business," she said at last, and he nodded.

"No, it's not. But don't deny you have shadows."

Harold chose that moment to stick his head through the gap between them—just to check that the world was okay in the front half of the car—and Jaron took a minute to fondle the old dog's ears and shove him back to where he ought to be. It also gave Annabelle enough time to get her face in order.

"Why did you move to Seattle?" he asked.

"I like Seattle."

"Hmm." He grinned. "Great weather."

"It is," she said defiantly. "Look at today. This is a real Indian summer. You couldn't get weather more perfect than today."

"We're not," he said carefully, still watching her, "actually talking about the weather. Tell me why you moved."

"I got a job as head of ER."

"You had a good job where you were."

"How do you know?"

"I checked up on you."

Her foot eased off the accelerator. "You did *what?*"

"I had you checked out," he said cheerfully. "As far as I was concerned, you were obstructing a case I was on and I wanted to know why."

"So," she said through gritted teeth, speeding up again. "Did you find out why?"

"Sort of."

"Great."

"There was a suicide," he said, gazing out at the highway before him. They were climbing into the woods on the outskirts of Seattle, leaving the city behind. It felt good—the air smelled great—but his senses were focused on Annabelle. "They say you were involved in caring for a kid who offed herself. You took it hard."

"I don't—"

"You got involved."

"I—"

"She was fourteen," Jaron said. "Pregnant. And you made the decision to tell her parents."

"How do you know all this?" Annabelle demanded angrily.

"I talked to your old boss. He's still worried about you. He said the parents reacted as if the daughter was filth itself. She was beaten—badly—and she committed suicide a week after leaving the hospital. You blame yourself for telling them in the first place—for assuming they were reasonable people when in fact they were cruel and vindictive. You'd referred the case to Social Services, but you hadn't followed through. With terrible consequences. So… After that, your boss said you refused to get involved with your patients at all. You did your job, you did it well, but you changed."

"Well, there you go, then," she said savagely. "You don't need to ask any more. You know all about me."

"No," he said thoughtfully. "I don't think I do. That's not saying I wouldn't like to."

"And pigs might fly." Her hands tightened on the steering wheel. "We take these photographs and you're out of my life, Jaron Dorsey."

"I don't think so."

"Why not?"

"I'm not sure," he said slowly, and he looked at her so long her color mounted. "I'm not sure at all."

TO SAY SHE WAS unsettled would be an understatement, Annabelle admitted to herself, but Jaron resorted to silence, and the drive up into the hills to Keith's cabin did something to restore her equilibrium.

Maybe buying a convertible, given Seattle's dubious weather, hadn't been the most sensible of decisions, but on days like today, with the hood down, the wind on her face and Harold's ears flying back like the sails on the Flying Nun, she felt as if she had life exactly where she wanted it. It was an illusion, she knew, but it was a great illusion and she'd hold on to it whenever she could.

Even the presence of the man beside her couldn't entirely spoil it for her. He made her mad, he intruded on her personal space, but he was…there. Since his revelation that he'd checked her background, he'd had the sense to shut up, and she found her fury evaporating as they got farther and farther from Seattle.

Harold rested his chin on Jaron's shoulder, and she liked that, too. She shouldn't. What had he said? He'd like to get to know her.

She didn't want anyone to get to know her, but she sort of liked that he'd said it. She liked the way he sat with his arms folded, not tense, the way some people crossed their arms, but as if he was a man waiting patiently for things to unfold.

Life had been tough on him, she thought, but it didn't show. Like his hands—he'd shrugged off the injury and gotten on with his life.

Why couldn't she?

She mused in silence and Jaron seemed content to let her do so. Apparently he had musing of his own to do.

THE COUNTRY where Keith had his cabin was gorgeous. The cabin itself was set lakeside, right in among the trees in what seemed absolute wilderness. If it had rained heavily over the last few days, her Noddy car never would have reached the cabin. By the time she pulled up by the front porch, Annabelle was so pleased Noddy had made it that the feelings of tension had almost dissipated.

Almost.

One thing was certain—Harold approved. He leaped out to follow scents a city dog could only dream of. Jaron unfolded himself from the car and watched him go.

"Seems he's a rabbiter," he drawled, and Annabelle flushed and wondered what on earth there was in his remark to make her flush.

She didn't get much time to think. Forewarned by Seth, Keith had been watching for them. He appeared on the porch almost as soon as she pulled up, with Shana close behind, holding the baby. They made a great-looking couple, Annabelle noted, trying to get her thoughts back to dispassionate. They were both in blue jeans—which seemed almost odd. Ankle-length skirts and button-up boots might be more suited to this setting.

"You guys only need coonskin caps, rocking chairs and a banjo to make a perfect picture," she told them. They grinned and came down the steps to greet her.

"I left the coonskins inside," Keith told her, "on the rocking chair. And if I produce the banjo, this good woman here would likely head for the hills so fast you wouldn't see her again anytime soon."

This good woman...

They looked tense, Annabelle thought as she let Keith's description sink in. She glanced from one to the other and decided they seemed...different. As if there was some sort of conflict.

She'd wondered how these two would get on, confined to a cabin for a weekend. It was the second day now, and there weren't any obvious cracks, but something was going on. She wouldn't ask any questions at this stage, but there was a faint tinge of color on Shana's normally pale cheeks, and the way Keith's body just brushed against hers...

Interesting.

"Did Seth tell you why we've come?" Jaron asked.

"He said Annabelle would be coming in the capacity of helpful hospital employee and photographer for Chris." Keith stood aside for Shana to carry the baby down the steps. Once more his body brushed against hers, and Annabelle watched as Shana seemed to flinch. More and more interesting. "I suppose you're here to make sure it's all done legally."

He sounded...brittle. Annabelle gave her friend a searching glance, but Shana's face was carefully impassive. She gave it up. There were all sorts of questions she wanted to ask, but she couldn't ask any of them now. Instead, she touched the baby's face as the men talked around her. "Is she feeding well?"

"Both ends are operating very satisfactorily," Shana said

dryly. "I think we're going to run out of diapers before the weekend is over. We'll probably have to pick up more. The way this one goes through them, it makes me almost feel guilty for not using cloth diapers. But it's just as well we don't have cloth ones, since Keith here doesn't have a washing machine."

"We have dish towels," Keith said, indignant at the implied criticism of his beloved cottage. "We could always use those. Besides, this is the West, my dear. Wild West women made do without washing machines."

"Okay, Billy the Kid," Shana retorted. "After we've used a few of those dish towels, you take your coonskin cap and a bagful of those makeshift diapers down to the creek for washing."

"You must be kidding," Keith said faintly. "The EPA would be on us like flies on—"

"I get the picture," Shana said quickly. "How about you trot off to town to buy another box of the disposable kind?"

"Your wish is my command. Just say when."

Annabelle was laughing. Maybe she'd only imagined the tension. This was great. You couldn't ask for better temporary parents than this pair. And if anything else was happening... She looked from one to the other again, trying to read what was unreadable.

She cast Shana an inquiring look, and to her astonishment, Shana was now blushing. Shana, the unflappable. This was getting more interesting by the minute. "Do you two have time for coffee?" Shana asked, as if preempting questions Annabelle hadn't even formed, and Annabelle's suspicions increased. "We have leftover muffins that Keith made for breakfast."

"Keith—muffins?" Annabelle stammered.

"There's no need to look so stunned," Keith said, wounded. He pleaded his case to Jaron. "We modern-day males can do almost anything. Don't you agree?"

Jaron was grinning. He turned to Annabelle. "What about it, Dr. Peters? Do we have time for a muffin by Chef Hewitt?"

She shook her head. There was something about this scene

that was almost claustrophobic. It was warm and tender and family. But there was still the tension. It wasn't real.

She wanted out.

"We'll just take the pictures and be on our way," she said, and if she sounded clipped, she couldn't help it. "I have things I need to do this afternoon, and I'm sure all of you do, as well."

Jaron did. Damnably, he did. He needed to collect the kids from his mother-in-law's at two, and woe betide him if he was late. "So be it," he said, but was it her imagination, or were his words tinged with reluctance?

No matter. It couldn't matter. Shana was unwrapping the baby from her bunny blanket and handing her over to Jaron.

"Okay, sweetheart," he told her, handling her like an expert. "Let's get you documented for posterity and let these people get on with their very busy lives. Then maybe you can go back to the important things in the world—like sleeping."

This time there was no mistaking it. There was a trace of sadness in his voice that made Annabelle wish she'd said yes to those muffins.

But she was right. She knew she was right. Take the pictures and get the hell out of here. Get back to her apartment, to her hospital. To her isolation.

THE PHOTOGRAPHY was magical.

An isolated and only child, Annabelle had been given her first camera when she was eight, and she'd used it as a shield ever since. "It's a new way of looking at the world," her grandpa had told her, and that was how she'd used it. No matter how dreadful her world became as her mother dragged her from one new "daddy" to another, behind the lens of her camera she was a spectator, not a vulnerable participant.

But today...somehow she didn't feel like that. She felt involved. She was being dragged out of her shell, whether she liked it or not.

There was a grassy clearing down by the creek. They headed

there with Chris, and Shana and Keith took turns holding her while the others tried to make her smile.

"It's likely gas," Annabelle decreed, only to be howled down.

"Gas!" Shana was practically speechless in denial. "I don't think so. Look at that beautiful smile. Isn't it the most precious thing you've ever seen?"

It was. If these pictures turned out half as well as Annabelle thought they would, they'd have the entire country clamoring to claim this baby.

"You should hold her, Jaron," Shana suggested. "It'll be perfect. Seth will get his sympathetic headlines with that one. Injured Officer Holds Orphaned Baby. Jaron, where are your bandages?"

"I don't need bandages. I agreed to keep this layer of gauze on, though, because it allows me to still use my hands."

"Wait." Shana grinned. "I've got it. Heroic Injured Cop Holds Orphaned Baby. What a guy! Annabelle, get this. Hero and baby. It's perfect."

They were all smiling, the tensions between them put on hold for the moment, but as Annabelle held the camera and tried to shoot, she found her fingers trembling. Things were changing. She was a part of this, like it or not, and it felt good. It felt almost indescribably sweet.

It also felt dangerous. It felt as if she was losing something it had taken her thirty years to build, and she didn't want to let it go.

Did she?

"I...surely we have enough now."

"I'll take this one." Keith took Annabelle's camera away from her. "Just one more. Doctor and cop—the team who saved the baby and who desperately tried to save the mother. Go ahead," he urged when Annabelle didn't move. "Seth will love it. Maybe you can hold Chris. Jaron, put your arm around the lady's waist like you're a family."

"He's right," Shana offered. "It'll be perfect."

Harold decided to nose in now. This place was so far out of

his city-dog experience that his old body was quivering in excitement. He loped over to Annabelle, put his face in hers and licked his pleasure—chin to forehead.

"Urgh…"

"A perfect family," Shana declared. And as Annabelle broke into reluctant laughter, Keith said, "Hold it" and shot, then shot again and again.

Their family photos were done.

THEY DROVE BACK to the city in silence. Annabelle was aware that things had changed, but she wasn't sure how. She wasn't sure what to do, but the safest thing seemed to be to retreat into silence.

And Jaron? For him, as well, silence was a shield. A defense against things he didn't know how to deal with. This lady had the world's biggest chip on her shoulder, and he wasn't even in the market for a lady, much less one with hang-ups.

So it was with a certain amount of relief that they arrived back downtown. She dropped him at the Station—there were things he wanted to check before he picked the kids up from their grandmother's. He climbed from her little car, gave Harold a farewell pat and lifted a hand in farewell.

"You'll get those shots to Seth?"

"Yes," she said stiffly.

There was nothing else to say. He nodded and turned away. Annabelle sat in the car, and her fingers clenched the wheel until her knuckles turned white. Until he disappeared into the station.

She didn't have a clue what was happening to her.

And neither did Jaron. He didn't turn back, but only he knew what effort it cost him to stay headed in the direction of work.

CHAPTER TEN

THE PICTURES were fantastic. Annabelle returned to her apartment, set up her little darkroom and uncovered the magic of her camera.

It *was* magic.

She couldn't believe it. She spread the developed prints on her dining-room table and looked at them with awe. The setting was lovely for a start—she couldn't have asked for better.

But the baby...

She was adorable. Annabelle stared at the little one's smile and felt her heart twist. How could this child have lost her mommy and daddy? How could she be so alone?

And how could Jaron think for a minute she'd withhold information that might keep this baby from her family?

He didn't. He was past it, she told herself. He believed her. Jaron...

She lifted the next picture and there he was, smiling down at the unknown infant as if she was his. He cared. You could see it in his expression, in the way his arm crooked around the tiny body, the way his chest sort of curved...

She found she was rigid with tension. Staring down at this man...

What was it about him? What was happening to her?

And then there was the last shot. The "family" shot. Keith had taken it, and maybe it didn't contain the same clarity, the same professionalism, as the shots she'd taken, but it was pretty good all the same. She and Jaron were sitting side by side on a fallen log, she was holding Chris, Harold was leaning over her shoulder gazing at the baby in canine astonishment, and

Chris was looking straight at the camera and smiling the most gorgeous smile.

But it wasn't Chris that snagged Annabelle's attention. It was Jaron. Keith had caught the moment just as Harold had completed his lick; she was laughing and Jaron was smiling at her laughter. The expression on his face made her breath catch in her throat. No man had ever looked at her like that.

It was an illusion, she told herself harshly. Photographs were an illusion. She forced herself to think back to the myriad "family" shots her mother had insisted on. Her mother and the latest "daddy," with Annabelle wedged between, endured by the guy in order to keep her mother happy. Her mother playing "happy families," where the words *for keeps* meant maybe until next Sunday.

Her mother had kept photo albums, and after she died, Annabelle had gone through and counted at least a score of such happy family shots. All of them lies.

Like this one.

She stared down at it and pressed her lips so hard together that they hurt. Then, carefully and deliberately, she tore the picture in two. Not so the images were destroyed. Just so she was alone again. Jaron was left with the baby and she was left with her dog. With Harold.

That was the way it had to be. Now and forever.

"We're okay, Harold," she told her dog, who, exhausted by the morning's activities, had taken himself to his favorite settee and was fast asleep.

He was no company at all.

She was so darned unsettled.

"I'll take these pictures down to Seth," she told the sleeping Harold. "And then I'll go to the market." She lifted the pictures and stared at them one last time.

The baby smiled back at her.

For a moment she was caught, aware suddenly of a twinge of uncertainty that hadn't been there before. What? She thought back to the mother's last anguished words.

Tell no one.

Tell no one what?

The woman had been so frightened for her child, yet she needn't have been. This little one was safe. Even if they couldn't find her family, they'd find someone who'd love her.

Annabelle had done all she could to see that she was safe. There was nothing else.

No. There was something. Something niggling…

It didn't add up. Over and over her mind replayed the woman's last frantic words. What had they meant? Did they hold any clue?

Maybe she should tell Jaron word for word what she'd said and let him figure it out.

But there was nothing to figure out. Annabelle had made a promise, and there was no need to break it. There was no information at all in the woman's whispered words.

Only in her own vague unease that there was something… something.

Nothing. *Make no assumptions, Annabelle* she told herself fiercely. *Keep out of what's not your business.*

She cast a last uncertain glance at the picture of the baby with Jaron, and then she slid all the photographs into an envelope to pass on to Seth. She didn't need to keep them. Not one.

The only one she wasn't handing over to Seth was the one she'd torn—the happy-families portrait—and that was in the wastebasket, where it deserved to be.

HALLOWEEN COSTUMES were hard to make, especially when your hands hurt. Jaron had bought crepe paper and was trying to fashion it into capes. He'd figured he could make witch and wizard hats with cardboard, capes with crepe paper, and then sprinkle everything with glitter.

It wasn't working. The tape he was using to fasten the cape was crinkling and warping the paper, and when he applied glue for the glitter, the crepe paper disintegrated into a soggy heap.

"We'll make them plain black," he told the kids. "Forget the glitter on the capes. Real witches and wizards wear black." He eyed the cardboard hats with doubt. "Maybe we can add a bit of glitter there."

"I want to be a pink witch," Tina said sadly in the tone of a pink witch who knew she was destined to be a plain black witch whose outfit would most likely tear the first time she wore it.

"Can we buy some red paper?" Ricky asked without much hope.

They both sounded pessimistic as hell. "Hey, these costumes are going to look great."

"It doesn't matter," Tina said, and walked over to the window. "It doesn't matter, Daddy."

Damn, it did matter.

"Maybe we can buy something." Yeah, right. Every kid in the city would have bought a costume weeks ago. There'd be nothing left. "Or maybe Grandma can help." Yet another hopeless thought. Cathy's mother would never help Jaron. She was "there for the children," she'd told him, but that meant she was there waiting for him to fail, for him to admit that he couldn't bring up two kids alone and hand over their entire upbringing to her.

"I'll get more crepe paper." Glue had crept into one of his burst blisters and it hurt. Hell, why was it sometimes so damned hard? *Cathy, where are you? Cathy...*

"There's Annabelle."

"What?" He glanced up from his pile of disaster. Tina was standing by the window, staring out at the street. When they'd bought this apartment, he'd worried that it was on too busy a road, but they all liked it—it made them seem less isolated. The kids watched passersby, instead of television, and Annabelle, it seemed, was passing by right now.

"She's on her bike." Tina seemed fascinated. "She has her doggy in a cart."

Annabelle. Jaron practically fell over himself in an effort to reach the window before she disappeared, but he made it in time, and Tina was right. There was Annabelle. She was in her shorts and short-sleeved blouse, her hair was flying free, she had a shopping bag strapped on her back...

And behind her bike she had a little wooden cart; Harold was being wheeled along in style. Jaron's apartment was on the road leading to the market, and as she rounded the corner and disappeared from view, he thought that was where she was headed. She had to be.

The market.

He could buy more crepe paper at the market. Or… something.

"Let's go," he told the kids, and they stared at him.

"Why?" Tina asked.

"We need to buy…"

But his son wasn't as reluctant as he was to voice the true intention. "We need to find Annabelle," Ricky said firmly. "She's fun."

HAROLD WAS an excellent shopping companion. He wasn't welcome in the food precinct, but that didn't bother Harold. Ever since Annabelle had built him his little cart, he'd loved market days. He'd sit up and let the wind billow his ears as she cycled along the city streets, regarding dogs being walked on leashes with scorn. Then, when they reached their destination, he'd assume killer-dog protection mode. Any burglar wanting to seize Annabelle's wheels would be licked into submission.

Feeling better for the long ride, Annabelle parked her bike, rumpled Harold's ears and left him to it. In truth there was little she needed at the market, but it was an excuse to be out, to be not thinking. Jaron had made her think too much, and she didn't like it.

She needed fruit, and maybe some cloth to make a skirt for winter. This Indian-summer weather had to stop soon.

The market was crowded and bustling, full of people enjoying a Sunday that wasn't followed by a workday. Everyone seemed happier than usual. Free. People were window-shopping, wandering and admiring. Serious food shopping was usually done on Saturday mornings. Sunday afternoon was for tourists and tire-kickers.

For couples and families.

Why was she seeing them everywhere? Where were all the single people?

Was she the only single person in the world?

"Hi, Annabelle." She turned to find Meg and Brody Taylor bearing down on her. Meg was a brilliant piano teacher as well as a singer and had been advertising for pupils when Annabelle first arrived in Seattle. The two had a piano lesson every week in Meg's sprawling family home. Annabelle always got the feeling that Meg would like to turn the pupil/teacher relationship into a friendship. But Meg, with her gorgeous husband, her mischievous twins and now her very welcome pregnancy, was a world away from Annabelle's isolated existence.

Friendship? She wasn't interested.

"Hi, Meg," she said. "How's it going?" She gave the couple a bright smile and moved on. This was a technique she'd perfected over the years. *Be superficially friendly, but don't get attached...*

But normally when she turned away, there wasn't this regret—as if she knew what she was turning away from.

Oh, for heaven's sake, what was wrong with her? This outing had been a mistake. She'd bike down to the waterfront and leave the fabric buying for another day. Leave the market to families.

JARON WAS HAVING his own problems. He had a kid on each hand and they were Annabelle-hunting...well, not really. Not... Who was he kidding? They were Annabelle-hunting. But families kept getting in the way.

First there was Detective Luke Sloan, a fellow detective and one of his best friends on the force, arm in arm with his new wife and their daughter, Emily. He and Abby looked gloriously happy, and they were in no mood to hurry. Abby was intent on Emily's getting to know Ricky and Tina.

"Why don't you bring the kids over for dinner?" she asked Jaron. "How about tonight? Luke's on cooking duty, so we'll be having his favorite. Hamburgers."

"It's not only my favorite, it's the only thing I can cook," Luke confessed. He was checking Jaron's hands. "You've lost the bandages?"

"They weren't my style."

"Then come and eat with us," Luke said, his concern showing through his gruffness.

"Thanks, but no," Jaron told them. "We have Halloween costumes to make."

Where was Annabelle?

The kids were tugging him toward the fruit stands.

"I think I see her over there." Ricky sounded as eager as he was. Damn, why was he eager? He'd only left her this morning. He'd probably see her and she'd tell him to get lost.

"Ricky! Tina!"

Sigh. It was Hannah Richards and Jack McKay. Wrong. It was now Hannah and Jack McKay. Jack was a parole officer Jaron knew well, and Hannah had been one of the founders of Forrester Square Day Care.

Another happy couple, with a nine-year-old son and a brand-new baby boy.

"Can we see your baby, please?" Tina asked politely. She knew her dad and her brother were eager to be going, but she had a woman's instinct of what was right. Showing interest in Hannah's new baby was definitely right.

"He's cute," she said doubtfully as Hannah pulled back the blanket to show her sleeping baby's face. "But he's squashed-looking."

Jaron grinned. "You looked squashed, too," he told his daughter. "So did Ricky."

"Not like this," Tina said. Then she looked up at Hannah and smiled. "He's very nice."

They all chuckled. "We think he's adorable," Hannah told her, not at all put out by the four-year-old's distinct lack of appreciation for her baby. "We've named him Kenny after my father, and if it's okay with you, we think we'll keep him."

"Well, okay. If you can't find a cuter one…"

More laughter. They moved on, leaving Jaron looking after them with a strange expression on his face. They were walking hand in hand, pushing the stroller between them, their older son beside his mother.

He'd done that with Cathy.

Where was Annabelle?
There!

TINA CALLED first. "Annabelle!"

At first Annabelle thought she was imagining it, but it came again. A high, shrill call. "Annabelle, over here!"

Tina. She recognized the voice before she turned around, and by the time she located Tina's small body in the crowd, she was already smiling. Okay, Tina might be attached to her very disturbing daddy, but Annabelle smiled all the same.

They were walking toward her, Jaron and a kid on each hand. It was only a couple of hours since she'd seen him, but her heart revved at the sight of him. They had three identical smiles, these three, and more and more she was...

No. She was not involved.

"We're here to buy crepe paper," Tina told her importantly as they came up to her. "We need more because the last bunch got soggy."

Paper. Soggy. Bemused, she looked at Jaron and found his eyes resting on hers with something...something she didn't recognize. It looked almost like hunger.

She was imagining things.

"I'm making Halloween costumes," he told her, his eyes on hers. There were things going on between them that had nothing to do with paper. Or costumes. "At least I'm *trying* to make Halloween costumes."

"With paper?"

"With crepe paper."

"They'll rip."

"They already have."

"You don't think," she said carefully, "that you might have more luck with fabric?"

"You can't glue fabric as easily."

"You can sew it." Around them people were pushing past with shopping bags, brushing their bodies. The group of four were blocking the aisle and getting more than a few irritated glances, but they were intent on each other. Very intent.

"I can't sew," Jaron said.

Annabelle took a deep breath. This was a watershed. A barrier she had to cross.

No. She didn't need to cross it. She could just smile apologetically and turn away, leaving him to his problems. Friendly but superficial.

"Where can we find pink paper?" Tina was asking. "I really, really want to be a pink witch."

Annabelle gazed down and saw Tina braced for disappointment, convinced her dad would say, sorry, he couldn't... Ricky was looking just the same.

"What color witch do you want to be?" she asked him before she could help herself, and Ricky swallowed.

"A wizard. I want to be a wizard."

"Of course you do." She smiled an apology. "That was stupid of me. Don't wizards wear black?"

"Harry Potter wears black," Ricky said, wistfulness personified. "But I want to be a red wizard, with stars." Then he looked at his father and pushed back his shoulders. "But black's fine," he said bravely. "If it sticks together."

Oh, for heaven's sake.

It was enough to break a stronger will than Annabelle's, and she was a wise enough woman to concede defeat.

"Let's head for the fabric section," she told them, with only the slightest of inward winces. *What am I doing?* "I know where we can find the best material for making witch and wizard costumes."

"But..." Jaron started. She forestalled him with a smile.

"I'm not just a neck with an attached stethoscope. I have a sewing machine and I can sew. Plus, I have a free afternoon." She glanced at her watch. "Well, a couple of free hours, anyway, so we can make a start and Halloween's weeks away. How attached are you to your idea of black crepe, Detective Dorsey?"

Jaron grinned. Something was lighting up inside him that hadn't been lit up for years. A neck with an attached stethoscope. That wasn't how he thought of her at all.

"Not attached in the least," he told her happily. "Not one little bit. Can you really sew?"

She eyed him speculatively. "I don't mend, I don't darn, and I don't make anything that's boring," she told him, very, very definitely. "Apart from that, yes, I can sew. When I feel like it."

"And you feel like it now?"

"Wizard and witch capes don't sound boring."

Of course not. *Boring.* How could he ever think that?

They bought fabric that was magic all by itself.

"How much can we spend?" Annabelle asked, and Jaron grinned and said, "The sky's the limit."

It didn't have to be. The crimson satin was the end of a roll and they bargained it down. The pink gossamer was more expensive, but Tina was so small they didn't need much. Then they searched for bits—bits of silver, bits of gold, tassels, buttons, bows, handfuls of wonderful, magical adornments.

"Because if I'm making costumes, I'm making *costumes,*" Annabelle announced, flitting from stall to stall like a fairy godmother as the kids watched, openmouthed. "Have we got everything we need? Off to my place, then. See you there, Detective Dorsey. Go slow since you're in your car and I'm on my bike."

"You're gonna bike?" Ricky asked, and Annabelle grinned.

"Of course I am. Cars are so boring, don't you think? Unless they're yellow."

Jaron gave an inward groan. He could just see himself spraypainting his family wagon, but Annabelle was already headed for her bike and he was left to follow.

He did go slow. He nosed his car into traffic and then, unable to resist, he put up with being honked at as they drove at bike pace behind Annabelle.

It was worth a few honks. Annabelle's neat backside was steady on the seat, her glorious hair flew out behind her, Harold was turned back to watch them follow, and Jaron could almost swear the old dog was grinning.

"We need a dog," Tina announced, and Ricky agreed.

"And a cart."

Great. Yellow spray paint. Dogs. Carts. Great! "Let's just

concentrate on costumes, shall we?'' Jaron said faintly, and found he wasn't concentrating on costumes at all.

THE KIDS LOVED Annabelle's apartment. They loved that it was in the hospital and she had to take her bike around to the service elevator to reach it. They loved the way she retrieved her key from under a potted plant beside the door and had Jaron demand incredulously whether she was out of her mind.

"Nope," she told him. "Didn't you see me punch the security code on the elevator? If I don't hit 927 then the elevator won't stop at this floor. All of us here are medics, we're all single, we all work crazy hours, and we all tend to oversleep. After a while you get so you'll even sleep through the phone. This way—leaving the key out—someone can come find you and splash you with cold water and get you ready for the fray again.''

"It's a crazy job," Jaron growled, and Annabelle nodded and looked at him speculatively.

"Something like being a cop?"

He had no answer to that. The kids were already in the door, whooping with delight, and he was left to follow.

Annabelle never promised what she couldn't deliver. They were no sooner in the door of her magic little apartment than she had her sewing machine set up and the cloth spread out on the floor, ready for cutting.

"Don't we need to measure before we cut?" Jaron asked faintly, and Annabelle regarded him with scorn.

"Measure? When you could have much more fun my way? Tina, lie down on your back on the cloth, spread out your arms like an angel about to take off, and let me cut around you.''

"Really?" Tina looked down at the shimmering cloud of pink Annabelle was laying out on the floor and almost shimmered herself.

"Yep. And keep very still." Annabelle was holding a huge pair of scissors, assuming an evil witchlike pose. "I have you in my parlor now, boys and girls. I'm a dangerous woman when I'm armed.''

That set the tone for the entire afternoon. Work and laughter and fantasy. Annabelle didn't believe in sewing while they watched. She involved them every step of the way.

"Watch," she ordered Jaron as she cut out Tina's costume, and then she handed him the scissors. "Now I've cut out Tina's, you get to cut out Ricky's."

"But…"

She raised her eyebrows, half-mocking. "What's the matter? Afraid?"

He wasn't afraid. No. Not afraid. He didn't know what he was.

The more the afternoon wore on, the more bemused he became. The kids were cutting stars and moons and every fantasy shape they could think of. Annabelle was fastening them as fast as they were making them, and attaching the buttons and loops and tassles.

His kids were falling in love, he realized, bewildered, and then thought. Hell.

So was he.

But this was dangerous territory. She might be a bubbly vivacious ball of fun, but she was a lady with a past. He didn't know her background, but he knew it could land him in uncharted territory.

He didn't want commitment.

Who the hell was he kidding? He wanted commitment more than he wanted anything.

He'd missed Cathy so desperately it was like a hunger. That ache had faded. Now it was no longer Cathy he wanted with all his heart, but he wanted someone. Someone to hold at night, to laugh with, to cuddle his kids. To cuddle him.

Annabelle wasn't the woman. Was she?

While his ill-assorted thoughts were jumbling around his head, there was an assembly line happening. The cloaks were becoming the most fantastic creations he'd ever seen.

Which added to his jumble of emotions.

"Enough," Annabelle finally decreed. "If we sew on one more thing, you won't be able to wear them. They'll be so heavy you'll have to wheel them behind you in Harold's cart."

The kids giggled. They were almost bursting with excitement. These cloaks were to die for.

It was time to be going, Jaron thought. It was getting dark. Dinnertime.

He didn't want to go.

"Why don't we order pizza and stay here?" Ricky suggested, and Jaron almost hugged him. Instead, he managed to look doubtful. A bit. Sort of.

"That's a fine idea, Ricky, but we might be inconveniencing Dr. Peters. I'm sure she has other things to do."

He was right. She did have things to do. He watched her face, and it said it all. She had a life to live. A solitary existence to resume.

But Tina and Ricky were both gazing up at her, their eyes full of hope. Jaron held his breath. Sometimes there were definite advantages to having kids.

"I don't think—"

"If you agree, then I'll order the pizza—and I'm paying," Jaron told her, and Annabelle glanced at him in astonishment. He looked as hopeful as his kids. Like one big cocker spaniel and two little ones.

The rat! This was an assumed expression, she thought desperately. She'd seen Harold strike exactly the same pose when he wanted something, and here Jaron was, a grown man...

But what an expression.

It was too much. Her lips twitched and a chuckle refused to be suppressed. She'd have to be superhuman to resist an appeal like this, and though the barriers she'd raised were high, she hadn't yet built them high enough to be totally impervious to a good-looking guy with two gorgeous kids who needed pizza.

Oh, for heaven's sake, even Harold seemed to be appealing to her to say yes. She held up her hands in mute surrender. "Fine. Great. You're very welcome to stay for dinner. I'm sorry I don't have anything here to feed you all."

"We'll provide it," Jaron told her magnanimously. "You and Harold supply the kitchen table, and we'll supply everything else."

THE PIZZA was excellent. So was the lemonade for the kids, the bottle of wine for themselves, the tub of double-chocolate ice cream with cherries and the box of chocolates to finish off. One thing Jaron had learned since Cathy's death was the complexities of ordering in food.

"Pizza's evil," Annabelle decreed as the last of the ice cream disappeared. "Pizza and ice cream is worse. Where does that leave pizza and ice cream and wine and lemonade and chocolate?"

"About as close to heaven as we can get," Jaron said, rising reluctantly from the table. They'd chatted over dinner almost like old friends—or maybe not old friends, but very new and interested friends. But now he couldn't extend the evening any longer. "It's time I took the kids home."

"But, Dad, *Buffy*'s on!" Tina protested. While Jaron and Annabelle had talked over ice cream, the kids had drifted into the sitting room. Now they were curled up on either side of Harold as they watched their favorite show, and they had no intention of leaving halfway through. "She's a witch, just like us."

"No, she's not. She's a vampire. And it's bedtime."

"It's a holiday tomorrow," Annabelle reminded him before she could stop herself, and then thought, *Why on earth did I do that?*

She knew why. She wanted him to stay.

Jaron was looking doubtfully at her. If she stayed silent now...

She should stay silent now. She should. But...

"I'm watching *Buffy*, too," she told him. "I've never watched her before. Is her costume as good as ours?" She plonked herself down on the second settee.

There was one place left. Beside her. Jaron stared down at her, stared at his kids and thought, *Why not? Why the hell not?*

And he sat down to watch *Buffy the Vampire Slayer.*

AFTERWARD, HE COULDN'T remember a thing about the teenage vampire slayer. All he remembered was the way Annabelle's long legs stretched out before him, the way her body just touched his, the soft citrusy scent of her.

Just *her*. Her presence. Her aura.

It must have been a boring Buffy. Or maybe it wasn't boring at all.

The kids were tired. They hadn't had a nap this afternoon. They'd eaten their fill of junk food. They were warm and they were happy and Harold was snoozing between them.

Four little eyes were drooping well before the end of the TV show. Buffy slayed her vampire with style, and the kids' eyes didn't even widen. The news headlines came on and Jaron should have risen immediately, but hey, the news was important, and before the sports wrap was halfway through, the kids were fast asleep.

As was Harold.

Kids and dog asleep.

Not Jaron. Nor Annabelle. They were both very much awake. Annabelle was so wide awake she felt as if an electric charge was running through her. She should rise and say firmly, "Good night. See you again, Detective Dorsey, like, next month sometime, and definitely not in the immediate future."

She couldn't.

The sports finished. Then the weather report ended.

She stared at the screen, not sure what she was staring at. Just…staring.

Jaron lifted the remote and hit Off.

The picture faded to nothing.

Annabelle turned back to Jaron, her eyes a question, and the question was answered. Of course it was answered. How could it not be?

There was only one course of action possible. He took her face in his hands and he kissed her.

CHAPTER ELEVEN

THEY'D KISSED before. That was nothing. Not compared with this.

The last time Annabelle had been kissed—seriously kissed by a man other than Jaron—she'd decided she must be frigid. Which was just as well, she thought. Given her life plan, frigidity was good. She'd work on maintaining it.

Frigidity had nothing to do with what she felt now. Nothing at all. What she felt was heat!

She'd felt it the entire time he'd sat by her. It was as if her body was warming from an arctic chill, thawing, so that when his mouth met hers and she felt fire spread through her body, it was an extension of a process that had already started. In fact, if she was honest with herself, it had started the moment she'd first set eyes on him.

The moment their lips met, something changed. Something...

Maybe their lips had intended to just brush. Maybe...

Instead, they locked. It was power meeting power, and it was something bigger than both of them. Holding forever.

FOREVER?

Forever was a good word. A great word. The word slammed into Jaron's mind and stayed.

Forever.

What the hell was he thinking?

He shouldn't think. He should just soak up this warmth, this wonder. This woman.

His hands were hauling her to him, pulling her so her breasts molded to his chest, letting the warmth and wonder of her fill him.

She was all wrong, he thought desperately with the last part of his mind that was capable of rational thought. If ever he wanted another woman he wanted a homebody—and a woman who was open to relationships. Not a career woman who swore the only thing she needed in her life was a dog.

Yet that wasn't who Annabelle was. She hadn't been truthful.

He could feel it in her body's response to his. She might say she was a loner, but her body knew otherwise. Her body was screaming its need. He could feel it in the way her mouth opened under his, surrendering her sweetness, aching, wanting.

"Annabelle..." Somehow he whispered her name, savoring the sweetness of it.

He wanted her.

SHE WAS on fire.

She didn't want a man.

Who was she kidding? She wanted him as if she was half of a whole and here was the other half. When he kissed her, it was as though the two halves of the whole had been rejoined. This day had been sweetness from beginning to end. Jaron...

He was a cop. He was big and tough. He lived in a world she knew nothing of, and he had strengths she didn't know. He'd buried his wife and raised his kids, and she knew by now that his reputation was that of one of the toughest cops in the district.

She'd never met anyone like him.

It wouldn't last. Couldn't. Tomorrow she'd go back to being on her own again. Someone like Jaron wouldn't want her for long—a one-night stand, maybe—so she should kick him out now.

Ha!

She couldn't kick him out. Not when his hands felt so wonderful. Not when his mouth was on hers and he tasted like pizza and chocolate-cherry ice cream and...well, he tasted like Jaron.

She loved the way he tasted.

And his hands...

They were sliding up under her blouse, under the soft fabric of her bra. She should push him away.

Push him away? Was she crazy?

She'd be thirty years old next birthday. She'd kept herself to herself, not for any maidenly ideas of virtue but because she didn't want to get close to anyone.

And now... She was close already, she thought, dazed beyond belief by what was happening to her. She could hardly get closer. Her body had made its own decision, and it had nothing to do with her head. Not with nice, sensible Dr. Annabelle Peters. Dr. Peters was no longer calling the shots. This was someone she hardly knew.

He was teasing her nipples, and she'd never felt anything so good. His fingers were roughly textured but oh, so gentle. Magic! Buffy had nothing on this sort of enchantment. Annabelle was responding in kind, driven by needs of her own. Her hands were under his shirt, feeling him, touching him, wanting him—and the broad, strong maleness of him was sending shards of desire right through her.

Jaron...

Maybe she moaned his name out loud—she didn't know—but he drew back then, just a little, so his eyes were searching hers, looking for an answer to a question they both understood.

"Annabelle?" he whispered, his voice hoarse with passion, and her whole body responded, ached, yearned toward him with something that might almost have been akin to love.

She loved the way he said her name. Annabelle... The way he said it was a caress in itself.

What was happening to her?

The kids were deeply asleep. She forced herself to look around and check. The three—dog and boy and girl—were a tumble of sleeping bodies.

She and Jaron might as well have been alone.

They couldn't. Not here.

Her bedroom was right through the door—and they were thinking as one.

"Hell, I haven't…" His voice was a groan and she knew at once what he meant. This was surely the time to pour cold water on the whole deal, the time for her to draw away and say good-night and slam the door on the lot of them.

Not with her body feeling like this.

"Didn't I tell you that I have everything I need for medical emergencies?" she whispered, teasing him with her eyes and glorying in the aching need she saw on his face. She was causing that. His need was for her.

"Don't tell me…"

"I already did." She was still melting against him. "I keep a complete medical kit in my bathroom. I'm equipped for medical emergencies from heart attack to snakebite, Detective Dorsey, and anything in between."

"You keep *condoms?*"

She was laughing up at him. "Yep. For professional need. Just like you keep a gun in your pocket, Detective Dorsey."

His wonderful mouth quirked into a smile of delight at that, and his kiss deepened. And when he drew away he was laughing down into her eyes with something that felt close to love.

"I have news for you," he drawled, and drew her even closer. "You must have seen the movie. That's not a gun in my pocket."

"No?"

"No." He stood then and swung her up into his arms as if she wasn't five feet eleven inches tall, but cute and little and adorable. And very, very sexy.

"You want to see what's in my pocket, Dr. Annabelle? It's not a gun. I'm just very pleased to see you. Now. We need to go past your medical kit. Fast!"

"Let's do it."

WOULD HE MIND?
Would he even notice? There was a part of Annabelle that was scared stiff, but it was overridden by this new Annabelle,

the Annabelle who knew what she wanted and wanted it right now.

She wanted Jaron.

She wanted his body. She wanted the hard, muscled firmness of him. She wanted the heat of him under her hands, the urgency of his fingers, the taste of him, his smell, the arrant maleness.

Had she ever imagined she could feel like this?

No.

She'd learned about relationships by watching her mother's boyfriends, one after another, and a couple of them had shown far more interest in her than they should have. She'd learned early to defend herself, to retreat into her shell, to slap away prying hands, to keep herself to herself.

So what was it about this man that was different?

It was the way he said her name. Like a prayer.

He was different. A big, rough cop with the heart of a lover. With the hands of a lover.

"You're beautiful," he murmured, and his hands were threading through her hair with a whispering intensity that made her want to cry out with pleasure. They were in her big bed, the bed she'd bought big to share with Harold, but was now too high for Harold to reach. So she was sharing it with Jaron. He'd carried her into the bedroom and laid her down on the covers like she was the most precious thing in the world.

Lord, it was a wonderful thing to be so precious in someone's eyes. In Jaron's eyes.

It wouldn't last. He didn't want her—not tomorrow. She wouldn't want him. Her life was one of independence. But for now...

She was unbuttoning her blouse and he was helping her, one button each all the way down, like some delicious tango. Then, as she put her hand back to unclip her bra, he stopped her.

"Let me."

And that was fine, too. The way he lifted the soft satin away and lay just looking, looking, and then letting his eyes drift back to hers so she knew it was the whole package he was appreciating. Not just breasts. Her!

She wanted him. She was so aroused she was close to screaming, and she no longer understood her need. She unfastened his shirt with much more recklessness than he'd shown with hers. She heard the cloth tear, but she didn't really care.

Who was she kidding? She didn't care at all.

And then they were naked. He was naked and he was…

What?

He took her breath away.

She'd seen men naked. Of course she had. She'd been a doctor for years.

She hadn't seen a man naked like this. He was like some Rodin sculpture but far more beautiful. Alive.

Hers.

She let a finger drift from the point under his throat where his breastbone started, then through the coarse hairs of his chest, down, down, until she was stroking upward again and he was hauling in his breath in ecstasy.

"Wait. Damn you, woman, wait."

She laughed, a delicious sound that broke over the pair of them and in some strange way bound them even closer. "Let me."

Her fingers carefully adjusted the tiny sheath of rubber, and he was groaning as her fingers brushed him, groaning and dragging her hard against him.

His fingers were doing their own exploration, finding her heat…

"Jaron…"

His body was suspended over her and he was laughing down into her eyes.

"Jaron…"

Slowly Jaron lowered himself, savoring the moment. His need was desperate, but he wouldn't hurry this. He wanted her so much, but she had to want him, too.

But she was arching upward, her body meeting his, urgent as he was, desperate for this joining.

"Please…"

And the moment of blessed surrender…

His body stiffened in shock.

"No!" She was holding him close, tight, drawing him into her, arching against him.

Hell, she wasn't…

"Jaron…"

He could hold himself no longer. Desire drove every thought from his head. He'd gone too far to pull back. Not now. There was only this woman, this moment, their need…

One.

"WHY?"

"Why?" They were lying entwined, exhausted with loving and sated with pleasure. Her wonderful hair was draped over his naked chest. She was curled into him and his arms were holding her in a gesture of possession. She felt…wonderful.

He'd forgotten how good it felt to hold a woman, he thought dazedly—or had it ever felt this good? It wasn't fair to compare, he decided, tugging her closer. Annabelle and Cathy. They were two different women. One was his past. The other…his future?

"Why didn't you tell me it was your first time?" he demanded gruffly, lifting a strand of her glorious hair and letting it drift through his fingers. The sensation was almost unbearably erotic.

She thought about it for a moment, her cheek pressed against the roughness of his chest.

"It's a bit absurd," she said at last. "To be a virgin at thirty."

"You're not a virgin anymore."

"No," she said on a note of quiet satisfaction. "I'm not."

"Hey." He was smiling, but his voice was a protest. "You sound like you just used me."

"For your body?" She was definitely smiling. "I did. And a very nice body it was, too."

That should have made him smile. But somehow…somehow

the thought that this might have been casual sex didn't cut it with him.

She felt wonderful. She felt so right, hooked into the crook of his arm. Her breath was warm against his cheek, and the fragrance of her was drifting into the warm night air. This wasn't just postcoital euphoria, he decided in a mist of wonder. This was…euphoria.

This was something he intended to pursue. A one-night stand? Not if he could help it.

"Why?" he asked again, his lips brushing the bare skin of her shoulder. Damn, she had no right to feel this good. To taste this good…

To be this wonderful.

"I never wanted to before now," she said simply, and his brow furrowed.

"Why not?"

"I've seen the hell my mother went through with her boyfriends. And they—her boyfriends…" Her voice faded.

But it was enough. He was a cop and he knew. "Ah, hell, Annabelle—"

"No." She shook her head in the darkness, knowing he understood what she'd been implying, and glorying in his instant outrage. He was some cop, this guy. "They didn't…interfere with me. But that's not to say they didn't try. I was born a fighter. I could scream the place down when I wanted, and boy, could I kick." She smiled a little at that. "Come to think of it, I still can."

"Good for you," he said unsteadily. "I hope you're not planning on demonstrating."

"Not if you're good."

"I'm good. I'm very, very good."

"Yeah, right…"

"Can you doubt me, woman? I'm the best!" Then as a fist punched into his solar plexus, he seized her around the waist and hauled her close. "Ow!"

But it was a conversation, once started, that should be finished.

They were laughing into each other's eyes, but the story needed to be finished.

"Parents," he said carefully, rolling her over, his arm tugging her in so her body curved against his. He cupped her breasts with his hands, and her back arched in a delicious *c* against his chest. "Parents have a lot to answer for. So these guys...they spoiled it for you forever?"

"They made me not want it." But the ghosts were fading. She was smiling into the dark. "They made me think it was sordid. I didn't know...until now..."

"That it could be as good as this?"

"I have a feeling it's not always like this."

"That sounds like a challenge." He tugged her around again so that she was looking into his eyes in the dim light. "Annabelle, we can make this work. You and me—"

"No." She placed a finger on his lips. "Not so fast. Let's just take this moment for what it is, Detective Dorsey."

"You mean there's no future for us? The hell there's not."

"I'm independent. It's the way I am."

"I can see that." His laughter faded. Of course. It wasn't just him, he thought grimly as he took a reality check. He had his kids. He had a past. What woman would want what he was offering? Him and the kids as a package deal? Ha! She had a great life right now.

"I have Harold," she said softly, voicing his thoughts almost exactly. "That's commitment enough."

"You could have me." But the offer didn't come out sounding very desirable at all.

She touched his lips again as if she couldn't help herself. "For now I do, and it's wonderful. But tomorrow..."

"Okay." He decided he'd go with her on this one. "For now let's not think about tomorrow."

She smiled. "Okay. Can you think of anything else we can think about?"

"I sure can," he said softly, and proceeded to show her.

IT WAS TWO in the morning before he stirred. Annabelle was asleep. The sensation of her body beside him was indescribable. The last thing he wanted to do was leave.

But his kids were asleep on the settee. If he didn't move, they'd awake in the morning and ask questions he wasn't sure he could answer.

Annabelle was an independent career woman. She'd made that plain. The future for them as a couple was uncertain.

So he needed to see to his kids. If he picked them up, took them home half-asleep, they'd assume he and Annabelle had watched television and then he'd taken them home as he'd done from friends' places countless times before.

But the wrench was almost unbearable.

He must.

He rose silently and dressed, then stood looking down at the woman in the bed for a long, long time. His woman, he thought, His woman for the night. She slept on, oblivious, as he stood there, soaking in the sight of her loveliness. The wonder of her.

He wanted her so much it was like a fierce hunger in his gut. He wanted her, and he wanted her forever.

Despite her damned independence.

Maybe because of her independence. He wouldn't change a thing about her.

Annabelle…

"JARON?"

She awoke murmuring his name, but he was gone. For a moment she couldn't believe it. Her hand groped the place where he'd lain, found the indentation of his head in her pillows, smelled the fragrance of him in her bedclothes…

But no Jaron. He'd gone!

She couldn't believe the way her body responded. It was all she could do not to scream.

Instead, she lay back and stared at the ceiling and let reality drift back.

He'd taken his kids home. Of course. He couldn't stay,

didn't want to have to explain to the kids why he'd woken up next to Annabelle.

Last night he'd spoken of their future, but there was no future. He was a cop with kids and she was an ER specialist with a dog.

"And never the twain shall meet," she whispered. She grabbed her robe and climbed from her bed, aware that every nerve in her body was tingling. It was as if she'd awoken from a dream, or as if a fog had lifted.

She'd never imagined it could be so good.

"I've had sex," she said with no small amount of wonder, and found she was blushing like a schoolgirl. Sex. It was something that, until now, she'd blocked from her life completely.

She'd thought it was overrated.

She was wrong.

Great. So what was she going to do now? Become available for the first time in her life? Look for more?

No, because it wasn't the sex itself. It was Jaron. She couldn't separate the two. She remembered how her body had felt, but it was Jaron's body that she remembered. Jaron's hands, his fingers, his mouth...

"So I spend the rest of my life trying to repeat that experience?" she asked herself.

"Who are you kidding?" she demanded as she headed for the shower. But then she paused. There was a note on her bedside table.

I had to take the kids home—I didn't think you were ready for their questions. But maybe I am. XXX. J.

As a love letter it left something to be desired, perhaps, but Annabelle stood and stared down at it for a very long time. What did he mean, *maybe I am.*

Did he mean he was ready for his kids to question him about their relationship?

No! This wasn't going anywhere, she decided, desperate in

her search for logic. It couldn't. She might have spent the past thirty years fighting shy of sex, only to discover it was somewhere between marvelous and magical, but that didn't mean she was in the market for a long-term commitment.

Did it?

Her eyes drifted to the wastebasket, where the photograph she'd taken the day before lay waiting to be cleared. The photograph which she'd torn in two. Jaron and the baby on one side. She and Harold on the other. She lifted the two pieces and laid them on the table, smoothing them into each other.

Families.

She and Jaron and dog and baby. And out of the frame, Ricky and Tina.

This whole setup was so far out of her ken that she felt almost claustrophobic. This wasn't going to happen. Not in a million years. She was a loner. Her whole life had been a striving for independence. And that was how she was going to stay.

He was a cop with a family. His kids needed a mother, and she had no idea how to be one. She'd struggled all her life to learn to live alone. If she got close, she'd hurt them. She must. How the hell could someone like her learn to play happy family?

But Jaron...

She looked down at his face and couldn't suppress a smile. All the tenderness in the world was in that face. He gave himself in bucket loads to his kids. He was willing to give it to this mystery baby.

And maybe he was willing to give it to her.

She wanted it!

She was going nuts. She cast one last glance at the picture, then moved to split it again. But something stopped her. Something...

She stared down at the photograph for a long time, seemingly lost in her own world. She was no longer looking at the photograph, but through it.

Tell no one.

Tell no one what?

Unbidden, the words echoed back. Annabelle conjured up the woman's image and then did the same with another image, one she'd prefer to block out.

And she focused again on the baby.

Hell.

"I'm going mad," she told Harold, who was still soundly asleep on the settee, where she'd left him the previous night. The old dog didn't stir.

Maybe she should phone Jaron.

Yeah, right. Phone Jaron? He'd walked out on her, and out was where he had to stay. She couldn't get any closer. Couldn't. Otherwise she'd go nuts.

She had some serious thinking to do and she needed time.

But what was before her had to be handled now.

"I'm imagining things," she told Harold, then sighed. "But it's just as well it's a holiday. How do you feel about another trip to the country?"

"WE NEED to go back to Annabelle's."

Ricky's demand was the first thing Jaron surfaced to, and it was so exactly what he felt like doing that he almost agreed without thinking. But he was waking up to Ricky and Tina jumping on his bed—the bed he'd shared with Cathy. The night was over. Common sense prevailed. Or did it?

"Um, why?" He was still half-asleep. He'd sat up half the night and stared out the window at Seattle traffic, thinking really, really stupid thoughts. Somewhere toward dawn he'd come to the realization that he was crazy. Annabelle wasn't the woman he needed. Annabelle was gorgeous and funny and clever, and she felt so damned good he could still feel her as part of him—but she *wasn't* what he needed. He *wanted* Annabelle, but he *needed* a mother figure for his kids. Annabelle was a professional—a doctor whose life was committed to her work.

That was his head working. Not his heart.

So where did he go from here? Maybe he should join a

support group for single parents, he thought grimly. That way he could meet someone in the same situation.

But all he could think of was Annabelle. He must be out of his mind. How could he even consider anyone else when Annabelle was there?

"We left our cloaks at Annabelle's," Tina was saying. "We have to go get them. Now!"

"Halloween's not for weeks." His objection sounded feeble, even to him.

"Yes, but we have to practice wearing them."

"Dr. Peters is probably working."

"Phone her, Daddy. Tell her we're coming."

"Can I have a shower first?"

"Yes, if you hurry."

WHEN ANNABELLE emerged from her shower, her phone was ringing.

"Breakfast?"

She blinked. Jaron's voice was deep and gravelly and unbelievably intimate. It did peculiar things to her insides.

"Pardon?"

"We were wondering, the kids and I," he said, as though he'd assumed she'd guess what he was thinking and was slightly surprised that she hadn't, "whether you needed breakfast. We wondered if we could have it together."

She looked down at her bare toes and thought about it. "I have cornflakes here," she told him. "Enough for one."

"That doesn't sound very companionable."

"No."

"Would you like to be companionable?"

She thought about that for so long she risked Jaron thinking the line was dead. Finally she responded. "No," she said.

His chuckle sounded down the line. "Scared, Dr. Peters?"

That was easy. "Yes."

"You have no need to be."

"I have every need. I have no idea why I did what I did last night…"

"Now that's a lie," he said softly. "You have every idea. We went into things with our eyes wide open, Dr. Peters. Two consenting adults having a very good time."

"So maybe that's where we leave it."

"After breakfast."

"Excuse me?"

"We forgot the cloaks."

The cloaks. She glanced around and there they were hanging over chairs, fantastic and amazing. "You left your cloaks behind! For heaven's sake! What were you thinking?"

"I can't imagine," he said with such a depth of meaning in his voice that she found herself blushing all the way to her toes. Good grief! The man was making her feel...

Making her feel what?

Beautiful.

And very, very desirable.

"The kids can't believe that we left them behind," he was saying, and she had to concentrate on stopping her body from reacting while she listened to what he was saying. She'd never felt like this. She was standing stark-naked by the phone and her whole body was blushing. Just from hearing his voice! "So maybe we could do breakfast."

"Not here!"

"Not if you only have cornflakes for one. How about Caffeine Hy's?"

Caffeine Hy's. She knew it. The whole hospital knew it. Caffeine Hy's was one of Seattle's best coffeehouses, and Hy himself seemed to be father confessor to half the hospital staff.

Even Annabelle wasn't impervious to Hy's easy sympathy and charm.

Maybe this was a good idea. Caffeine Hy's was hardly the place for an intimate rendezvous, she thought, and Hy made great hotcakes.

"You're bringing the kids?"

"For breakfast on a public holiday? Of course I'm bringing the kids."

"Great." She was rescheduling her day in her head. A fast

breakfast, offload the cloaks, then head out to Keith's cottage. Via the mortuary.

Maybe she should tell Jaron what she was intending. What she was starting to suspect.

No. Her suspicion was just a tiny niggle in the back of her brain. Maybe she was being stupid. If she was…well, she'd lose nothing by investigating herself.

Tell no one. And don't get involved.

She shouldn't even go for breakfast.

''I'll see you in half an hour,'' she said before her sensible self could make any more sensible suggestions. She didn't want to hear one more word from her sensible self. Not one.

CHAPTER TWELVE

SHE WAS LATE—or maybe they were early. Jaron ushered the kids into Caffeine Hy's and looked around him. The mismatched chairs, the scarred old tables, the beaded floor lamps and paper wall sconces...the place had a bohemian feel to it that he normally loved.

Today he didn't even appreciate it. Where was Annabelle?

"Well, well, if it isn't the good detective and Trouble One and Trouble Two. Hi, guys. What can I do for you this morning?" Hy himself was standing over them, beaming down at the kids.

Jaron visited this place often. Hy's was a kid-friendly venue for emergencies when there wasn't anything to eat at home. Or when he was just too tired to cook. Or too lonely. "You're out early this morning," Hy was saying, and the kids were bursting to tell him why.

"We're collecting our cloaks," Tina said importantly.

"From Dr. Peters," Ricky added. "We stayed at her place last night, but we went to sleep and we forgot to take them home with us."

Great! Hy's eyebrows were hitting his hairline and Jaron could see the gossip-cogs working overtime.

"Annabelle Peters?" Hy asked without looking at Jaron, and Jaron gave an inward groan. "Do you kids mean Dr. Annabelle Peters? Dr. Peters of the amazing hair?"

Tina beamed. "Annabelle has lovely hair. Daddy thinks it's lovely, don't you, Daddy?"

Another silent groan from Jaron. Discretion wasn't in Tina's vocabulary. He'd have to start teaching the kids survival skills. For *his* survival.

"She has the superest car," Ricky added. "It's yellow and she puts the hood down so we can let the wind blow on our faces."

"And she has a dog named Harold who licks us and lets us sleep on his couch," Tina put in for good measure.

Hy was looking more and more intrigued. Jaron caught his friend's eye and tried to frown him down.

"Nothing," he said warningly, and got another lift of the eyebrows.

"Nothing?"

"If you know what's good for you, you'll say nothing," Jaron growled.

"Discretion is my middle name." But Hy was laughing and Jaron thought, Yeah, get real. If this wasn't all over Seattle by midday, it'd be a miracle.

"So did you say Dr. Peters is coming here?" Hy asked. "For breakfast?"

"With our cloaks." Tina and Ricky were beaming identical smiles. Things were right in their world. Very, very right. "Daddy says we can have hotcakes."

"A pile of hotcakes? Maple syrup? Whipped butter?"

"Yes!"

"Coming right up." Hy's great chuckle rang out over the coffeehouse. "A pile of celebration hotcakes with trimmings. You guys and Annabelle Peters. Well, well and well."

THE ENCOUNTER had affected Jaron.

He hadn't been teased about a woman since he'd married Cathy. Hy's look, his laugh... It hit home suddenly that he was being unfaithful. It felt really, really strange.

Was he being unfaithful to Cathy?

His wife had been dead for two long years, he told himself harshly. She wouldn't be standing over him reminding him to grieve. *Get a life,* he could almost hear her saying, and was absurdly comforted.

And then Annabelle walked in and he forgot about feeling strange. He forgot about Cathy. He forgot about everything but Annabelle.

Had she been this beautiful last night?

No. It wasn't possible. She'd changed in some indefinable way...matured...grown. She seemed almost to be glowing. Casually dressed in sweatshirt, jeans and sneakers, she practically bounced across to their table. Her hair was pulled casually back, not in her normal tight braid but in a wild, bunched ponytail of curls. She looked all of sixteen.

Except for her eyes, he thought, dazed. And her mouth. Her mouth looked full, bruised even. Kissed. She smiled and she was every bit a mature woman.

Gloriously mature.

It was all Jaron could do not to stand and take her in his arms right then and there. The memory of last night came flooding back, the feel of her, the taste...

What the hell was he doing in Caffeine Hy's? They could take the kids to Round the Clock and...

But she was sliding into a seat, her beaming expression embracing the kids as they whooped over the cloaks she'd brought.

"Hi. You guys must have alarm clocks or something."

"Did we wake you?" His voice sounded strange. Croaky. She cast him a glance he didn't understand.

"Nope. I just got out of the shower when you called." She met his eyes at last and she was laughing. "I woke up chilly. All my bedclothes seemed to be on the floor on the other side of the bed. I can't imagine how that happened."

He blushed, just like a silly kid. Good grief.

"Maybe you had a bad dream," Tina said helpfully, and Annabelle nodded.

"Maybe. Or maybe it was a good dream. What do you think, Detective Dorsey?"

What did he think? That was easy.

"A good dream," he said definitely. "The best."

Their eyes met and locked. It was only for a moment, but felt much longer. As if the earth in some incomprehensible way had made a quantum shift, and when it stopped, things weren't the same.

And it wasn't just Jaron it was happening to. Annabelle

opened her mouth to speak, but nothing came out. She looked winded. As if she'd run a marathon.

As if she didn't know what on earth was happening to her.

"Here's breakfast." Hy placed a plate of steaming hotcakes before them. He was grinning, his eyes asking all sorts of questions, which were being answered very satisfactorily, thank you very much. "If I'm not interrupting anything?"

"What would you be interrupting?" Jaron managed to say.

"What would I be interrupting? Now there's a question. I suspect it's one that only you guys can answer." Hy put plates down before Tina and Ricky and smiled broadly at the kids.

"Should I bother giving plates to Annabelle and your dad? Do you think they're hungry?"

"Of course they're hungry," Ricky said, reaching for his first pancake. "Who wouldn't be hungry when there's hotcakes?"

"I guess it depends what else is on the menu," Hy said enigmatically, and then at the look in Jaron's eyes, he held up his hands in mock surrender. "Okay. Okay. No questions. I'll leave you to your breakfast. I'll leave you to whatever."

IT WAS A GREAT breakfast, followed by a great morning. Full of pancakes they took themselves for a walk.

"Only for an hour," Annabelle told them. "I have things to do."

"Like what?" Jaron asked. They were walking along the waterfront, the kids between them. They were linked like a family, Annabelle on one side and Jaron on the other. Okay, so they were separated by two kids, but it sure didn't feel like that. It felt as if the current of warmth was flowing right through.

It felt…great.

"Work," Annabelle told him, and he frowned.

"I thought you were off duty for the whole weekend."

"Mmm. But there are things to do."

"Same with me." He'd promised to head into the station and make a few calls. He had men in Vancouver looking for missing people. Despite his preoccupation with Annabelle, the baby's plight still weighed heavily on his mind. "Speaking of which…"

There was a newspaper stand right beside them. Jaron paused and picked up the top copy. Annabelle's picture of tiny Chris beamed up at him. The paper had run it as a headline: Mystery Orphan—Help Us Find Her Family

"Powerful stuff," Jaron murmured, looking at the photograph. There were more pictures on page two and three—the ones of him and the baby, and Keith and Shana. "This should get the media off Seth's back. Great job."

"Did you take these pictures?" Ricky asked, staring at the newspaper, and Annabelle nodded.

"Yes."

"So you can find out who the baby's mommy is?"

"The baby's mommy died," Annabelle said gently, and Ricky nodded.

"Oh, yeah, I forgot. Like ours. Our mommy died."

"Now we're trying to find her grandma and grandpa and her aunties and uncles."

"She'd rather have a mommy," Tina said flatly, and walked away from them. They all gazed after her. Her four-year-old shoulders were set and braced, as if she was pushing through pain.

"Hell," Jaron whispered, but there was no end to it. He knew Annabelle saw the bleakness in his heart. He knew she wanted desperately to do something. Anything.

But to reach out and touch him was a gesture that was beyond her. For to reach out was to join the circle, to say she wanted to move past this last boundary and be a part of this little group.

To be part of a family.

She couldn't. Not yet. All her life she must have been alone. For her to take this one last step…

"I…" She glanced at her watch. "I need to go."

Jaron heard what she was saying. Really saying. He stilled, his eyes searching hers. "Really?"

"Yes."

"You really do have to work?"

"Yes."

Of course, Jaron realized. She was a professional. A doctor. She had no part in their lives and he had no right to try to include her.

"We haven't made our hats yet," Ricky said urgently, tugging her hand. "Don't you remember? Last night you said maybe we could make hats. Daddy's terrible at making hats."

Annabelle managed a smile, but it was a weak one. "How about I make them for you?"

"It'd be more fun to make them together."

Tina was listening. She'd turned back and was watching the interplay, her small face thoughtful, as if she knew what Annabelle was about to say before she said it.

"I don't have time," Annabelle said, and the child's face shut down. Yep, she'd expected it.

"You'll never have time," Tina said.

"I meant I don't have time for us to make them together," Annabelle told her. "But I'm sure I have all the things I need to make excellent hats. What if I do them myself and then drop them off to your daddy at the police station?"

"Maybe we could have breakfast together again," Ricky suggested, but Jaron was shaking his head and swooping his little boy up into his arms. As if protecting him.

"No. Dr. Peters is a busy lady. We can't keep interfering in her life."

Damn, what had happened? It had gone from light to dark in an instant.

"I'll see you later," she said uncertainly, and turned away before the bleakness in three sets of faces could reach her any further. Before she took that one final step that obviously scared her silly.

AFTER SHE LEFT them, Annabelle didn't return to the hospital right away. Sure, she had things to do. Sure, the hospital was calling, but for now she paced the waterfront and tried to work out what was happening.

She could fall in love with Jaron in an instant. Maybe she already had.

And she could fall in love with his kids. In a way, that was much, much easier. They were great kids. They needed stability and love and cuddles and someone to make them wizard and witch hats.

It was an enticing call. It would be so easy to take this next step forward. Commit.

Yeah, right, as if she knew the first thing about commitment. With her background? It'd be an unmitigated disaster. She didn't know anything about raising kids. She didn't know the first thing about loving.

She was a doctor. Her life was her job. She needed no one and no one needed her.

Except Harold. She had a dog waiting for her back at the hospital, and a suspicion about a mystery baby to be confirmed or proved wrong.

She had things to do. She didn't have time to spend wandering the waterfront, thinking of impossibilities. Thinking of families.

But she was.

WHAT HAD GONE wrong?

Jaron took the kids the long way home past the waterfront carousel. The kids loved it here. He could keep handing money to the man in charge and let his confused mind think while the kids rode up and down and whooped on the dappled horses.

Last night had been amazing. Annabelle had given herself to him in a way he'd never dreamed possible. She was a virgin. The knowledge had stunned him, but she'd opened to him, welcoming his body, meeting him and merging with him like two halves of a whole.

Last night had felt like a marriage. It hadn't felt like a one-night stand. It had felt like forever.

And this morning? When he'd seen her, it had felt the same. Just plain wonderful. His body had reacted to her in a way he'd never known his body to react before, not even with Cathy.

And the kids liked her. They loved her! They thought she was a truly amazing human being—which she was.

Annabelle...

So what had made her pull back?

It had been too fast, he told himself as his daughter bobbed up and down in front of him on her white horse, and waved her ice-cream cone at him. He'd moved too fast, had been too damned eager. Hell, he was going to have to learn this dating business all over again. He'd scare off a woman like Annabelle. Breakfast with the kids, Hy gossiping all over town—that had been just plain stupid. And he'd only known her since Friday.

That was it. It was too fast.

Maybe if he backed off a little. Just a little. Maybe he could start again.

But then he thought of Annabelle's face as she'd retreated. Her expression had bordered on panic.

He'd be lucky to get within twenty feet of her, he thought grimly. He'd blown it. She was a doctor, single and smart and well paid. What the hell would she want with a family? *For an intelligent man, Dorsey, you're an idiot.*

ANNABELLE'S FIRST STOP was the morgue. Her suspicions, once aroused, refused to be suppressed.

"There've been no inquiries?" she asked the morgue attendant, and Linda shook her head.

"Nope. Looks like Jane and John Doe might be with us for a while. I'm trying to arrange transfer to the city morgue."

There was more storage space at the city morgue than at the hospital, Annabelle knew. There had to be. The city was full of dead unknowns. Kids on drugs. Hit-and-run victims. People who'd died homeless. This pair weren't the only John and Jane Does in the city. There were too darned many.

And she hated it that the parents of little Chris had joined the list of unknowns. The transfer to the city morgue was the first step in losing their identity even further.

"I don't want them moved until tomorrow," she said, and Linda nodded.

"We can't get transport on a public holiday, anyway."

"Fine."

But it wasn't fine. Annabelle slid the cadavers out of their storage spaces and stared down at them, one then the other.

The man's face was burned beyond recognition. Only his bone structure remained. And the woman...

She looked at her longer.

Tell no one...

"If I have to tell your secret then I will," she whispered. "If I can figure it out. If I'm right...I'm sorry, but your secret isn't safe with me. Not if you've done what I think you've done."

She bit her lip and then turned to ask the attendant to run a few more tests.

Like it or not, Dr. Annabelle Peters was involved. In more ways than one.

JARON TOOK the kids into Round the Clock and left them.

"Why can't we go to Annabelle's and make hats?" Tina demanded, but Jaron shook his head.

"You heard Annabelle. She has to work. Just like I do."

"When you finish work, will you take us to Annabelle's?"

"It'll be too late."

"Please, Daddy."

"It sounds like you're being coerced like all good daddies." Jill Jamison, a local celebrity, was dropping off her son, Todd, and she was laughing at Tina's pleading tone. "Are you another of the unlucky ones who get to work on public holidays?"

"You know cops," Jaron told her. "No such thing as business hours." Jill was the face and spokesperson for Mother Nature skin-care products. Jill kept the fact she had a son a secret from the general public and wore various wigs and disguises whenever she came to Round the Clock with Todd. The staff and the parents who knew of her situation did their best to help her protect her privacy. Alexandra Webber had once tried her hand at matchmaking between Jaron and Jill when both were using Forrester Square Day Care, but things hadn't fizzed between them. Nothing had fizzed for Jaron. Until Annabelle...

"Business hours are not for models, either," Jill told him.

"I have a photo shoot for a charity today. Thank heaven for Round the Clock."

Todd was certainly a live wire. In fact, four-year-old Todd had the reputation of being the most challenging child in day care. Even now he was reaching out for a pair of scissors on the reception desk.

"Todd!" The scissors fell with a clatter as his mother's stern voice rang out. But Todd's bright little eyes immediately moved on, searching for another source of mischief.

Jill must have eyes in the back of her head, Jaron thought, and thanked heaven for his well-behaved kids. But then, his kids had had a couple of years of Cathy's calming influence. Jill had done it on her own from the start.

"I'm sorry, we can't go back to Annabelle's," he told Ricky and Tina, ushering them into the playroom. "But she's told us that she'll make the hats."

"It's not the same as helping."

It wasn't, but he had to move on. He couldn't afford to think about Annabelle all the time. Or any of the time.

"I'll see you guys later," he told them. "Before dinner."

"Okay." Normally they were delighted to be at Round the Clock, but something had changed. Two sad pairs of eyes followed him to the door.

Things had changed, for his kids, as well as for him.

ANNABELLE DROVE up to Keith's cabin, feeling very peculiar indeed.

Maybe she should be with Jaron.

It would be so easy, she thought, to drop into the police station and tell him what she suspected. He'd be with her now.

Which was exactly why she hadn't done it. She didn't want to be sitting beside Jaron. She needed to get her thoughts in order. Last night her world had shifted on its axis and she badly needed it to resettle.

The ride in the country was the perfect remedy. Soon Indian summer would end, and autumn—or winter—would begin in earnest. But for now she'd let the wind blow in her hair and she'd enjoy every minute. Harold was sitting beside her. She had her dog. She had her car. She had her life.

What else did she want?

Jaron. And Tina. And Ricky.

"Don't be a fool. You didn't know them before Friday."

"I can't wind the clock back and change things."

"No. But you can be sensible."

She was talking out loud, and Harold was looking at her with a puzzled expression on his gentle face. She gave him a quick stroke and sighed.

"You don't want a family, do you, boy? You're happy with me?"

But the image returned—the picture of Harold with Tina and Ricky draped over him as they all slept in front of the television. Harold wouldn't mind a family at all.

"THERE'S NOTHING."

"What do you mean, nothing?"

Luke Sloan had been sifting through a mass of paperwork when Jaron arrived. "We've reached a blank," Luke told him. "Our guys have been up to Glacier and absolutely nothing has turned up."

"Define 'nothing.'"

Luke sighed and shrugged. "Okay. The car was stolen weeks ago. It belonged to a couple with four young kids who'd left the car for only minutes. The car was unlocked with the keys in the ignition."

"Stupid."

"Yeah, but understandable. Dad takes the older kids in to choose ice cream, leaving Mom and baby in the car. There's a queue, so he's longer than expected. The baby starts crying. Mom picks up the baby and follows him in, not realizing her husband left the keys in the ignition. Two minutes later they see their car disappearing down the street. So that's it."

"There's no response from the publicity?"

"No." Luke lifted the newspaper and stared down at the baby's face. "Maybe we won't get anything. All kids look the same at this age."

"You wait until you have your own," Jaron said, and watched his friend's face tinge with something that might almost have been pleasure.

"Actually..." Luke began, and the look on his face said it all. Jaron stared, and then grinned in delight.

"You're kidding."

"Nope. There'll be a little Sloan baby seven months from now."

"Congratulations. No wonder you were looking so smug at the market yesterday. You'll never say all kids look the same again."

Luke hesitated. "I guess I won't. But it doesn't help our case now, though. We need to focus on this one."

Jaron nodded. "So we have a couple who stole an unlocked car with the keys in the ignition. Impulse steal?"

"I'd guess." Luke handed over the vehicle description. "Helped also by the fact that the owners had attached the mounts for a baby seat. Real handy."

Jaron thought about it and winced. "Nothing else?"

"Nope. The car seat you hauled out of the fire is a standard job—it could be one of thousands, which explains why the straps fitted. But that's all we have. Opportunistic theft. Maybe panic theft, but we don't know why. You'd think if they were planning on driving all the way to Seattle, they'd steal something in better condition."

"Unless, as you say, it was just a chance opportunity that couldn't be ignored. A car available with everything they needed right when they needed it. But why did they need it?"

"You tell me."

"Hell." Jaron lifted the mound of paperwork and groaned. Missing-person reports. Phone calls from helpful members of the public. Tips from sources. With such an appealing story, chances were they'd have hundreds more such leads before the end of the day.

"Mom and Dad and a baby missing from somewhere near Glacier." He mused. "You realize there might be an older kid waiting for them to come home. The mother's given birth before."

"I don't want to think about that," Luke said flatly. "I can't work any faster than I'm doing right now. The chief's put me on this with you. The child molester is taking precedence—he's becoming a real nightmare. But let's find this kid a family."

UP IN THE CABIN the baby in question had all the family she needed and then some. She'd had the undivided attention of both Keith and Shana—well, almost undivided attention, but that was another story—and now she had Annabelle. And Harold.

Harold was the only one not interested. The old dog was delighted to be back at the cabin and was totally focused on rabbit sniffing.

Which left Annabelle free to concentrate on Chris.

"Why are you here?" Shana asked when Annabelle arrived, and Annabelle shrugged in some embarrassment. Why was she here? Good question.

"A hunch."

"What sort of hunch?"

"I'm not really sure," Annabelle admitted. "Can I see her again?"

So now she sat on Keith's sofa with tiny Chris fast asleep in her arms, and what had seemed possible back at the hospital now seemed stupid.

"I was imagining things. Thank heaven I didn't tell Jaron."

Shana sat down beside her and looked at her friend in concern. "What didn't you tell Jaron?"

Annabelle stared down at the baby and the doubts she'd had back in the city seemed more and more ridiculous. She looked up at Keith who was wiping down the counter. "He's quite domestic, isn't he," she murmured, but they all knew she was just buying time. Trying to figure out what to say.

"I've been stupid," she said at last into the silence.

"You want to tell us why?" Keith was wiping a saucepan now, increasing the impression of domesticity.

Keith and Shana. Annabelle glanced from one to the other.

On the surface this setup seemed terrific. But there were undercurrents. The way they didn't quite look at each other...

She needed to concentrate on the baby. On the reason she was here. "I just..." She frowned and stared some more at little Chris's rosy cheeks. "I thought the couple who died...they're fine-boned, lean. And this little one...well, she's round-faced and chubby. It was just a momentary impression." She shook her head as if trying to clear it. "It was nothing, I suppose."

"I was round-faced and chubby," Keith told her. "Michelin man—or Michelin baby—that was me. I think I was born with three spare tires. But look at me now." He flexed a bare arm in the sunlight and grinned. "Pure muscle."

"I think maybe you'd better stick to your kitchen chores," Shana said dryly, and at the look on his face, both women burst into giggles. Tension dispelled in one fell swoop.

"I believe I've just been insulted." Keith huffed, and the giggles increased.

But the laughter didn't last long. The tension slammed home again.

"Annabelle, we're all upset about this," Keith said gently as she bit her lip in distress. "We're worried about what will happen to the baby. But you can't read anything into a baby's parentage by the way she looks at four weeks old. Or not much, anyway."

"I know."

"What are you thinking?" Shana asked slowly.

"I'm not sure."

"That the couple who died weren't the baby's parents?" Keith asked, his face intense. "I thought you said there was evidence the woman had just given birth."

"There is. She had."

"So..."

Annabelle tried to think it through. Out loud. "They were running for a reason," she said slowly. "They'd come a long way after stealing a car. The police have found no reports of crimes that would indicate this couple as suspects. But there had to be something that sent them fleeing."

"It's early in the investigation yet," Keith countered. "These things take time."

Annabelle shook her head. "I know it sounds stupid. It was just…I looked at the photograph I'd taken and she seemed so chubby, so different from the couple. But you're right. Looking at her now… There's no reason to doubt her parentage, I guess."

Keith nodded. All eyes were on the sleeping baby. "It would definitely complicate matters if the child wasn't a biological match with the couple."

"That's why you're here," Shana whispered. "You're not sure. You had to have another look."

"I…"

"Just tell us what you need, Annabelle," Keith said, still watching the baby. "We're your friends. You can tell us."

"I thought perhaps a blood test would be in order. Nothing complicated like DNA profiling—that can wait—but just a simple blood test. If they're not compatible…"

"You really think you're onto something, don't you." Keith was looking at her now, and her fear must have shown. He sounded appalled, which was how Annabelle felt.

"I…I didn't say that," she told him. "But having thought it, having wondered…well, what would it hurt? Maybe I should do the blood test and find out."

CHAPTER THIRTEEN

KEITH AGREED to the blood test and it only took a moment. A pinprick. With the tiny vial of blood safe beside her, Annabelle drove back into the city thinking she was losing her mind. She was becoming paranoid.

Why on earth did she suspect the couple had done something worse than steal a car?

Tell no one...

It wasn't just the words, she thought. It was the way the woman had looked at her lovely, healthy little girl—and stared right through her.

You don't understand. He made me do it. She's not... He said... Tell no one. But she...she's going to die. My baby will die.

And...

My baby. My baby. Oh, God, what have I done? I want her so... Find her for me. Don't let her die. Please.

The whole thing didn't make sense. The woman had died of a ruptured aorta. She had only minor head injuries. She'd been conscious. Sure, she'd been suffering massive blood loss and internal bleeding, but that shouldn't have made her blind to what she was seeing. Her daughter.

Unless it wasn't her daughter.

Oh, God, maybe she should have told Jaron exactly what the woman had said. Word for word. Thinking it through now, with these awful suspicions in her mind, she felt appalled that she hadn't.

"It's none of my business," Annabelle told Harold as she turned her car into the hospital parking lot. "It doesn't concern me. Have I learned nothing? Keep my nose out of what's not my affair.''

But the look on Jaron's face as he'd gazed down at the baby came flooding back to her. It was a look that had the power to change Annabelle's world.

Jaron had lost his wife. He had two small children who were dependent on him and a mother-in-law who hated him. He, more than anyone else, should have learned to hold the world at bay. He should have learned not to get involved.

But yesterday, as Annabelle had held the camera, he'd looked down into the baby's face and he'd cared.

He was a caring man.

He could care…for her?

"Yeah, and pigs might fly," she said angrily as she drew to a halt. "Because I'd have to care back. And I don't. I can't."

But she could at least do this one thing. Get involved this much.

One blood test and that would be the end of it.

ONLY IT WASN'T an end to it at all. The blood test raised more questions than it answered. Annabelle sat at her desk and stared at the results in front of her and felt sick.

Mother AB.

Father A.

Baby O.

She stared blankly at the results for a long, long time.

Okay, what did she have here? The test results meant the woman definitely wasn't the baby's mother and the man probably wasn't the baby's father.

There were a million kids in the country right this minute whose parents didn't match their blood group, she thought. Dad remarries. Mix and match families.

But the words came back again to haunt her.

You don't understand. He made me do it. She's not…

And…

My baby. My baby. Oh, God, what have I done?

She couldn't ignore this. She couldn't sweep this under the carpet.

Damn, damn and triple-damn.

Sighing, she reached for the phone to contact Jaron. She knew he wasn't going to like it.

To SAY HE DIDN'T like it was an understatement.

"She's *what?*" Jaron had made the trip to the hospital faster than she'd thought possible. Now he was standing in the doorway of her office, staring at her incredulously.

"According to the blood groups, our baby can't be the woman's biological daughter. The chances are strong that she isn't the man's daughter, either."

"You're kidding."

"No."

Silence. He didn't seem to know what to say. Where to start. So she had to start. Somehow.

"I've been out to Keith's cottage," she explained. "I took a sample of blood from the baby and compared it with samples from our John and Jane Doe. They don't match. The mother's AB, the father is A, and they have a type O daughter. It doesn't fit."

He was visibly forcing himself to stay calm. "The woman who was killed in the accident is not the baby's mother?"

"No."

He was almost frighteningly still, Annabelle thought, but somehow she made herself go on. "The father's blood type is A, which means he can still be the baby's father, but it's unlikely, and since the mother's not the birth mother, though she's recently given birth...well, it's almost discountable. I've sent samples for DNA testing, but I'm almost sure I'm right."

Jaron didn't move. He couldn't. For a moment, anger threatened to overwhelm him. The emotion of the night before had dissolved—or maybe it was still there, making him feel as if this was a personal betrayal.

"What made you do the test?"

It seemed an innocuous remark, but Annabelle shivered. She

knew this man well enough to realize there was a depth of care behind his words. A depth of fury.

So what had made her suspect? What was making her almost sure she was right?

"I just wondered…"

His eyes weren't leaving hers for a second. "You wondered enough to go all the way to Keith's to take a blood sample."

"Yes."

"Yet you didn't tell me."

"I'm telling you now."

He flexed his knuckles until they cracked. Once more she had that impression of emotion barely contained.

He was standing in the doorway watching her, but his thoughts were obviously back at the scene of the wreck. "I saw the lady scared stiff about her husband," he told her. "I saw her terrified for her baby. She gave birth four weeks ago and the baby's four weeks old. To say it's not hers… It's crazy. What made you suspect otherwise, Annabelle? *What?*"

Annabelle. The way he said her name made her shiver. Last night it had been an endearment. Today it was nothing of the kind. "I—"

"What?" He walked forward and slammed his hands on her desk so hard that the papers in front of her jumped half an inch off the surface. His anger was no longer contained as he towered over her. "What the hell? You treat her and you don't say a word. You tell me she didn't say anything that might help. You spend two days stalling, and all the time…you suspect *this*. You think maybe she's not their baby. Female intuition? I don't think so. You tell me what she said, Dr. Peters, or I'm going to cross this desk and wring every last word out of you. Now!"

She tried for a smile, but it didn't quite work. "There's a professional warning, I don't think."

"Hang professional. There's nothing professional about what's between us. I don't sleep with my colleagues. I don't make Halloween costumes with witnesses or with suspects. I trusted you and I was just plain stupid. This has gone far beyond professionalism—witness lying to cop—and you know it. You've lied to us. You've lied to *me*.''

Anger came to her aid then, and thank God for it. It enabled her to meet his gaze, be defiant, instead of remorseful. ''I haven't lied to anyone,'' she snapped.

''Tell me what she said.'' There was an element of weariness in his tone now—and an element of something else. As though he'd moved on.

As though she'd killed something that he really wanted.

''She didn't say—'' she started, but he interrupted.

''She did say and I want to hear it.'' He was speaking slowly, as if she was a sandwich short of a picnic. ''I want every single word with every last intonation. This is a child's life we're talking about here, Dr. Peters. You spit the whole truth out. Now.''

''I—''

''You can't get any more involved than you are right now,'' he told her, lowering his voice to just plain threatening. ''I can do it the hard way if you like—get a subpoena and take you to court and drag it out of you bit by bit. But you don't want that and neither do I. So stop being so damned stupid and tell me.''

Silence. They were head-to-head. He was so close. She could feel his anger emanating in waves.

''I didn't mean—''

''I know you didn't mean,'' he cut her off. ''You didn't mean to get involved. That's your style. Caring's for the rest of the world, not for you.''

''I didn't say I didn't care.''

''No. You showed it.''

''Look—''

''Just tell me, Annabelle,'' he said wearily. ''Just tell me.''

So she did.

It was nothing. Or she'd thought it was nothing but the woman's fear for her baby and husband and fear about a stolen car. But now, as she sat at her desk and gazed at the angry eyes of the man in front of her, she could see that it wasn't nothing at all.

First there was the fact that the woman hadn't seemed to see the baby.

"I noticed that," Jaron told her, his anger giving way to intense concentration. The cop in him was taking precedence. "I thought she'd suffered a head injury."

"She hadn't. Yet she was looking right through the baby. Past her. She was sobbing terror for her child, yet her baby was right there. No matter how we reassured her, she didn't seem to hear. And then…"

"Then?"

Annabelle thought back. She closed her eyes and let the whole scene resurface. The moments before the administration of the anesthetic. It was all still horribly real. She let herself drift back, speaking the remembered words out loud.

"My baby. My baby." The whispering was almost frantic.

"Your baby's here."

"You don't understand. He made me do it. She's not… He said… Tell no one. But she…she's going to die. My baby will die."

"Your baby's healthy, well cared for…"

"My baby. My baby. Oh, God, what have I done? I want her so…"

And then the woman's hand clutched hers.

"Find…find her for me. Don't let her die. Please."

"I won't. We'll find her and look after her."

Annabelle was holding the baby in her arms right there and then.

"You'll keep her safe? You'll tell no one. What I said?" The woman's hand clutched Annabelle's in terror.

"I'll tell no one," she agreed, and the woman's terror lessened.

"My husband…he'll be so angry. But…keep her safe."

"I'll keep her safe."

Annabelle paused. That was all there was and she'd related

it aloud exactly as it had been said to her. It was little enough, but she felt drained. Ill.

A vision came back, the memory of a young girl being wheeled into the morgue because Annabelle had broken a promise. Dear God, let this not have similar repercussions.

Jaron was staring at her, a strange look on his face. As if he couldn't figure her out. He'd sat down on the far side of her desk, watchful and wary.

"That's it?"

"That's it."

"It's not exactly a betrayal," he said mildly, watching her face, "to tell me that."

"I promised."

"And the last time you broke a promise, a kid lost her life."

"I...yes." She tilted her chin.

"But this time there's a baby who needs a life. Without your help she has nothing." He leaned over the desk and took her hands in his. Not as a gesture of comfort. More with a sense of urgency, as if he was trying to shake some sense into her. "It seems you're not exactly working on intuition, but you're not working on facts, either. She could simply have been confused."

"Yes."

"But you don't think so."

"No." She shook her head. "'He made me do it,' she said. Do what? I didn't understand then and I don't understand now. But I'm starting to feel sick to my stomach."

"So am I." He was still holding her hands. The feeling was strange. It wasn't a feeling of comfort or strength. It felt almost claustrophobic, as if he was hauling her into this web of concern whether she liked it or not.

She withdrew her hands from his, the feeling of nausea increasing by the minute. "I don't know what to think," she said honestly. "We have a mother who's delivered at least two children. She delivered the last baby a month ago and the first baby maybe two years back. The child with Keith and Shana fits the age of the baby she most recently delivered, but she doesn't fit the blood group. This is not her baby.''

''They could have adopted.''

But Annabelle had already thought that through and found it wanting. ''If the mother hadn't recently given birth, then I'd say that's what must have happened. I'd say they must have adopted or else they're caring for someone else's child. But what are the odds? Where's her own child? Her body's not fully recovered from the birth. She's driving a stolen car with a baby in the back seat who's not hers.''

''She's stolen the baby?'' Jaron demanded incredulously, and Annabelle nodded.

''Maybe. Sometimes when a baby dies, parents become unhinged. Grief makes people do stupid things.''

Jaron was thinking fast, coming to terms with the horror. ''That'd fit, except there's no stolen baby. It'd be all over the country by now if a child had been kidnapped.'' He took a step back from the desk and stared down at her, baffled. ''I need to move on this.''

''And do what?''

''Check out adoption records.''

''No organization is going to adopt out a baby to a mother who's so recently given birth.''

''That's supposition.''

''Phone Keith and ask him. It's a reasonable supposition.''

His mind was racing. ''Maybe their baby died so a family member...I don't know, a sister or someone with more kids than they knew what to do with said, 'Take one of mine.' It's been done before.''

''Maybe.''

''But you don't think so.''

''It's the timing. For her to have a baby die and have a sister say, 'I have one exactly the same age—take mine'... What's the chance of that? Or what's the chance of someone saying, 'I need someone to care for my baby—your baby's dead so here you are.' It wouldn't happen. Then there's the fact they were driving a stolen car. And why did she say her husband made her do it? Do what?''

Silence. Then, ''They lost a baby,'' Jaron said flatly, accepting the unthinkable. ''So they took one.''

''And no outcry?''

''They were running scared. They were terrified when I pulled up behind them in the patrol car. That's why they ran the lights.'' He hesitated, but it needed to be said. It was what they were both thinking. ''Maybe they did something to the mother to stop her from talking.''

''Dear God.''

''If we'd known earlier... Why the hell didn't you say anything?''

''I didn't know. I couldn't guess.''

''But you're guessing now.''

''Yes,'' she said bleakly. ''Or maybe I'm not guessing.''

HE LEFT HER then, wheeling away to set an investigation in place that Annabelle didn't want to think about. His anger stayed with her.

In a moment she'd have to find the strength to go and tell Seth about the public-relations nightmare about to crash over his head. But not yet.

She felt sick. Alone.

She felt so damned—

There was a knock. It had to be Seth, she thought. Jaron would have gone straight to him. She hauled her features into some sort of control, but it was Shana whose face appeared around the door.

''Hi.''

''Shana.'' Annabelle regrouped, sort of, and tried to put her thoughts in order. ''Why...why aren't you up at the cabin?''

''We needed diapers, and I thought one of us should find out what's going on. May I come in?''

''Of course. But aren't you coming back to town tonight, anyway?''

''We'll be coming down tomorrow morning to work and to

sort things out,'' Shana said diffidently. ''We still have to figure out the details.''

The details of what? Annabelle looked into her friend's face
and even her own misery couldn't stop her from seeing what
was clearly written there.

''Shana…''

''Don't ask any questions,'' Shana pleaded. ''Because I can't
answer them. Not yet. Right now I'm too confused. I only
know that things are happening I don't really understand, but
I'm going to give them every chance they have of working out.
I have to.''

''You and Keith…''

''Haven't slept together. Not yet, anyway.'' It was an answer
to an unspoken question—maybe more along the lines of what
Shana was thinking than what Annabelle was wondering—and
Annabelle blinked in increased astonishment.

But Shana had moved on. She plopped into the chair Jaron
had just vacated and looked across the desk at her friend. Really looked at her. ''You look like hell, by the way,'' she told
her, and Annabelle winced.

''Gee, thanks.''

''Don't mention it. What are friends for?''

''To boost my spirits?'' Annabelle tried for laughter. ''To
tell me watery is the newest look in makeup?''

Shana's eyes narrowed. Annabelle's flippancy wasn't fooling
her for a minute. ''Watery isn't a look I would associate with
you.''

''Why not?'' Annabelle was suddenly tired of pretense.
''When I cut I bleed.''

''Like the rest of the human race?''

''Yes.''

''You don't usually admit that the human race has anything
to do with you,'' Shana said thoughtfully. ''Or vice versa.''

''So…''

''It's Jaron, isn't it?''

''It's the baby.''

But Shana wasn't listening. "I saw the way you were with each other. It's definitely Jaron. Oh, Annabelle."

Annabelle sniffed and glared. "Oh, Annabelle nothing!"

"Definitely something. Have you slept with him?"

Annabelle's face must have said it all. Shana's eyes widened and she sat back in her chair and stared at her friend in amazement. "You have! He probably hasn't been near a woman since his wife was killed. And you... Have you even dated anyone since coming here?"

"It's none of your business." Heck, how well did Shana know her? They'd lived next door to each other for months, but Annabelle had always made sure she kept to herself. Now she was wondering just how transparent she'd been.

How thin was her armor?

"Tell me what's happening with the baby," Shana said, her tone gentling in the face of her friend's distress. "What did the blood test tell you?"

"That the couple killed weren't her biological parents."

There was a silence. A very long silence.

"Whoa," Shana said at last. "Does Seth know?"

"Not yet."

"And Jaron?"

"I've told him."

"Which is why you're so soggy?"

"Shana..."

Shana held up her hands as if in defense. "Hey, I know I'm making assumptions here, but I'm right, aren't I?"

Annabelle tried. She really tried to keep her face forbidding and cold. It didn't work. "He thinks I'm such a loser," she whispered. "I should have told him before. I could have said..."

"Said what?"

So Annabelle repeated the whole story. *Tell no one.* Ha! That was a joke. The way she was going, she was close to telling the whole world.

But when she was finished, the judgment Annabelle expected wasn't written on Shana's face. "I think maybe I would have done the same thing,'' Shana said thoughtfully, and Annabelle stared.

"You would?''

"You found out the car was stolen. That was enough to explain the 'My husband made me do it' remark. There wasn't anything in that to anticipate something as awful as a stolen baby.''

"But—''

"And she was dying. She was practically incoherent. You couldn't have expected this sort of thing, and the moment you even vaguely wondered, you took steps to check. I think you've done the right thing, and if you'd like, I'll say so to Jaron.''

"I don't think he'll listen.''

"Then he's a fool.'' Shana hesitated, then came around the desk and crouched in front of Annabelle. "You're a very nice person, Annabelle Peters. I don't know what you're running from, why you're holding yourself back from the human race, but I do know that you've got integrity and courage and you care. None of this is your fault.''

Annabelle tried to hold herself back even now. She tried, but Shana wasn't having any of it.

"You need a friend here, Annabelle,'' she said softly. "You need someone to take you out and buy you amaretto and ice cream and chocolate-filled Oreos. In bulk.''

Annabelle stared. She sniffed and searched wildly for a tissue, then sniffed again. Where was her self-containment now? She didn't cry. She wouldn't! "What about Keith?'' she asked, and Shana managed a grin, albeit a shaky one. Shana was involved here, too, up to her neck, and maybe she needed a break from drama, as well.

"Keith can wait. Would we let a man get in the way of us and Oreos? No way. There are some things even more important than sex, and the combination of amaretto and Oreos is one of them.''

"THE KID'S not theirs?'' Seth was in his office when Jaron found him. He'd been elbow-deep in paperwork, and at Jaron's bald statement, the document he was working on dropped to the floor. "What the hell...?"

Jaron outlined the problem to him, and Seth ran his hand through his hair in disbelief.

"Have you any idea what this will do to the hospital? Doctor holds back identity..."

"She didn't hold back the identity," Jaron said, but Seth was in no mood to be placated.

"They'll have our asses. She'll have to go."

"What, fire her?" Jaron's brows snapped together. "You can't do that."

"No, but the powers above me can, and what else are they supposed to do? We can't have our medical team interfering with police investigations. Firing her is the only way to get the press off our back."

Firing her...

Jaron felt sick. A vision of Annabelle's face as he'd last seen it came flooding back. White. Shocked.

Bereft.

Damn the woman, but she'd gotten under his skin. What was he supposed to do? Defend her?

"I don't think it warrants firing."

"She withheld information."

"Yeah, but she had her reasons. Patient confidentiality and stuff. The woman made her promise."

"The woman's dead and now we've got this kid on our hands. The press will have a field day."

"Not if we don't tell them."

"What, keep it under wraps?"

"No. Just say that further information from the autopsy reveals a nonmatch."

"You think they'll buy that? After the leaks there've already been? They're not fools."

"And Dr. Peters isn't a criminal."

"I want her out of my hair," Seth growled. "Damned woman—"

"No. You want this problem out of your hair. It's not going to go away by losing one of your best doctors."

"How do you know she's any good?"

"Are you saying she's not?"

"No." Seth shook his head and raked his hair again. "Okay, so she's good at what she does, and one of the reasons she's good is that she stays impersonal. It's essential in the ER. If you get upset, things start falling apart. Concentrate on the job. That's what Peters is good at."

"And this time?"

"She was a bit *too* impersonal."

"It's not a capital offense."

"Maybe not." Seth groaned and leaned over to pick up his scattered paperwork. "Okay. I won't advise firing her. Yet." He gave a lopsided smile. "Maybe the board wouldn't, anyway," he conceded. "We get more than our money's worth from your Dr. Peters. She's strong and she's competent and she gets things done. She's the one who's always available to be on duty. When anyone's sick and off work, she's there to fill in. There are huge advantages in employing socially isolated doctors."

Socially isolated doctors.

Jaron thought about that and didn't like it. Damn, once more he felt like going in, boots and all, to her defense.

He couldn't.

Socially isolated.

Yeah, she was that, he thought. For just a while, for a few short hours last night, he thought he could make her human.

Not now.

He found he was clenching his hands into fists, but it was frustration, not rage, that made him feel like this. He wanted her. Damn, he wanted her so much!

But he wanted what she could be. Not what she was now.

"I CAN'T EAT all this."

"Not only can—will." Shana plonked a grocery carton

down on the floor and shooed Harold away. "And no sharing with your dog. This is for you, girl."

"I don't want—"

"You do want. In times of deep personal crises, there's really only one answer. And that's chocolate."

"This is not—"

"A deep personal crisis? You know, I'm pretty sure it is." Shana ripped open the package of Oreos and offered Annabelle one. "You've betrayed a patient's trust, albeit a dead one, and you feel real bad about that. What's more, you've made a gorgeous male mad at you." She bit into an Oreo and grinned at her friend. "In fact, in one short weekend you've joined the human race. Welcome, to the real world, Dr. Peters."

"I can't—"

"No," Shana said wisely. "And you don't need to. For the rest of the day, block out the world. Drown it in amaretto and smother it in chocolate. You won't feel any better in the morning, but you'll sure as heck feel better now. I promise."

CHAPTER FOURTEEN

SOMEONE WAS THUMPING the side of her head.

Annabelle thought about it, trying to figure out a way to make it stop. She groaned and hauled a pillow over her head, but the noise just got worse.

Maybe it wasn't the side of her head. Maybe it was just marginally farther away.

Harold licked her hand and barked—louder than he'd ever barked in his life. *Ouch.* The sound made her wince.

Maybe cheering herself up with amaretto wasn't wise.

The banging didn't stop. She'd have to do something to make it go away.

What?

Get up?

Yeah, right. How did one get up? She put a hand to her head and rose, very, very slowly.

Her clock said it was late afternoon. She'd only slept for an hour or so.

She wanted to sleep for much, much longer.

The banging was on her front door. Right. Fourteen steps away. She started counting—carefully. Somehow she made it, flung the door wide—and Jaron was right there.

"Dr. Peters."

She must look like hell, she decided dazedly as she stared at the man in front of her. She sure enough felt like hell, and the way he was looking at her...

"Go away," she told him, but it didn't work.

"What's the matter?" He was over the threshold, gripping

her shoulders in his big hands, supporting her body as it threatened to sag at the knees. "Hell, Annabelle, you haven't…"

Haven't what? What was he thinking? There was fear in his voice and she was even more confused.

"What?"

But his trained eyes were scanning the apartment and he found what he was looking for. With a sigh of relief he propelled her over to the settee and pushed her down. Then he lifted the amaretto bottle.

It was still more than three-quarters full.

"Is this your first bottle?" Jaron asked, puzzled. This amount of alcohol was hardly enough to have her in the state she was in.

"Shana bought it for me," she said with such an attempt at dignity that he almost laughed. The relief he felt was overpowering. "Shana said welcome to the human race. She said I needed amaretto and Oreos."

"Yeah, well, I can think of better ways to welcome you to the human race." But he was smiling. When he'd opened the door and seen her so out of it…well, his mind had immediately gone to worst-case scenario.

The combination of the stress of the weekend and Seth's threat to dismiss her had scared him stupid. He'd seen enough overdoses in his time to almost expect it.

But this… He glanced at the bottle again and thought, Nope, not even close to death.

But she was certainly wobbly.

"How much do you normally drink?" he asked, and Annabelle lay back on the settee cushions and thought about it. It was very hard to think without her head falling off.

"Lots," she said at last with another attempt at dignity, but there was no way it was going to come off. Spinning head, oversize pajamas, fluffy slippers…

It was not yet dinnertime, but at some point after the third amaretto, Annabelle had decided it was bedtime. Bed had seemed the safest place to be. It wasn't going to happen now, though. Jaron needed her and he needed her sober.

"You drink lots." Jaron grinned. She might be tipsy, but she was still gorgeous, and her attempt at dignity was wonderful. "Like, coffee, tea and cola maybe? But hard stuff?"

"Hard stuff?" She seemed to be finding it really, really hard to focus.

"Wine. Beer. Amaretto?"

"I don't drink," she insisted. "My mother drank. Not me. But Shana said I should."

"Bully for Shana."

So she never drank, Jaron was thinking. Three glasses of amaretto must have practically knocked her out.

And now…Luke was waiting down at the station to see her. The powers that be were having forty fits that this very public affair had been so badly bungled. Annabelle had to be interviewed. He couldn't protect her from that. By rights he should just frog-march her out of her apartment, prop her in the back of his patrol car and take her in as ordered. In her wonderful pajamas.

He couldn't. Not Annabelle.

"We need to get you sober," he told her.

"Sober?" She was evidently having the greatest difficulty figuring out what he was talking about. "I'm not not sober…"

"You know, I'm almost sure you are."

THREE CUPS of strong black coffee didn't cut it. There was only the tried-and-true method he'd used many times before.

A shower. A *cold* shower.

He'd done this with drunken buddies, stripping them and dousing them with cold water. It was cruel, harsh—and it worked like a charm.

But this was Annabelle.

"Can you shower yourself?" he demanded, and she grinned and nodded and swayed.

"Of course I can."

Yeah, right. She'd slip and knock herself out on the shower taps.

He propelled her into the bathroom and turned on the taps.

"Strip."

"Who, me?"

"I've seen you naked already," he said, and then at the look on her face he relented. "Think of me as another doctor."

"I can't."

"Then we'll shower you in your pj's."

She thought about that and decided against it.

"I can do it." She sat down on the bathroom stool and thought about it some more. "In a minute."

"Right." He knelt and unbuttoned her pajama top. He should be impersonal, he thought. Impersonal, ha! All he could think about was how gorgeous she was.

Whew. He just had to touch her and he needed a cold shower.

He just had to think about her!

"Tell me why I'm having a shower?" She seemed to be floating in some vague euphoric fog. She fumbled with her pajama bottoms and swayed backward on the stool. He caught her and held her while she tugged the flannelette from her legs. Her face was against his thighs as she tried to balance. Her breasts were molded to him.

Maybe they should both take a cold shower. Together.

Come to think of it...

He had to cut this line of thought right now, he told himself desperately. He was here to do a job. He needed to get her sober and down to the station. Fast.

Her pajama bottoms were gone now, kicked out in front of her, and she was standing, leaning the full weight of her body against him. He was holding her close, smelling the perfume of her hair, feeling the warmth of her skin and the faint beat of her heart against his chest. She was wonderfully, gloriously naked.

The shower. Right, the shower.

"In." He propelled her into the shower stall and held her by the shoulders as he turned on the tap. Cold water sprayed her breasts.

She squealed.

When she reared back he held her tight. She spluttered and fought him, but he held fast.

"No!"

"Yes."

"Let me out."

"When you're sober."

"I'm sober."

"Count from a hundred backward."

"A hundred," she said defiantly. Then, "Ninety-nine."

"Faster."

"I can do it." She tilted her chin. "I just choose not to."

"Then I choose to hold you under the shower."

"This is police harassment."

"It's better than letting you sober up in a cell."

That seemed to bring her around all by itself. "A jail cell?" she said uncertainly, and he adjusted the shower head so she could breathe and speak without the water making her splutter.

"That's right."

"You're planning on arresting me?"

He had no such intent. In fact, his only desire right at this minute was to pick her up, sodden or not, sober or not, and cart her through to the bedroom and—

Dorsey! Cut it out!

"You need to come down to the station and answer some questions."

"I told you everything I know." She was sobering up by the minute.

"I know you did, but it's out of my hands now. This is getting close to being a federal case. If the baby's real mother has been killed…"

"She wouldn't," Annabelle said distressfully, the last vestiges of alcoholic fog disappearing. "Not the lady I treated."

"How do you know?"

"I don't." She turned in his hold so she was facing him, water streaming down her naked body. All traces of the amaretto had gone. She was naked in his hands, but her state of dress—or undress—was unimportant. "The woman I treated wasn't a killer. She wasn't."

"You saw her for a few minutes at the end of her life. You never met her husband."

"But she said…"

"She said what?"

This was the strangest conversation, he thought. He was wet himself now. He'd been standing out of the shower cubicle, but she was leaning into him with urgency, and her hair was streaming against his chest.

"She said?" he prodded again.

"She said, 'She's going to die. My baby will die.' She didn't say her baby had already died."

"She was dying herself. She was confused. We've been thinking about it. The most likely scenario is that the woman's baby dies and the husband steals another. They come from somewhere up north. God knows where the baby they stole comes from, but if they had it for a while and it wasn't reported, then we have to assume the worst has happened to the real mother. Our couple bring the stolen kid south—maybe they're scared the mother's body will be found. We pull up behind them in the patrol car, and they panic so much they run the lights."

"You really think they murdered the mother?" Annabelle's eyes were drenched in horror. She'd apparently forgotten completely that she was naked. She seemed to have forgotten everything but the tragedy surrounding the baby and her unknown mother.

"We don't know," Jaron told her. He jostled her out of the cubicle and started toweling her dry. It was the most intimate of acts, yet they were being businesslike with each other. Maybe the reality of what they were speaking of was too much for either to comprehend.

Jaron should be case-hardened by now, he thought wearily. He wasn't. The human capacity for evil could still shift his foundations.

"I can't help you any more than I have already," Annabelle

said, immeasurably distressed. She turned in his arms so that she was looking straight up at him, her eyes meeting his and demanding that he believe her. "I'm not holding anything back. You must believe me, Jaron."

"I believe you," he told her, and put her gently away from him. He handed her the towel. She was sober enough to take over here, and he had to give himself some breathing space. "But you'll have to make a full statement. I can't keep you from that. Get yourself dressed and come with me."

SHE FELT ILL and it had nothing to do with the effects of the amaretto. Annabelle pulled on jeans and a sweatshirt, caught her still damp curls into a knot and stared at herself in the mirror.

What had she done?

She'd hindered a police investigation. Because of her reluctance to get involved, this discrepancy in blood types hadn't been discovered earlier. The police could have been looking for the real mother three days ago.

It was Monday night. She'd delayed things since Friday.

"They wouldn't have guessed any more than I did," she whispered to her reflection. "If I'd told them everything..."

They might have guessed, her reflection seemed to accuse.

"I promised."

It was stupid to promise. Stupid to try to stay uninvolved.

"But I'm stupid to be involved now."

Jaron was waiting for her in the living room, and the thought of him made her feel even worse. She'd hurt him, she thought drearily. She'd shoved him away in her distrust.

She'd hardly had a choice.

"I hurt everyone I touch," she whispered, and she leaned forward and let her face rest against the cold glass of the mirror. "I can't get it right. No matter what."

Maybe if she learned to trust herself?

Yeah, right. Learning something like that didn't come easily after thirty years of hard knocks.

"Just get this interview over with and get on with life," she told herself flatly. "By yourself."

JARON DIDN'T sit in on the interview. He was too close. He couldn't stay dispassionate, so Luke kicked him out.

"Your face gives you away," Luke told him as he closed the door on the interview room, shutting Annabelle in. "I don't know what's between you two and I don't want to know." Then he grinned and corrected himself. "Or maybe I do, but that's for finding out later, over a beer after knock-off time. Meanwhile, you do some legwork. Find out what's happening in Glacier. Bring the boys up there up to speed. Let me and Gary do this."

"You'll be okay with her?"

"Meaning, are we going to lean on her?" Luke's smile died. "Yeah. She's our only source of information. The only person the woman spoke to at any length. We need every single thing she has and she doesn't leave this room until she's given it."

"She's told all she knows."

"That's what she said on Friday night. How do you know she's telling the truth now?"

"I know."

Luke searched his friend's face and nodded.

"Definitely a beer after work," he said softly. "But meanwhile, take yourself off, pal. Like I said, you're too damned close."

IT TOOK an hour. Jaron spent most of that time on the phone, but his mind wasn't on what he was doing. It was on what was happening behind the closed door of interview room four. When the door finally opened, he was on his feet before Luke even appeared.

"What—"

"Relax." Luke closed the door behind him. "She's just signing her statement. She'll be out in five minutes and then you can take over guard duty."

"I'm not…"

"Interested? Yeah. You don't intend to so much as look at her. Pull the other leg. It plays 'Jingle Bells.'"

"What was the outcome?"

Luke grimaced. "As you said. Nothing. We had to give it a shot, though."

"You gave her a hard time?"

"We just made sure." Then at Jaron's look, he shook his head. "Don't give me that. You know as well as I do that we suspected she was holding back information that might impede a possible murder investigation. We had to go in with both barrels."

"And now?"

"The lady's feeling a bit sorry for herself."

The amaretto wouldn't be helping, either, Jaron thought ruefully. Not a good day for Annabelle.

"So there's nothing new?"

"No." Luke shook his head. "We have a four-week-old baby who doesn't belong here, but she doesn't seem to belong anywhere else, either."

"So?"

"So we look at birth records for hospitals around the location where the car was stolen. We look at babies who were born around that time and we check on each and every one of them."

"We need to look for deaths, too," Jaron said. "Deaths of tiny babies or still births."

"Yeah." Luke looked sideways at Jaron. "You don't want to head north yourself?"

"Not unless I have to." If absolutely necessary, Jaron could leave the kids with Cathy's mother, but he hated doing it.

"Then we might send Gary." Luke grimaced. "Like you, I'll go if I have to, but I sure as hell don't want to leave Abby right now."

Jaron knew the feeling. He thought back to how he'd felt whenever he had to leave Cathy, and the old longing surged again. To have a woman in his bed…

Only it wasn't Cathy he was longing for now. It was Annabelle.

This sort of talk was getting them nowhere. He couldn't leave his kids. Luke or Gary would have to go. Both of them knew it. "Let's hope this is wrapped up fast."

"I don't know how the hell it can be," Luke said honestly. "We don't even know what we're looking for. No thanks to Annabelle."

"She can't help that."

"No."

Jaron glanced up at him. "You don't still think she's holding something back?"

Luke chewed his bottom lip and glanced uncertainly at his friend. "No, I don't," he said at last. "At least, I don't think she's holding back information."

"Then what do you mean?"

"She's holding back herself. The lady's a self-contained block of ice. I don't know what's going on between the pair of you, but I don't like your chances of getting her to thaw."

SHE LOOKED SICK.

Annabelle emerged from the interview room, and it was all Jaron could do not to take her in his arms right there and then. The normally bouncy, full-of-life Annabelle had been replaced by a wan-faced little girl.

"Annabelle—"

"I've finished." Her voice was flat, emotionless. "Where can I call a cab?"

"I'll take you home."

"You needn't bother."

He didn't answer, just took her arm and ushered her out to his car. He directed her into the passenger seat and she went without resisting. She'd made a mistake. Another one. She was internalizing it and hating herself for it, he thought, and he put his hand on her cheek in a gesture of reassurance.

She pushed his hand away and stared straight ahead.

"Annabelle, I'm sorry."

"So am I." She shook her head and let out her breath in a long sigh of regret. "What a mess. Everything I touch—"

"It's not your fault. You did what you had to do."

"No." The old Annabelle surfaced then with fleeting anger, but the anger was directed at herself. "I did what I figured I had to do. Just like I did last time. Last time I ended up with a dead kid. Now…a dead mom? A baby without a mother forever?"

"You don't know that." He wanted to do something. Anything! He wanted to haul her out of the car and hold her and comfort her and kiss that glorious flaming hair…

Her body language said she wanted no such thing. She was hunched into herself, regrouping. Finding the old independent Annabelle who nothing touched.

So for want of an alternative, he got into the driver's seat and headed back toward the hospital.

They drove in silence. He glanced at her and found her face stony. Closed.

No! This was all wrong. She was so much…fun? She had so much to give.

To him?

No. He gave himself a mental shake. She'd let him take her to bed and it had been a gift. A glorious affirmation of life. But he was a widower with two dependent children, and she needed him the way she needed old luggage. How could he take things further than he already had?

She was a loner. She'd told him that, and he believed it. What was happening now would only affirm that loneliness, but she had the right to keep her life as it was. She had Harold and she had her career.

But hell, what a waste.

"Have dinner with us tonight," he said, but she went on staring out through the windshield at the oncoming traffic.

"No," she said at last.

"You're supposed to say no, thank you very much," he remonstrated.

She bit her lip. "No, thank you very much."

"And give a reason."

"I have to spend the night with Harold."

"Harold's invited, too."

"I don't want to."

"Because you're afraid?"

"Why would I be afraid?"

"Because you're getting involved."

"Wrong!" she snapped, and there was another surge of anger in her voice. That was okay, he decided. Anger was better than apathy. "I've become involved and I've caused trouble. Now I'm getting uninvolved as fast as I can."

"You know," he said softly, and it was suddenly as if he wasn't speaking to Annabelle, "if I hadn't loved Cathy, then I wouldn't have lost her. I wouldn't have almost gone out of my mind with grief. But if I could wind the clock back and not start that relationship...hell, I wouldn't for a minute consider that."

"It's not me who hurts when I get involved," Annabelle said bitterly. "It's other people."

"You've been unlucky."

"Yeah, right. Unlucky. I was born unlucky, then. Stay away from me, Jaron. I'm a walking disaster."

"You don't think you might be just the tiniest bit overdramatic?"

"No."

"Really?" He was still driving, still concentrating on the road. But there was suddenly the faintest note of teasing in his voice.

"Cut it out."

"You're enjoying wallowing in self-pity?"

She glowered, refusing to rise to the bait. "I'm enjoying nothing of the kind."

"Hey, if I'm not wallowing, I don't see why *you* should. I didn't speak to the lady, either. I didn't demand her name before they lifted her into the ambulance. And I've lost a wife, remember? So...who's got more grounds for wallowing? Me or you?"

"I am not *wallowing*."

"It looks like wallowing from this angle. Hangover from too much amaretto and too much self-pity."

"Will you cut it out?"

"Only if you do. And if you agree to come back to my place and eat dinner."

"You need to collect your children."

"So I do," he said cordially. "That's why this car is pointing to the hospital. If I didn't need to collect my kids, I'd whisk you straight back to my apartment and bounce any trace of self-pity right out of you. Right now."

She gasped. And tried to think of something to say. And couldn't. There was a tiny surge of something breaking through her self-pity. A desire for...*bouncing?*

Surely not.

"You want it," he said, and she glowered some more.

"I do not!"

"What'll we have for dinner?" he asked, changing tack. "Pasta?"

"I—"

"Or baked beans. They're my specialty, apart from pasta. Pasta one night. Baked beans the next. Ben Jessup tells me they're two healthy meals to give kids, so I have 'em down to an art form."

"I don't want to come back to your place for dinner."

"Sure you do." He knew nothing of the kind, but he was darned if he'd let her go back to her apartment like this.

What sort of childhood had she had, he wondered suddenly, to produce armor as thick as this? What little she'd told him sounded appalling. There was no basis of trust here. No expectation that life could be good.

That was the difference between him and Annabelle, he decided. Sure, life had dealt him some knocks, and maybe it would again, but in between there'd been good times. What he and Cathy had built had been great. His kids were great. His mom and dad had thought that he was the ants' pants.

He grinned and discovered that Annabelle was looking at him as if he was slightly off balance.

"Hey. I haven't lost my mind. There's no need to look at me like that. Have you decided yet? Baked beans or pasta?"

"Why are you grinning?" she demanded, and he thought about telling her. And decided he would.

"I was just remembering," he told her, "how my dad once told me that he wouldn't swap me for a Cy Young baseball card."

"Yeah?" She was still looking at him strangely. "Cy Young, hey? Hmm…what's that got to do with the price of fish?"

"Everything," he told her. "Has anyone ever told you that?"

"That I'm more valuable than a baseball card?"

"A *Cy Young* baseball card. Or similar," he said expansively. "Girls' equivalent."

"I don't know what you mean."

"There you go, then. No one ever has. And that's why you distrust the world."

"Jaron—"

"You're better than any baseball card," he told her, his voice softening. "Any one at all."

"Jaron—"

"For a start, you're a damned sight more beautiful."

"Was it me who drank the amaretto?" she demanded. "Or you?"

"You. Baked beans or pasta?"

"I don't know. I don't care. I'm not coming…"

"Yes, you are," he told her soundly. To heck with her professionalism and the fact that someone like her couldn't possibly stay involved with a widower cop with two dependent kids. To heck with everything. "Yes, you are," he said again. "Even if I have to pick you up and carry you."

CHAPTER FIFTEEN

IN THE END it was easier to go along with him, she decided.
She was too tired to argue.

Too darned intrigued at the thought of bouncing...

No!

At least the kids had energy to spare. Jaron towed her beside
him up to Round the Clock, and Tina and Ricky met her with
squeals of delight.

"Can we go back to Annabelle's and finish the hats?" Tina
pleaded, but Jaron shook his head.

"Nope. It's dinner at our place tonight. We'll just stop over
at Annabelle's and collect Harold."

"Is Harold coming?"

"Of course he is." Jaron swung Tina up in his arms while
Ricky clung to his legs, hanging backward and trying to spin.
"Where I go, you guys go, right?"

"Yep."

"No argument. 'Cause we're a family. So where there's Annabelle, there's Harold. Same thing."

"Excellent," Ricky said, and Annabelle didn't disagree with
him for a moment. She couldn't.

Her family was Harold.

Only Harold.

Bouncing?

THEY ATE neither baked beans nor pasta, because once Annabelle faced the inevitable, she decided she might as well stir
herself to go all the way. The kids whooping around her made

her feel alive again, interested, as if there might be life after this awful day.

Bouncing...

No. She managed to force her thoughts back to dinner. Somehow. But the concept of bouncing had had its effect. As they collected Harold, her apathy fell away. She grabbed a handful of ingredients from her freezer, and when they arrived back at Jaron's, she headed for the kitchen.

"I'm cooking."

"Hey!" Jaron frowned. "I do the best baked beans this side of the Rockies."

"I'm sure you do." She gave him her very nicest smile, and if she'd known the effect it had on him, she would have been out of there right now. Or maybe not. "So if you tell me that you'd much rather have baked beans than chicken cacciatore, then I'll move over and let you cook right now."

He looked at her sideways, as if he was trying to decide, and the sight of him looking at her like that...well, it was enough to knock a girl sideways.

Bouncing.

They had kids to care for. They had to behave.

"I'll sort the laundry then."

"You do that."

So while she fried chicken and chopped vegetables, he sorted underwear and socks into three neat piles, and they both tried desperately to concentrate on what they were doing. The kids were hanging over the kitchen bench "helping," scraping carrots and eating as much as they scraped, licking the bowl of the chocolate pudding she'd decided to whip up, because how could she just make one course for this crew...

The whole scene was unbelievably domestic. Unbelievably good.

Unbelievably erotic?

He was folding socks. What was she thinking?

She knew exactly what she was thinking.

It was all so...right. Harold was lying by her feet—every time she moved she had to step over him—but it was part of the feel-good time they were having. She had Harold. She had everything she wanted right here in this room.

If she let them any closer, she'd cause disaster.

She should run right now, she told herself, but Jaron was holding up one Mickey Mouse sock and another sock with Strawberry Shortcake on it. How could she run when he seemed to have encountered the nation's worst crime?

"These are all I have left," he announced in the tone of someone who had just found a body beneath the stairs. "Will someone please explain?"

"That's how I wore them, Daddy," Tina said with patience. "I like them that way. I had Mickey on one foot and Strawberry Shortcake on the other."

"So there's two clean socks in your drawer—one Mickey and one Strawberry."

"I put Strawberry with Goofy," she told him. She held out her feet for inspection. "See? I'm wearing them now. And I put the other Mickey in the garbage. His ears are too big and I don't like wearing all those ears."

Detective Dorsey considered. Annabelle could practically see his policeman's mind ticking. "So we have a spare Goofy sock."

"Teddy's wearing Goofy—it's his sleeping bag," Tina told him with exaggerated care, and Annabelle grinned, caught by the patience of this big, rough cop and his gorgeous daughter.

And she couldn't help putting in her two cents' worth. "Honestly, Daddy," she told him. "You're a detective. You'd think you'd have been able to figure that out all by yourself."

A bundle of Strawberry/Mickey socks hit her on the nose. Before she could catch them, the socks landed in her bowl of chocolate-pudding mixture. Annabelle retrieved them and held them up, dripping chocolate.

"Well, that's a problem," she told the kids, refusing to look at Jaron. "The rest of us will have chocolate pudding for dinner, while your daddy has chocolate socks."

"But Daddy's never had chocolate pudding before," Tina

said, suddenly anxious on her father's behalf. "I don't think chocolate socks tastes good."

Annabelle was shocked. "You've never had chocolate pudding!" What sort of family was this?

"Grandma says pudding's bad for us," Ricky said sadly. "And Daddy can't make it. He's good at brownies, but that's all he's good at. Now we just go to Hy's. Daddy says we can't get enough insurance on our house to cover his cooking experiments."

"Oh, dear." Annabelle choked on laughter, barely suppressed. Her eyes flashed involuntarily to Jaron's and held. He was laughing back at her, but his look... It was such a look! There was tenderness and laughter and...

Desire.

He wanted her. She could see it. There was no disguising the hunger in his eyes.

It could be for any woman, she told herself desperately. He was hungry for companionship and sex and women in general.

"No," he told her, and it was as if he'd read her mind. The laughter suddenly faded. "Not anyone," he said softly, for her ears alone. "Just you."

SHE WASN'T SURE how she managed to finish cooking dinner after that, but somehow she did. They set the table and used a real tablecloth that Tina had hauled out from a long-forgotten store because it was such a special occasion. Jaron and Annabelle sat opposite each other, the kids between. The kids glowed and chatted while they ate, as if they were being given a treat more special than any birthday present they could ever think of.

"I love your chocolate pudding," Tina announced as she finished her second helping.

"I like Annabelle's chicken better," Ricky said. "What do you think, Daddy?"

"I think I like Annabelle best of all."

Whew.

With a face the color of fire, Annabelle helped clear the table and then found the courage to take the next step.

"It's time for me to take Harold home."

But… "Read us a bedtime story. Please, please, Annabelle?"

How could she resist? Not when the alternative was an empty apartment and a bottle of amaretto. The kids had bounded into their pajamas as she and Jaron cleared the table, so they were standing looking absolutely adorable, each in pin-striped pajamas, clutching battered teddies and a dog-eared book.

"You put them up to this," she muttered, but Jaron gave her his most innocent look.

"I have 'em well trained. Dinner, pajamas, bed—in that order. We do showers in the morning in this family, because often by the time we get home, we're asleep on our feet."

"Very wise." But she found she wasn't concentrating on the domestic arrangements of Jaron's family. She was concentrating—or trying really hard not to concentrate—on just how close Jaron was to her.

And just how…intimate this family made her feel.

"So…will you read to them?" he asked.

Tina was holding out her book. "It's called *Harry the Dirty Dog*," she told her. "I think Harold will like it. Do you think so?"

How could she say no? She couldn't. Not with the three of them watching. Even Harold had his head to one side, as if he was thinking she'd be a fool to reject this offer to share in a tiny part of their lives.

It was so sweet. So enticing. Like the song of the Sirens, it was drawing her ever closer. She couldn't resist, but oh, she knew she should.

So she sat on the end of Tina's bed and read about Harry's adventures while Jaron sat on the end of Ricky's bed and watched Annabelle, and her color grew a deeper and deeper crimson by the moment. As did her disquiet.

Bouncing…

Finally the story was finished. Two weary little pairs of eyes were closing, and as Jaron tucked them in, Annabelle couldn't resist. She leaned over and kissed them both on their noses. Tina put her arms up and clung to her.

"We like you here," she whispered. "We like your chocolate pudding. We like your dog. We like you."

Annabelle managed a smile, but when Jaron switched off the light and ushered her out of the bedroom, she found there were tears in her eyes.

"I...I'd better go. Can I call a cab?"

"Will a cab take Harold?"

Damn, she hadn't thought of that. "Oh..."

"And I can't take you now." Jaron didn't sound the least put out. He even sounded cheerful. "Not now that the kids are asleep."

"Can I leave Harold with you, then?" she asked. "Maybe you could drop him off when you take the kids to Round the Clock in the morning."

"I could do that." He was leaning against the wall, watching her. The light was dim. They should return to the living room, but he didn't move. She should push past him, but she didn't move, either.

"Or you could stay," he said gently, and watched her face.

"I...I don't think that's wise."

"Why not?"

"Because..."

"Because?"

"Jaron, you don't want to get involved with me," she said harshly. "I'm no good at relationships."

"You haven't done relationships until now. You need to take a few risks if you want the good things in life, Annabelle. You have no solid background of caring to make you see that even though bad things happen all the time, so do good things. Just because Cathy died," he said softly, not moving his eyes from her face, "just because I lost her, doesn't mean I won't love again. I've got my kids. I have great friends. I've met this fantastic dog-cum-doormat who promises to be a part of my life from now on. And I have a woman right by me now who I want to kiss more than anything else in the world.''

"Jaron…"

"Are you saying I can't kiss you?"

"No, but—"

"Because I intend to," he said, and proceeded to do just that. Which silenced her very effectively indeed.

SHE HAD TO MOVE. She had to break away, but he was holding her so sweetly that it was all she could do not to melt into him.

What was she thinking? She was dissolving into him. He was so big. So male. So…Jaron.

Everything she wanted in the world was right here, she thought dazedly. This man…

Dear God, she loved him.

How could she know that she loved him after only four short days?

She'd known that she loved him after four short minutes, she decided as his mouth claimed hers, as his hands pulled her into him, as her breasts pressed against his chest and she felt herself merging, wanting, aching, loving…

Jaron.

Here was her home. Her life. Her peace and her future.

Her lips were opening under his, her tongue was tasting him, her hands were holding the rough fabric of his shirt, glorying in the maleness of him. She'd never known she could feel like this. She'd never dreamed…

She closed her eyes and let herself sink into him, savoring the wonder, savoring the hope…

His kiss deepened, claiming her. Glorying in her. Behind them his children slept. Harold was on guard duty between their beds.

This was Jaron's and her time. Their…destiny?

"I…" Somehow she pulled back. She wanted to see him. She wanted to be sure that he wanted her as much as she wanted him.

But Jaron mistook what she needed. The thought came out of left field and cleared his mind.

She'd been a virgin. The last time they'd made love—was it only two days ago?—she'd been a virgin.

Making love to this woman wasn't something to do lightly. Because now, suddenly, he was sure.

So instead of seeing desire on his face, Annabelle saw much more. There was a measure of peace and certainty and joy that almost blew her away.

"Annabelle…"

The love in his voice made her gasp.

"I…"

"This isn't a one-night stand," he told her softly, releasing her so that he could take her hands in his. His eyes held hers with so much love that she knew what was coming before he could say the words. Before she could stop him. "Annabelle, I want to marry you."

Marriage.

I want to marry you.

The words drifted around in the darkness, increasing in speed, like an echo becoming louder all the time. Her eyes widened and she took an involuntary step back, freeing her hands from his.

I want to marry you.

"You don't know what you're talking about," she said at last, and he laughed, though it was a pretty shaky and uncertain laugh.

"I think I do."

"We've only known each other since Friday."

"You made my kids Halloween costumes." It was a stupid thing to say, Jaron decided, trying to make his fuzzy brain focus, but there it was. Until then he'd seen her as a doctor, as someone whose life could never be entangled with his. But she'd made costumes…

And it couldn't have been the wrong thing to say. It had made her smile, even though she was shaking her head.

"You can get costumes professionally made from Tara the Tailor down the street. Marry Tara."

"If Tara's the lady I'm thinking of," he said cautiously, "she's close to sixty, give or take a few years. Probably give. If you don't mind, I'd rather marry you." He was smiling at her with the killer smile that had the capacity to knock her sideways. Which was just how she felt. "Besides, I bet Tara doesn't make chocolate pudding."

"I'm sure she's an expert at making chocolate puddings. Almost everyone knows how." Annabelle was trying desperately to keep the mood light, but she was having enormous trouble with her breathing. For a mechanical function that had been operating satisfactorily for thirty years, breathing had suddenly become a skill she didn't seem to have.

"*I* can't," Jaron said, and she had to focus on what the heck he was talking about.

"You can't what?"

"I can't make chocolate pudding."

"You can't marry someone just because they make chocolate pudding."

"Well, to admit the truth, I've fallen for your dog," he said, catching her hands again. "He makes the best floor rug. It's a real decorator item. The only way I can get your dog is to propose to you."

"Will you...will you please be serious?"

"Do you want me to be serious?"

"Yes. *No!*" Damn, her breathing had stopped again. She had to pause and think about the muscles required to fill her lungs. Even then she didn't do a very good job. Maybe there wasn't a great deal of oxygen available.

Maybe he was too close. Was that the problem?

But he was serious, anyway.

"I want to marry you because of you," he told her, and the world stood still. They stood, hands locked, in the dim corridor, while outside the world spun on its axis. Outside—somewhere, but not here—people went about their ordinary lives as if this wasn't a watershed.

A turning point.

"I love you, Annabelle," Jaron said, so softly she had to strain to hear it. "Even when I'm mad as hell at you. Even this morning when I thought you'd lied to me. Even when you turn away from me and become like a tortoise, retreating into its shell because the world hurts...

"You're beautiful, you're smart, you're funny. You're warm and you care. You care so much you withdraw into yourself for fear of hurting people. Yet you have all this love to give."

"I don't."

"You just don't know it," he told her. "Annabelle, trust me. This thing between us..." He pulled her into his arms, brooking no opposition. "You know as well as I do that there's this pull. This...I don't know. This feeling that we're meant to be.

"You can feel it," he went on roughly, kissing her hair. "I can feel you feeling it. Sure we've only known each other since Friday, but I felt it in minutes. And so did you."

"I didn't."

"Liar."

She was so out of control she let herself fall against him. But the emotion surging through her now wasn't desire.

It was terror.

That was how she felt—terrified. As if she were hanging over an abyss and one false step would see her plummet.

Or all of them would plummet.

A memory slammed back with such sickening force that it was almost real. It was of one of her mother's boyfriends, but this time a nice one. Dave, the man who'd given her Harold. It had been the only Christmas of her childhood that she remembered with any trace of enjoyment, and at the end of the day she'd hugged her mother and said, "Marry Dave, Mom. He's the best."

Her mother had stared at her as if she was stupid, and the next morning Dave was gone. "If you think I'm letting men suck up to me through my daughter, you have another think coming,'' her mother had snapped at her. ''And you can get rid of the dog, too.''

She'd held on to Harold, fought a thousand fights to keep him, but she'd never seen Dave again.

If she'd just shut up…

This was crazy. It had nothing to do with now. It had nothing to do with Jaron.

But if she said yes…

She couldn't. The yawning chasm was still there. She'd learned the hard way, over and over again, what happened when that step was taken.

It wasn't herself who hurt most. It was others. Her mother's lover. The teenager she'd tried to help with her pregnancy. The mystery baby.

Tina and Ricky? Maybe.

Jaron.

What sort of wife would she make? she wondered wildly. She wasn't sure, and she wasn't about to take a chance on someone she cared about as much as she cared about Jaron.

''No,'' she said so flatly it made him release her.

''No?''

''You don't want to marry me.''

''I'm thirty-two years old,'' he told her. ''I've been a cop for ten years. I've been married, widowed, and I'm raising two kids. You think I'd know by now what I want and don't want.''

''You don't know me.'' Her tone was without inflection. What he was offering was like some incredible, wonderful gift, a gift so far out of her reach, she knew she must be dreaming. ''I'm a loner.''

''You don't want me?''

There was nothing she wanted more. But… ''No.''

''Is it the kids?''

''I don't want,'' she said carefully, ''to hurt your kids.''

''How on earth could you hurt my kids?''

''I don't know. I just…don't know anything about them. I never dreamed of having them. I don't want…''

So that was that. It was the kids, Jaron thought drearily as her voice faded. Hell, of course it was the kids. Why had he ever dreamed he could ask a woman like Annabelle to marry him? He'd known it was impossible, so why had he tried?

She was a doctor. She had a great career. He was a widowed cop with two kids.

But this thing they had…

It wasn't enough. Her body language said it all. Sure, she had issues, sure, she had a past that made her afraid of commitment, but was it fair to push her?

Not when he was pushing his two kids as well as himself onto her.

It wouldn't be easy. Parenting was just plain hard. He could keep the major load for himself, but every time she came home, the kids would be there. Another woman's children. What woman wanted that?

"I need to go," she whispered. "Please…"

"You really want to?" But he knew what she was about to say before she opened her mouth.

"Yes, Jaron," she said bleakly. "I really want to."

SHE LEFT HAROLD behind. He was sound asleep and he wouldn't awake before morning. He wouldn't even miss her.

"I'll drop him off at your apartment after I leave the kids at Round the Clock in the morning," Jaron told her as he helped her into a cab.

"That'd be great. If I'm not there, you know where the key is."

"Fine."

Only it wasn't fine. It was the end, she thought bleakly as the cab made the turn and headed for the hospital.

The end.

CHAPTER SIXTEEN

WHAT HAD HE BEEN thinking, to ask her so soon? Jaron lay in the dark and stared at nothing and called himself every name for fool he could think of. He'd rushed it and he'd blown it.

Or maybe rushing wasn't the problem. Maybe it wouldn't have made any difference if he'd waited for years. He'd seen the look of terror in her eyes. To ask if she'd join a ready-made family, to attempt to saddle her with two kids, a cop as a husband...

Hell, he bet he earned a lot less than she did! His hours were appalling. His kids needed a mother, not a high-powered doctor. His mother-in-law would cause as much trouble as she could. Hazel wouldn't accept any replacement for Cathy. She was the nightmare in the background.

The whole scenario was a nightmare.

"If I was Annabelle, I wouldn't marry me," he told himself. "If I was anyone, I wouldn't marry me."

So where did that leave him?

Alone.

Forever?

He had his kids, but there was little comfort in that thought tonight. He lay in his too-big bed, and sleep wouldn't come. Finally, at about three in the morning, he rose and stared bleakly out the window rather than at the darkened ceiling. After an hour of that, he was going crazy. He climbed back into bed—and a vast warm body landed on top of him.

Harold.

"You're missing your mistress, boy?" he asked, and Harold gave him a slurping lick from chin to forehead.

"Ugh."

It didn't matter. It was better than sleeping alone. He put an arm around the animal's midriff and tried again.

Sleep was nowhere.

"How am I going to convince your mistress I have anything to offer?" he demanded of Harold, and got another lick for his pains.

"No," Jaron said definitely. "As a suggested lovemaking technique, it lacks a certain finesse. I don't think that's going to work."

What would?

Nothing.

ANNABELLE DIDN'T even try to go to bed. She sat at her kitchen table and cradled a cup of coffee that had long gone cold, knowing it wasn't foolishness that was holding her back.

It was cowardice. Panic. She'd fallen for him so hard, but then...*he'd asked her to marry him?*

He was offering her the world. Two fantastic kids. Warmth, love and laughter. Companionship.

Himself.

What woman would refuse Jaron? Even the thought of him, the sound of his name, the way he smiled and the way he touched her.

He'd never hurt her.

No. She'd hurt him and she couldn't bear it. She had no idea what it was to play happy family. He was a cop. She'd have to face shift work, and the kids would depend on her, and maybe Jaron would be hurt at work and she'd be alone and...

"And maybe the world will end or we'll be taken over by aliens," she told the night sky. "These are bogeys, Annabelle. You're a big girl. Stop scaring yourself."

Easy to say. Impossible to do. What was it here that was scaring her senseless?

She began talking out loud to herself.

"Coward."

"You need time."

"You don't need time. You're never going to be more sure than you are at this minute."

"So I'm not sure. Where does that leave me?"

"Here. And he's there." She bit her lip and a memory came back. "He promised to bounce the self-pity right out of me," she said to the dark. "So why is he on the other side of the city?"

Why indeed? Only she had the answers, and she didn't understand them any better than he did.

SHE'D ALREADY LEFT for work when Jaron dropped Harold off at her apartment the following morning. He'd taken the kids to Round the Clock first, so if she was there, maybe he could talk to her by himself.

But she wasn't. She'd be down in the ER, already doing what she did best. Living life without him.

He let himself in with her hidden key and watched as Harold made himself at home on the settee. He and the kids had taken Harold for a stroll in the park first thing, so the big dog was well prepared to spend the day snoozing.

"Do you ever get lonesome?" he asked Harold, and Harold gave him a look that said he didn't know what on earth Jaron was talking about. Which made sense. Jaron wasn't sure what he was talking about, either.

Lonesome...

"I have two kids," Jaron murmured, looking around at the wonderful little apartment with its music and its pictures and its dog. He could imagine all this transferred to their home, filling the aching void of loneliness that had been his for so long.

Two kids weren't enough. Dear God, he wanted Annabelle so much it was like a physical hunger.

"What can I do?"

Harold had no answers. No one had any answers.

Work was waiting. Work was always waiting. If he couldn't have Annabelle, maybe he'd best concentrate on finding a family for the tiny mystery baby. Finding someone to love her.

He wanted someone to love him.

He wanted Annabelle.

"YOU LOOK like you've had a rough night." Luke was assessing his friend with concern. "Your hands troubling you?"

His hands. He hadn't given his hands a thought. He stared down at them with detachment. There were still a couple of blistered patches. They were tender, but they didn't hurt. What lay inside hurt.

"No."

"Then what?"

"It's nothing."

"Is it Annabelle?"

Jaron flinched. "I said it's nothing."

"It *is* Annabelle," Luke said with conviction. "Women. We can't live with 'em and we can't live without 'em."

"Are you saying you can't live with Abby?"

"I'm a lucky man," Luke said with some complacency. "I just hope you end up as lucky as me."

"ANNABELLE?" Ben Jessup came up behind her and made her jump about a foot. "Sorry," the pediatrician said as she turned to face him. "Where were you?"

"A million miles away."

"You gonna tell me about it?"

"No."

Hmm. Ben surveyed his colleague. He'd been hearing about the mystery baby and Annabelle's role in the fiasco, and knew that concern was written all over his face.

Annabelle held herself aloof, but that didn't mean Ben didn't worry about her. Many on their tight-knit medical team were doing the same. They appreciated how good she was at her job, but fretted that the tension inside her would finally make her snap. Maybe that time was now. Talk of the mystery baby was all over the hospital.

There'd been a kid admitted through the ER with an asthma

attack, and Ben had been called down to help. The kid was on his way up to the ward now and Ben should follow, but the shadows in Annabelle's face made him pause. "Sometimes it helps to talk about it," he said mildly, and waited.

"Nothing will help."

"You did what you thought was best," he said gently. "No one expects you to do any more than that. In this job you make a call and you stick with it. If it's the wrong call, then you face the consequences and get on with it. But forgive yourself. You're not God, Annabelle."

She closed her eyes. He understood. "Hell, Ben, I screwed up."

"All of us do."

"Not you."

"Even me," he told her, his voice gentling still further. "All of us. It's called being human."

"No. It's just me."

"That's where you're wrong." He was watching her, his calm eyes understanding. "You and the detective. It's not just the baby drama that's making your eyes blank like this, is it."

"How…" She shook her head in confusion. "How did you know?"

"Keith's been talking."

"Keith has no right—"

"To be concerned? How can he not be concerned? You have friends, Annabelle, whether you want us or not."

"I don't need—"

"You do need," he said. "You can't exist alone."

"I can."

"I think you're wrong," he told her softly. "Be kind to yourself, Annabelle. You're a damned fine doctor and a damned fine human being—if only you'd let yourself see it."

IT WAS ONLY for a second. A fraction of a second.

Todd was being naughty again, but then, Todd Jamison was always naughty. The kids weren't permitted out in the reception area. There was a self-locking door with a kid-proof latch up high, so only adults could open the door from the reception area into Round the Clock.

But Shana was just inside the door, cradling the mystery baby and talking to Alexandra about her, and there was a huddle of moms clucking around her, wanting to see. One mom had paused for a moment, holding the door open while she gazed down at the tiny baby in Shana's arms. There was an old guy in the elevator, keeping the Open button pushed while he watched the tableau of kids and moms. The adults were clustered around the door, all eyes on the baby, and it was all the time Todd needed to dart out.

By the time they noticed his escape, Todd was in the elevator, the doors were sliding shut and he was heading down.

Alexandra was yelling for the closest mom to stop him. Shana was by the door to Round the Clock, which was still swinging wide. But she turned and rushed to the phone on the desk...

Tina was right there in the muddle of moms and babies and chaos, and she knew where she wanted to go.

If Todd could do it...

The doors from reception were wide open. Shana was on the phone at the front desk and Alexandra was by the elevator, using her cell phone. If she went that way, Tina thought...

No. When Daddy took them home, sometimes they took the stairs. "It'll keep us fit," he told Tina when she asked him why.

No one was looking at the door to the stairwell.

So no one noticed at all. The little girl took a deep breath, slid the stairwell door open just far enough for her small body to slip through the crack and headed in the direction she wanted to go.

Todd was collected by a beefy security guard as he emerged from the elevator two floors down.

Back at Round the Clock, he wasn't the least bit repentant. He'd caused excitement, and the security guard who'd caught him had been wearing a uniform and carrying a gun. The old guy and the little girl in the elevator with him had looked really scared.

All in all, Todd thought, it was very exciting. Now he settled down to play with his building blocks like the angelic child he occasionally was.

Alexandra collected her breath and thanked her lucky stars it hadn't been worse.

Now, as she always did, sometimes even in her sleep, she counted heads.

Fourteen.

She frowned. Surely there should be fifteen.

"Someone's missing," she told Shana, and both women gazed around at their little brood.

It took ten whole seconds before they figured out who wasn't there.

"Tina. Tina's gone."

"BEN?"

The pediatrician was still with Annabelle, but when his cell phone rang, he made an apologetic gesture and lifted it from his belt. He should be in the kids' ward right now, not down in ER talking to Annabelle. Work was bound to catch up with him sooner or later.

But it wasn't work. It was Alexandra, his fiancée and head of Round the Clock.

"Hey, slow down," he told her. Alexandra Webber, soon to be Alexandra Jessup, was normally one very collected lady, but her panic sounded down the line. Her fear reached Annabelle, who was standing close enough to hear. "What's up?"

"We've lost a child." Alexandra could barely get the words out. "Half an hour ago. We've had security scour the hospital, but she's gone. There's someone...Ben, there was a guy in the elevator. An old guy, and we're afraid... Can you come up, please? Ben, I know you're working, but I need you."

"I'm coming," Ben told her, not waiting to hear more. "Who's the kid? Todd?" He knew all about Todd Jamison.

He'd put Todd's limbs in plaster three times now because of the child's addiction to trouble.

"No. It's not Todd, though Todd caused it. It's Tina Dorsey. I have to ring Jaron now. Oh, Ben—"

"I'm coming."

How COULD she stay in ER after that? Annabelle cleared her absence with the rest of the team—thankfully at this hour of the morning, the ER was pretty calm—removed her white coat and headed up to Round the Clock.

They were all there. Alexandra and Shana. Keith and Ben. The kids. Ricky.

No Tina.

"What's happening?" she asked, and Shana looked as if she was about to burst into tears. She was hugging the mystery baby to her breast as if she needed the contact. The warmth.

"One of the moms was holding the door open, and that's when Todd escaped," she told her. "When we got Todd back, we realized Tina was missing."

"She's run away?" Annabelle asked.

Shana shook her head. "Why would she run away? She loves it here."

"There were all sorts of people around," Alexandra said distressfully. "One of the mothers had her two cousins here, showing them the center. By the time we realized Tina was missing…"

"You think someone may have taken her?" Annabelle stared at her, appalled.

"No. No, but…why would she run away?" Alexandra was ashen-faced. "Why?"

Why indeed? And a vision of Seattle's newspaper headlines over the past few weeks came flooding back. The mystery baby had taken over the front page for a couple of days, but the major story had been more dreadful.

Child molester…

Children missing…

"There's more," Alexandra whispered. "There was someone in the elevator with Todd. He was up here when Tina went missing. One of the moms said he came up with her in the elevator, but then just stood…looking. An old guy in a shabby suit. The security guard brushed right by him when he was grabbing Todd, and he said he had a little girl with him.''

''Tina?''

''We don't know. The security guard was looking for Todd and not focusing on anyone else. The elevator stopped before it reached the ground floor and there were other people in there. We asked Todd, and he says maybe it was Tina, but he can't remember.''

Annabelle stared, appalled at what she was saying. At what she was implying. ''Dear God.''

''Where's Tina?'' A tiny voice sounded at her side, and Annabelle looked down to see Ricky clutching her skirt. ''Annabelle, where's Tina?''

''Oh, Ricky.'' She bent and gathered him to her, and she held on as if she was drowning.

TWO MINUTES LATER Jaron burst through the door. He stopped dead at the sight before him. Alexandra was on the phone at the desk, Keith was barking instructions on his cell phone, and Seth was striding through the doors behind him. Shana was clutching Chris and trying to organize the remaining children into a circle on the mats to hear a story. To distract them from the chaos.

Annabelle was sitting on the floor holding Ricky.

''What…?''

''We don't know where she is,'' Alexandra said, putting down the phone and hurrying toward him. ''Oh, Jaron, I'm so sorry.''

He stared at her without comprehension. ''You *must* know.''

But there were no answers in her face. ''The police are on their way,'' she managed to say. ''We've notified everyone. We've searched the hospital—security's doing a second search now. We can't—'' She broke off.

Jaron stared wildly around. Then his gaze fell to Ricky. His son was staring up at him with eyes that were vast in his little face. Ricky, who'd lost his mother. Who still remembered that ghastly sequence of events. Ricky, who already knew far too well what horror in adult voices meant.

Ricky was cradled in Annabelle's arms. He stared up at his father, but he didn't move. He didn't need to.

Jaron was down on the floor beside him in an instant, hugging his son to him, and if in doing so he hauled Annabelle into his arms as well...

Who could blame him?

WHAT FOLLOWED was maybe the longest day Jaron could ever remember. Even the day Cathy had died hadn't been this long, he thought. Cathy's death had been dreadful, but it had been almost instant—a vicious blow that left them reeling. This was like slow torture, growing more excruciating by the minute.

Where was she?

Everything was so confused.

"I remember the guy," the mother who'd traveled up with the man in the elevator told the police. "I don't think he had a child with him on the way up. I don't think...I just didn't take any notice. There were nurses with us."

But the nurses couldn't remember seeing anyone.

"You're sure he had a little girl with him when he left the elevator?" the security guard was asked, and he looked miserable.

"Yeah," he said. "He was holding her hand. She was only waist-high, but I don't remember anything else. I was trying to grab the kid who escaped. A real little wriggler."

So no one had seen anything except the mother who'd shared the elevator with the man—and she could describe him.

His description fitted the man the entire Seattle police force was looking for.

The police closed Round the Clock. The staff were too distressed to continue and everyone was being interviewed. Alexandra organized the remaining children to be taken to Forrester Square Day Care for the day. This was no environment for children to be in. The police were crawling all over the hospital. Every adult who'd been near the place was being located and brought back in for interviews. In the back of everyone's mind were those headlines. Somewhere out there...

Somewhere out there...what?

"If it was Todd, I'd say he was probably hiding," Alexandra whispered for about the fiftieth time. "But Tina wouldn't hide, would she?"

No. They all knew it. Tina and Ricky were inseparable. For her to leave her brother was unthinkable. To run away...

But the alternative was that someone had taken her, and thinking that was the way of madness.

Jaron was going quietly crazy. He was desperate to do something. He wanted to be out on the streets actively searching, but he was made to see how useless that was.

"We have every cop in Seattle searching," Luke told him. "The mystery-baby problem has become priority two. This takes precedence over everything." Luke had arrived at the child-care center minutes after Jaron, and his role seemed to be to calm Jaron down. "We've canceled all leave and even the guys on night shift are coming back in to help. Jaron, what we need from you is a complete description of everything she's wearing. We need pictures. I'll take you home now and you can find us a good likeness."

"We'll come, too," Annabelle told them, lifting Ricky and still holding him to her as if he was hers. She was right by Jaron, her body touching his. She could do so little, but she could give him that.

The comfort of her body. It was so small a thing compared with what was lost. Tina...

THE DAY dragged endlessly on.

Annabelle sat in Jaron's kitchen and held Ricky while the world spun around her. There were people everywhere. Half the world seemed to know about Tina's disappearance and they all dropped in—mostly for a couple of minutes in the midst of their searching, enough time to hug Jaron and assure him that they, too, were looking and that everything that could be done was being done.

So many people.

People who cared.

Ricky was almost comatose. He lay cradled against Annabelle's breast, turned in an instant from a confident five-year-old to a terrified baby. Often Jaron held his son himself, and that was fine by Ricky, but when things became too much and Jaron insisted on being in a patrol car driving up and down Seattle's streets—uselessly, endlessly—Annabelle stayed with Ricky nestled in her arms.

Finally, exhausted, he slept. Her cheek rested against his soft curls, and as he slept, she found he was a part of the prayer she kept repeating to herself.

"Keep this little family safe. Keep Ricky from more sadness. Keep Jaron with those who love him."

He'd lost so much already. How could he lose more?

Toward evening, Jaron's mother-in-law arrived, a hard-faced woman whose immediate reaction was anger that they hadn't been able to find her sooner. She'd been out playing bridge and had come home to learn that her son-in-law had been "stupid" enough to lose her granddaughter. The friends surrounding Jaron faded away in the face of her fury. Only Annabelle stayed. She listened to a tirade of abuse flow over Jaron's head, and as he sat, ashen-faced and defeated, adding his own blame to the blame Hazel was heaping on him, she had to defend him.

"Round the Clock's the best child-care facility in Seattle," she told the woman. "Jaron can't be blamed."

"Who the hell are you?"

Ricky stirred then and twined his arms around Annabelle's neck. "Annabelle's our friend. She has the best dog—"

He was ignored. "I'll make dinner," Hazel announced, and then stared at Annabelle with dislike. "Maybe it's best if you leave. The child's exhausted. He's best with just family."

Jaron shook himself at that, stirring out of his misery with something akin to anger.

"Annabelle is…"

But Annabelle wasn't. They all knew it, and now wasn't the time to be changing anything. Annabelle looked at Jaron's strained features and couldn't bear to add to his worries.

"I do have a dog," she said softly, and kissed Ricky on the nose. "He's been alone all day so he needs me. I'll go home now and feed him while your grandma feeds you."

"You'll come back?" Ricky said, a hint of desperation in his voice, and Annabelle looked up and saw exactly the same desperation written on Jaron's face.

She nodded. Then, not caring one bit what Hazel thought, she put Ricky down and crossed to take Jaron's face in her hands. She kissed him. Not with passion, but with all the love in her heart. With her need, as well as his.

"I'll come back," she told them. "I promise."

"Because you're family, whether you like it or not," Jaron whispered, and Annabelle closed her eyes.

What had happened to her?

She loved. She didn't have a choice in the matter. She stood looking into Jaron's eyes and knew things had been taken out of her hands. She loved.

This was her man. This was her family. They were a part of her. Tina's disappearance—it was as though a part of her had been torn from her body. There was an aching, desperate void that couldn't be filled by anyone but Tina. And if Jaron were to leave…or Ricky…

These were her people. Her family. Her love. She couldn't be a part of them any more than she was right at this minute.

Hazel was still watching her with hostile eyes, but it didn't matter much anymore. Nothing mattered but the fact that Tina was missing and her family needed her. Annabelle's family.

"I'll collect Harold and I'll be right back," she said out loud. "I promise."

LUKE WAS pulling up in a squad car as she came out the front door. One look at his face told her there was no news.

"Nothing?"

"No." His face was set. Darkness was closing in, and the situation was becoming grimmer by the minute. Luke was a hardened cop. He'd been around enough to know what they were up against. Annabelle read his expression and she felt sick.

"You're leaving for the night?" he asked, and she shook her head.

"I'm going to get my dog and come back."

"I can get one of my men to feed your dog," he told her, but she shook her head.

"Jaron's mother-in-law's in there just now. She...she needs space."

Luke had met Hazel. He nodded, understanding completely. "I'll drive you home, then. I'll wait and bring you back if you like."

"Weren't you going in to see Jaron?"

"I don't have any news," he said bluntly. "If Hazel's there...I'll wait."

"You should be searching."

"Every cop in Seattle is searching," Luke said wearily. "Plus about half the citizens. We're almost out of options."

Out of options. Dear God.

"I don't..." She couldn't force her desperate mind to think. "I can catch a cab."

"You don't want to be alone, though, do you?" Luke asked, and watched her face.

How did they know her, these people? she wondered, dazed with the speed at which things were happening. This time last week she didn't know anyone at all, and now they all seemed somehow...

Her people.

Her protective armor had shattered and fallen away in a million pieces. She no longer had anything to protect herself from this pain. She closed her eyes, and when she opened them, Luke was putting his arm around her and helping her into the patrol car.

"Come on, Annabelle," he said softly. "Let's take you home."

Home?

Home was no longer her hospital apartment, she thought as they turned away from Jaron and Ricky. Home was back here.

Home was with her family.

"Who is she?"

"What?" Jaron wasn't taking anything in. He was staring at the telephone, willing it to ring. Damn it, why didn't it ring? Why wasn't there news? He was going nuts. He needed to get out of here. He needed to do something!

But his mother-in-law was insistent. "The woman, Annabelle. Who is she?"

"A doctor at the hospital."

"She seems very familiar."

"I don't think you know her."

"I don't mean familiar to me," Hazel snapped. "I mean familiar here. Sitting here with Ricky like she belongs."

He thought about it. What had Hazel said? *Sitting here like she belongs.* He looked at Annabelle's empty chair as if it had personally betrayed him. Where was she now? Annabelle's presence had been the only thing that had kept him sane, and now that she'd gone, he felt as if his hold on his sanity was slipping.

"Have you been seeing her?"

"Hazel…" He stared up at his mother-in-law. Was she out of her mind? Tina was missing and she was focusing on Annabelle?

"Do you know anything about her?"

"What the hell do you mean?"

"Well, it seems very odd. You start seeing some woman and your daughter disappears."

He shook his head, trying to clear the fog. Unsuccessfully.

"Where's her family?"

Ricky looked up at that. Hazel had served him a plate of spaghetti, and he was stirring it around rather than eating it.

"She's only got Harold," Ricky said with a sideways glance at his father. "And us. Dad and me and Tina."

Then he choked on a sob and balled his fist into his eyes.

"And Tina," he repeated, and fled to his bedroom.

LUKE ESCORTED Annabelle all the way to her apartment.

"For heaven's sake, I don't need a police escort." But he wouldn't take no for an answer.

"We'll collect your dog and I'll take the pair of you back to Jaron's," he said.

"You don't need to."

"I know I don't need to," he told her. "But it's something I can do and I'm desperate."

Desperate?

Annabelle looked into his face and saw he spoke the absolute truth.

She thought back to the whispered words of the dying woman. *Tell no one.* All her life that was what she'd been doing. Telling no one. Admitting no one.

Loving no one.

And here…here there was life. At such a time…

Oh, God, where was Tina?

She sagged on the thought, and Luke's arms came out to support her. "Come on, Annabelle," he said. "We can get through this. Together."

Together.

"Dear God, we must find her," she whispered. "We must." If Tina…

No. She mustn't think like that. She mustn't.

"Where is she?"

SHE WAS SITTING on the floor of Annabelle's apartment. Tina Dorsey was making her third hat, and when Annabelle opened the door, the little girl beamed up at her and Luke as if she'd conjured up her very nicest surprise.

"Hi," she said.

Annabelle stopped dead. Luke, coming in behind her, bumped right into her.

"Tina!"

Tina's smile faltered a little. "You sound funny. Is something wrong?"

Was something wrong?

Annabelle was down on the floor in seconds, gathering the little girl into her arms. Tina was covered in glue and sparkles and pieces of cut-up paper; she was wielding Annabelle's sharpest pair of scissors. She was covered in poster paint—and Annabelle didn't care in the least.

Tina was against her heart.

"Where have you been?"

"Here," Tina said, surprised. "Harold and I were waiting for you to come home. I remembered the number you put in the elevator, and I know where you keep the key. I even made myself a sandwich, but it wasn't a very good one. Do you like my hats, Annabelle?"

CHAPTER SEVENTEEN

AFTER THAT, things got a little blurry.

Luke was shouting into his cell phone. "No, you're not to drive yourself, Jaron. There's a car on the way to collect you. No, she's safe. She's fine. She's covered with bits of cloth and glue—and Annabelle... No, she's covered with Annabelle. I meant, Annabelle's hugging her. Yeah, the dog's here, too. She's fine, I tell you, Jaron. She's fantastic."

He dropped the phone, and then because it was all too much for a hardened cop to take in at once, Luke was picking the pair of them up and spinning like a crazy person, probably tearing every muscle in his back in the process.

"Hey, you're a cop," Annabelle spluttered through laughter and through tears. "Is this the way to behave?"

"Yeah, it is." His own eyes were shimmering as he set them down on the settee on top of the long-suffering Harold. "You think in this game that you've seen everything and maybe you have, and you're so damned afraid, and then something like this happens."

They were grinning at each other like idiots. Waiting...

There was the sound of sirens in the street below. Hell, every squad car in the city must be descending on the hospital to share in this happy ending.

"Do you want to help me make more hats?" Tina asked from her squashed position between Annabelle and Harold. Annabelle smiled tremulously through her tears.

"I might just wait for your daddy."

There was the sound of running feet. Luke had the door open, waiting.

Jaron was at the door. Jaron, devouring his daughter with his eyes. Turning to look at Luke in disbelief, as if wanting to see confirmation of his right to joy on his friend's face. And then Annabelle...

He looked at Annabelle for a long moment—and then walked forward like a man in a dream and gathered his daughter to his heart.

SHE WAS WEEPING. Stupidly, Annabelle, who never cried—never!—was weeping and she couldn't stop. She rose and backed away from them, toward the door, but there was a cop coming through the door with Ricky by his side. Trapped, she edged sideways, but Jaron was turning back to her, Tina cradled in his arms.

"Annabelle."

Dear God. The look on his face. The end to such suffering. And she'd caused it.

"She...she came to find me," she said falteringly. "It's my fault. Oh, Jaron, I'm so sorry."

And he saw in an instant where she was coming from. He knew.

"Annabelle, Tina came to find you because she loves you," he said so strongly and firmly and jubilantly that every person in the room could hear and even those outside, the gathering crowd of onlookers. "She came to find you because you're a part of our family. And it highlights the problem. Our only problem. What Tina needs is one home. Not two. One home with two kids, a mom and dad and a dog. And one heart."

"Jaron, you don't know what you're saying." Annabelle's voice was a thread of a whisper.

But Jaron was scooping up his son in his free arm so that he was holding both his children, and he was looking at her with all the tenderness in the world shining out of his eyes. He'd seen her holding Ricky throughout this long day. He'd thought he couldn't push her to have the kids, to be part of his family, but his grief and terror had been hers. He didn't need to push. His kids already had hold of her heart.

"Me and the kids need you," he told her. "Don't we, guys?"

"Yeah," Tina said. "Annabelle, my hats don't work properly."

It was never going to get any better than this, he decided. Her defenses were down. Tears were slipping down her cheeks. And she loved his kids. She *loved* his kids, he thought exultantly. He'd seen her pain and her joy.

She loved his kids.

Hell, at this moment anything was possible. He'd never known such joy, and she was standing in the doorway wavering.

She had to take that step back. To him.

"Marry me, Annabelle," he said gently, and the whole world held its breath.

The hallway was getting more crowded by the minute. So many people. Shana and Keith. Ben and Alexandra. Seth. Luke. Abby. Where had Abby come from? There were more cops than you could count. Doctors, nurses, janitors…

There was even a security guard towing a bemused old guy with a little girl at his side—a child who'd turned out to be his granddaughter. It seemed they'd been amusing themselves riding elevators while the little girl's mom had been having an outpatient procedure.

Despite the misunderstandings, despite the fact that the security guard had collared the pair when he recognized them, they were quite happy to join in. Everyone was joining in. In this bad-news world here was a glorious happy ending, and no one was missing a minute of it.

Marry me…

Maybe there'd be another happy ending right now.

"Marry us," Jaron revised, and Ricky hugged his dad's neck, looked shyly at Annabelle and added his own pressure.

"If you marry us, Tina won't run away again," he told her.

"I didn't run away," Tina said scornfully. "Not away. I ran to Annabelle."

"You see what I mean?" Jaron said gently. He was smiling

at her, and such a smile! It made her catch her breath in awe. That such a man could look at her like this.

Independence at all cost…

But how could she set store by her independence when such a man was looking at her as if she was the most precious thing in the world? When Ricky was looking at her with love and Tina was demanding more hats?

Even Harold was looking at her with affection, though that was probably just because it was his dinnertime.

Around them were their people. People who cared. She looked across at Shana, who was still holding the little mystery baby who'd started all this. These people cared so much. They became involved, they loved, and sometimes it ended in disaster. But the alternative *wasn't* to love, and how much worse was that?

There'd be a happy ending for this baby, Annabelle knew. It didn't matter that she didn't know what that ending was. The important thing was that people cared—that they loved.

Could she?

She looked back at Jaron, his smile slipping a little in the face of her hesitation. He didn't know, she thought joyously. He didn't know that she loved him. He wasn't sure.

"Jaron," she whispered, and it was an answer all by itself.

She took a step toward him and he took a step, too. And then she wasn't sure how the rest of the distance was covered, because they were suddenly entwined, a man and a woman and two children hugging and kissing and laughing and crying, with Harold nosing in between.

Around them was a laughing, applauding crowd, but they didn't hear. They couldn't. Because something very important was happening.

One man and one woman, one little boy, one little girl—and one big elderly dog—were becoming a family.

From this day forth.

IT WAS THE END of a long, long day. Soon they'd slide into sleep, but for now they were content to lie entwined in Jaron's big bed and feel each other's heartbeats. The moonlight was playing over the bed. In the next room the children were fast asleep in one small bed with Harold draped across four small feet.

God was indeed in his heaven.

"We need another place to live," Jaron said sleepily, tracing an auburn curl that was lying entrancingly over his chest.

"We have two apartments."

"We need a house. With a yard for Harold."

She thought about that and liked it. "How about another couple of bedrooms while we're at it?"

"Another...?"

She hesitated. Maybe. Maybe not. But she wanted to say it just in case.

"Maybe we could fill them."

And maybe she was right. He was raised on one elbow, looking down into her face with an expression of such blazing joy that surely she must be asleep and dreaming. "You'd have a baby? You'd have my child?"

"If...if you don't think two's enough."

"Four," he said definitely. "We'll go for four and then we'll see. And the kids have been agitating for a puppy. Do you think Harold could stand a friend?"

"Harold will love everyone who comes along." She was drifting in a haze of love and joy and a desire so great it was threatening to overwhelm her. "Just the one puppy?"

"We don't want to get carried away." He hesitated. "Your work...Annabelle, you're a wonderful doctor."

"And you're a wonderful cop."

"You think...maybe if we both went on four-day weeks. After the babies come, that is..."

"Four-day weeks sound terrific to me," she said contentedly. "And not just after any babies come. I think four days' work sounds fine right now. As long as our three days off coincide. I'm not married to my work, Detective Dorsey. I intend to be married to you."

"Ditto." But something else was bothering him. "Annabelle, you earn…"

"Heaps," she said cheerfully. "Squillions. Which is just as well if we have to buy all this dog food."

"It won't bother you that I'm a cop and you're a doctor?"

"Bother me?" It was her turn to sit up now and she did, staring down in astonishment. "Bother me? A cop and a doctor. You and me?"

"I just thought…"

"That we're a perfect combination?"

"I was worried about the money."

"Why would we be bothered about money when we have us?"

He thought about it. And couldn't come up with a single reason.

Hell, she was naked and she was looking down at him with such love and such laughter…

She was so beautiful.

It was too much. With a groan he hauled her down to him and found her mouth, running his hands through that glorious flaming hair, loving her, aching for her, knowing that she was his.

As he was hers.

"Four babies?" he whispered, and sighed in ecstasy. His fingers were driving her wild. His mouth, his body, his…

"At least," she managed to say. "And two puppies…"

"Then what are we waiting for?" he breathed as her body merged into his and a myriad of stars exploded around them. "Just what are we waiting for, my love? Let's start now."

WHERE HAD SHE come from?

Shana had settled baby Chris into her crib, and now she came downstairs to join Keith. But her thoughts were still on the baby.

The little one was so beautiful. So…perfect. There must be a happy ending out there for her somewhere. Jaron and Annabelle had their happy ending. They'd found their family. So where did this baby belong?

"Why do you think the woman kept insisting that Annabelle tell no one?" she asked, and Keith moved over on the back step so she could sit beside him. But it took him a while to answer.

"I don't know," he said at last, staring out over the woods into the starlit night beyond. "Maybe we never will. But on a night like this…anything is possible. It's a night of miracles."

He shrugged and then he smiled.

"A night of miracles," he repeated softly. "'Tell no one'? Look up at that sky, Shana, and tell me that there are any real secrets at all."

Tell no one…

"Someone knows," he whispered. "Somewhere, someone knows."

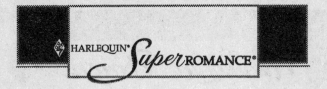
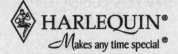

HARLEQUIN®
Makes any time special®

Upbeat, All-American Romances

Romantic Comedy

Harlequin® Historical

Historical, Romantic Adventure

HARLEQUIN®
INTRIGUE

Romantic Suspense

Capturing the World You Dream Of

HARLEQUIN® *Presents*

Seduction and passion guaranteed

HARLEQUIN® *Super* ROMANCE®

Emotional, Exciting, Unexpected

HARLEQUIN® *Temptation*

Sassy, Sexy, Seductive!